PRINCE

OF THE PALISADES

Books by Julian Winters

As You Walk On By
How to Be Remy Cameron
Right Where I Left You
Running with Lions
The Summer of Everything

PRINCE
OF THE PALISADES

Julian Winters

VIKING

VIKING
An imprint of Penguin Random House LLC
1745 Broadway, New York, New York 10019

First published in the United States of America by Viking,
an imprint of Penguin Random House LLC, 2024

Visit us online at PenguinRandomHouse.com.

Library of Congress Cataloging-in-Publication Data is available.

ISBN 9780593624425

1st Printing

Printed in the United States of America

LSCC

Edited by Dana Leydig
Design by Kate Renner
Text set in Strato Pro

For the ones who were told they weren't "worthy"
or "enough"—you're more than deserving just as you are.
Wear your crown proudly.

For James Akinaka, who said he'd love to see me write
a queer royals story—thank you, King.

You have to decide who you are
and force the world to deal with you,
not with its idea of you.

—James Baldwin

ROYAL GONE ROGUE

by Kip Davies

Not everyone is meant to sit on the throne. Prince Jadon of the beautiful Îles de la Réverie proved just that last Saturday night.

In a three-minute video that has since gone viral, the visibly sloshed seventeen-year-old royal was caught inside GOLDRUSH, a trendy Los Angeles night club, ranting about his country's beloved Prime Minister Barnard. He's quoted calling PM Barnard "an unforgivable, worthless waste of oxygen," among other expletive-filled declarations *The Dish and Chips* refuses to print. Footage also shows empty shot glasses, questionable pill-shaped items, and HRH Prince Jadon's best mate: Kofi Baptiste, son of an international hotel developer and a BAFTA-winning actress.

Experts inside of Centauri Palace have yet to identify the video's unknown source. No official statement has been released from King Simon, who's only in his eighth year as monarch following the death of his father, King Jacques III, from a lengthy battle with leukemia. Crisis talks have forced Crown Princess Annika, 21, to return early from a European tour.

This isn't the first time Prince Un-Charming has

been caught behaving poorly. Remember Mayhem in Marseille? *The Worst Supper* in Milan? Royal insiders noted the recent breakup with model Léon Barnard, who also happens to be the prime minister's son, as the probable cause.

Elsewhere, *Crown Chat* reports Prince Jadon's outburst was "most likely influenced by his American roots." King Simon's union with California-born Queen Ava marked the first time a monarch married outside of Réverie.

After this latest scandal, all eyes are on Prince Jadon's next move. The biggest question remains: Is this Rebel Royal truly fit to carry the weight of his birthright?

A ROYAL RUNAWAY?

Since his viral incident last weekend, insiders report Prince Jadon has gone MIA. Earlier today, Crown Princess Annika was snapped arriving at LAX with a small entourage. Has she come to stop the prince's royal rampage?

Never believe the headlines.

It's Royal Etiquette 101. Almost everything you read online or see on the news is dramatized for viewership. "Facts" is a loose term in the world of celebrity journalism. A lesson I learned while teething. And yet here I am, literal seconds from tossing my phone into the Pacific Ocean after watching the latest clip of everyone's favorite soul-devouring, trash-eating bad-take journalist, Kip Davies.

"The video is *treasonous*," he says in his condescending British accent. "Drugs, underage drinking, foul language. How is anyone supposed to respect him?"

He flashes a hyper-white smile all over BBC News. I bite so

hard on the inside of my cheek I nearly draw blood.

A few vital details Kip left out:

One, those were *Pez candies*, not drugs. My best friend—correction: former best friend—Kofi is obsessed with them. I brought some as a gag gift.

Two, I wasn't *that* drunk. I only had two shots of the vile peppermint vodka the club was serving. We were celebrating Kofi's birthday. He's the one who suggested we come to LA. Who kept inviting total strangers into our roped-off VIP section.

Three, I did what any other pissed-off teen would after a long week of stress and arguments and overhearing conversations he shouldn't have: got caught on camera sharing his most private thoughts. It's ridiculous. No one filmed Kofi doing body shots off some hot young influencer's abs. Just me ranting about that asshole Barnard.

I don't regret what I said. It felt good to finally exhaust the fire raging in my chest. I'm more annoyed that it's everywhere. That people like Kip Davies won't stop talking about it.

"Prince Jadon," he continues, "is a truly *awful* representation of the Crown." He smirks pretentiously. Like he has something to be proud of.

Congratulations, you ruined a teen's reputation.

Still, his words echo next to the ones Papa said to me two days ago over a video call:

Is this who you are now? A rebel? A walking headline? Do you care how this makes our country look? Our family? What's the cause of all this?

My first mistake was not answering him. The second was

4

looking at my mom. Watching the frustration bloom across her face, as if this is completely my fault. She has no idea what I heard inside the palace. The foul things that spilled from Barnard's mouth.

They don't belong here.

I don't want to tell her—or anyone—what he said. Would they believe me if I did? Now that this video is out?

Kip's voice startles my attention back to my phone. "Are we really blaming the prince's failed relationship with Lé—"

"Nope," I say, swiping to another video before he can finish. I don't want to hear my ex's name. See his face. Relive the way our last conversation ended. Our breakup has nothing to do with why I'm officially *stuck* in California.

As the next clip loads, I think back to Papa's final words:

D'accord! Since you can't explain yourself. Since you love making a mess of your legacy. Stay in America! You're banned from returning home until you prove you're the kind of prince Rêverie deserves.

"Hot take, but—"

My eyes snap to the new video playing.

Five American cohosts sit around a glass table. A thirty-something woman with warm, reddish-brown skin and a silver stud in her left nostril is talking: "He's *seventeen*. He's made mistakes. What does Rêverie—the world, for that matter—expect from him?"

A lot, apparently, I want to tell her.

A hand blurs across my vision, snatching my phone away. My sister, Annika, glares at me. "Ça suffit!" *That's enough.* We only use French with each other when we're annoyed.

I offer her a weak, apologetic grin.

In the background, attendants rush around with luggage. The house we're staying in is a gated three-story modern architectural jewel set in the hills of Pacific Palisades. Seven bedrooms, ten bathrooms, a heated pool, and a bunch of other amenities I can't remember. Hardly as lavish as Centauri Palace, but I don't have much room to complain. It was rented on short notice.

The gourmet kitchen's lighting accentuates how many of our parents' features Annika and I share. Papa's height, his full lips and round jaw. Mom's medium brown complexion, strong eyebrows, her thick, curly hair. Despite recently traveling five time zones, Annika's curls are impeccably pinned up with pearl clips, showing off her high cheekbones. My own hair is shaved on the sides, the top long enough for springy curls to hang over my forehead.

"Jade," Annika sighs out.

"Hmm?"

"I didn't fly twelve hours for you to watch this *trash*." She waves my phone around.

The corners of my mouth inch up. "You came for the authentic California rolls, right?"

She rolls her eyes in that *obviously* way she does.

"Fine, fine." I raise my hands, surrendering. "Wow, jet lag makes you uptight."

"*It's not the jet lag,*" Luc coughs into his elbow while passing behind Annika. Without looking, she flips him off.

My sister's Royal Protection Guard is slightly taller than my 1.85 meters. His buzz cut draws attention to his hazel eyes, gold-brown skin. If he weren't guarding the literal heir to Réverie's throne, he'd probably have a career in high fashion ads.

"The videos are for research," I tell Annika.

She looks unimpressed. "Is that why I'm here instead of living my best pumpkin spice life in New York City?"

"Respectfully, Princess," Luc says, fixing the cuffs of his black Oxford, "we live on an *island*. We're warm weather people. You can't survive a New York winter."

"He's got a point," I say.

"First of all, it's only *September*." Annika cocks her chin at Luc. "Second, is that a challenge?"

His lips purse. "You wouldn't last thirty days in their conditions."

"I'd last longer than you."

"How much are you willing to bet?"

"When the crown princess finally murders you, Luc," a voice interrupts, "I won't tell anyone where the body's hidden."

I snort as Ajani, my Royal Protection Guard, steps into the kitchen. While Luc is still young and new to his position, everything about Ajani is sharp and experienced, from her low-fade haircut to the tailored black pantsuit and boots. She's been by my side since I could walk. With golden rays from the sunset glazing over her rich, dark brown skin, she completes routine security checks around the house.

"No one's killing anyone," Annika asserts. "Not until we get my little bro back home."

She turns to me. "What's the plan, Jade?"

I try not to frown. My fingertips trace along the black induction cooktops. I study the double oven, the stainless steel refrigerator and walk-in pantry that have been fully stocked with supplies by the house manager. I miss the palace kitchens, the air scented with powdered sugar and melted butter and warm pastries. The stool I'd climb on as a kid, sidled up to Papa's side.

Life was easier then. Before my pépère died. Before Papa became monarch.

On quiet mornings, we'd roll out dough for palmiers. Bake sugary gâteau au yaourt or flip crêpes. Now, I see more of Papa on TV, giving speeches. Coming and going from meetings. Every second of his day is dedicated to the crown.

Eyes flitting around, I say, "I'm going to . . ."

"We're going to show the world His Royal Highness is a charming, down-to-earth, charitable prince," Samuel announces. He strides in, carrying a phone in one hand, a tablet in the other. Royal Liaison Mode fully activated. He's short with a stocky frame. The lavender of his shirt pops against his cool umber complexion. "Instead of—"

"Spoiled and surly?" Annika suggests. "Moody and poorly dressed?"

"Hey!" I pinch her shoulder. "I'm very stylish."

"We're going to prove," Samuel continues, resting his phone on the counter, screen up, "he's not *this*."

There it is. Trending at number one: #RebelRoyal.

It's Kip Davies's weakest effort yet. #ProblematicPrince was right there. He's been "reporting" on my family since before Papa's ascension. Every little lie and fake scandal he can create for clicks and likes.

Next to me, Annika chews nervously on her lower lip.

Between us, she's the calm, optimistic one. I'm more of the "burn shit down, ask questions later" variety. But I don't plan to let anyone see *that* Jadon while I'm here.

Not if I ever want to get home again.

"Samuel's right," I say, straightening my shoulders. "I'm going to be as normal and unproblematic as possible."

I ignore Annika's loud snort.

"We'll start with His Royal Highness attending Willow Wood Academy, a prestigious private school," Samuel notes, reading from the itinerary he forwarded me yesterday. "It's more of a formality. Her Majesty insists on a proper education while we sort out his . . . unfortunate situation. Mingling with Willow Wood's illustrious student body will help our cause."

I resist the urge to roll my eyes. New friends? No thanks. I won't be here long enough to remember anyone's name. But I respect all the effort Samuel's put into this, so I don't comment.

"I'm also working on a few low-profile appearances," Samuel says, scrolling. "Small but noticeable events that'll encourage the press to change their narrative. As well as media appearances for you, Crown Princess."

Annika shrugs. "Anything to make this loser look better."

I pinch her again, scowling.

"*Oh*," Samuel says, beaming, "and we're confirmed for the Sunset Ball in early December!"

My jaw tightens. The Sunset Ball is California's equivalent to the Met Gala. A big, glitzy party. It's also an emergency, final effort to win over Réverie's approval. If I'm trapped here until December, I might throw *myself* into the Pacific.

Samuel says, "The organizers have agreed to Prince Jadon giving a speech"—I can practically hear Annika's eyes popping out of her head—"which is the perfect opportunity to prove he's not who the world thinks."

"Perfect," I parrot.

"And if that doesn't work?" Annika asks.

"It *will*, Anni," I say, pretending like I haven't second-guessed this plan six times in the last twenty-four hours. "A few smiles. An interview or two. One silly speech, and then we're back to Réverie."

Where I never have to deal with things like this, I don't add.

Annika's mouth opens like she's about to argue, then closes.

Instead, Samuel says, brow wrinkled, "I do wish we'd been given a slightly larger entourage to work with."

It's true. I'm used to a bigger group whenever one of these situations happens. There's no team of royal media specialists making calls. No chamberlains running around. Not even Dion, my royal stylist, ready to dress me in the right look for the cameras.

I'm lucky to have Samuel, a bargain Annika made with Mom.

But it's fine.

"We've got this," I assert. I smile widely, extending my arms out to either side. "Who needs all those extra bodies? All I want are the four people right here."

And maybe a prayer. Or for a meteor to suddenly destroy the Earth.

My new bedroom is . . . *adequate.*

Forest-green walls and a high ceiling. Various shades of gray furniture. A wide bed tucked between two floor-to-ceiling windows. Inside the walk-in closet is the luggage Annika brought from Réverie for me. In addition to clothes, she— begrudgingly—packed two Gucci suitcases full of sneakers.

Do my parents expect me to live months without my Jordans?

While a rotation of soft R&B music plays from my phone, I pace around. The space is *almost* homey. But there are no framed photos of me, Annika, and our parents laughing on Réverie's western shore. No stack of leather-bound notebooks where I scribble all my favorite recipes. Even the sounds from the Pacific Ocean are wrong.

Noisy, restless. Nothing like the tranquil sea surrounding Réverie.

Our island rests in the central Atlantic Ocean, west of Africa. It's not large, but it's warm and beautiful, the people content. We've survived on one strict policy: *neutrality.* We never involve ourselves in others' conflicts or wars. We preserve strong relationships across the world while keeping a manageable distance.

Policies I don't always agree with.

Ninety percent of Réverie's population comes from generations of families who originated on the island, centuries ago.

Then came Mom. Now my sister and me.

They don't belong here. She's not one of us. Never will be!

Fragments of Prime Minister Barnard's words churn in my skull. I know he isn't the only one back home who feels differently about my mom. It's in the headlines too. How Mom's "American roots" influence my actions, but they don't.

My playlist and my thoughts are interrupted by a new notification. A DM to my finsta account. From @RoiDesLions.

King of the lions, also known as my ex.

I'm tempted to open the message. I've ghosted so many people lately, I might as well start a paranormal support group. It's only been a month since our breakup. Less than two weeks since he walked away when I needed him.

My chest tightens. How can you simultaneously want to punch someone in their pretty, perfectly angled face and miss the way they'd press a sleepy smile into the crook of your neck late at night? Why are first loves the worst?

Before my finger does the wrong thing, someone knocks at my door.

I toss my phone like it's a grenade. Annika leans in the archway, smiling suspiciously. "Am I interrupting? Were you watching por—"

"No!" My face wrinkles. "Why would you think that?"

"You're the one who threw your phone across the room!"

True.

"I'm not judging you," Annika says, barely holding in a laugh.

"Stop! I wasn't—you scared me. That's it."

She lets it go, sitting on the bed before checking her manicure. Annika's aesthetic is understated glam. She's wearing a Burberry turtleneck, dark denim skinny jeans, and runway-ready black heels. I can't keep up with how many Best Dressed lists she's appeared on, among other royal-approved headlines.

I flop down next to her, hands tucked behind my head. There's an appalling light fixture in the middle of my ceiling.

"So," Annika says, "a speech? At the Sunset Ball?"

"Don't start," I groan.

"I wouldn't dare. I just think it's a bold strategy considering—"

"I'm so bad at public speaking?" I insert. "Since I have a history of saying all the wrong things?"

She shrugs, not commenting. I know what she's thinking.

Annika's the perfect princess. Never needed an army of professionals coaching her on what to say, when and where to be herself. She was born for this life. Meanwhile, I force myself into whatever prince mold people expect until I'm either bored or annoyed.

Then, well. Shit happens.

It's not who I am, but I know it's who I'm supposed to be.

"It's just a speech," I say, grinning. I have one advantage over Annika—irresistible dimples. "How hard can it be?"

She pointedly doesn't return my gaze, her mouth puckered.

I laugh. "Anni, I didn't invite you all the way to California to lose faith in me before things even get started."

"I volunteered," she reminds me.

Not that I needed it. Annika's here to watch over me. To make sure I don't fuck things up so severely that Papa permanently bans me. Don't get me wrong, I'm grateful, but there's an island-sized guilt floating in my chest. Réverie's crown princess should be doing a million other things instead of helping me fix my mistakes.

But I'm happy she's here.

Since her eighteenth birthday, we've seen each other less and less. She's always traveling, like our parents. It's nice having more than five minutes with the only person left in my life that *gets me*.

"Well." I hear the teasing smile in Annika's voice. "Are you taking a *date?*"

I blow out a long breath. "*Non.*"

"Why not?"

"What for?"

"Hello!" Annika swats my chest, the sting forcing me to curl up like a dying rodent. "To show everyone—including your dickish ex—that you've moved on? Also, because you *can?*"

"Valid points," I reluctantly admit, "but I have no interest in asking a random boy to a silly ball I don't even want to go to."

"Wow. *TeenBuzz* really named *you* one of their most adorable singles?"

"Isn't it obvious?" I smugly flash my dimples.

She smacks my chest again.

"Stop being so invested in my love life," I huff after recovering. "Go get your own."

Annika hums. After she turned sixteen, everyone decided to play matchmaker for her. From politicians and nobilities, down to royal staffers. Boring, forgettable boys treating the future queen's heart like a game of chess. Annika's focused on her own goals, a relationship far from in the picture.

"It can't hurt to be *friendly* with someone new," she advises.

I snort. "As if any American boy's worth it."

She crosses her arms, disappointed.

"Look, Anni," I say, "I'm not wasting valuable time chatting up someone I won't even see past December. I'm here to prove something. To show Papa I'm not the prince from that video."

"Jade, are you sure—"

"Boys are out of the equation," I insist.

Annika sighs. "Okay. Message received!"

We sit quietly for a moment. Low music fills the spaces. My forgotten phone still lies face-down on the area rug. I'm not avoiding boys because of Léon. They're just another unwanted distraction.

I have more important things to resolve.

"Hey," Annika says softly, "I could survive a month in New York, right?"

I roll my eyes. Have I mentioned my sister's competitive streak?

"Of course," I reply without sarcasm. "You're a badass. You could survive anywhere."

"I know. Thanks for confirming." She pats my knee before standing. "Get some sleep. School starts tomorrow."

On her way to the door, I yell, "I also didn't invite you here to mom me."

She pauses, one hand on the knob. "I'm here to spend all day at the beach. Hit up Rodeo Drive. Smile during interviews. Make *you* look like a competent prince."

I laugh as the door clicks shut. A weight lifts from my chest.

Annika has my back. By the Sunset Ball, I'll prove Papa—the world—wrong about me.

Whatever it takes.

My phone buzzes on the rug. I roll and stretch to scoop it up. The first notification is a new article.

I click on it. The headline hits me in big, bold, capitalized letters:

THE GOLDEN STATE WELCOMES RÉVERIE'S GOLDEN BOY!

EXCLUSIVE: From Shore to Shore, Royalty Joins California's Elite

Surprise! America just got a lot more regal as Prince Jadon, 17, is staying stateside—and going to school! "It has always been His Royal Highness's intention to go abroad and spend quality time in the area his mother, Queen Ava, spent her youth," Centauri Palace tells *People*. Princess Annika, 21, is confirmed to be accompanying her brother.

The news comes after Jadon recently made headlines for a controversial video. Palace officials assure, "His Royal Highness is eager to move past any unfortunate narratives about him or the crown. He's looking forward to acquainting himself with America and his peers."

Before she was queen, my mom was simply Ava Gilbert from Long Beach. Photographic evidence confirms she was an ambitious teen. Prom queen and debate club president and valedictorian. She attended her dream college, the University of Southern California. But one trip to Paris, a graduation gift from my grandparents, changed her entire life.

"I was gonna be a teacher," she told me, years ago. "Then I met your papa and, well."

It's insufferable—the way Mom gets when she tells the story. Shimmering eyes, heart in her throat while describing their meet-cute: a last-minute amateur baking class they both signed up for. Papa approaching her with flour-stained cheeks, a shy smile.

Gross.

But *here*—this is where Mom discovered who she was.

We've taken family trips to California. When I was much younger. My grandparents have since moved. Papa bought them a farm in Arkansas where they could escape the constant attention, start fresh. They visit us twice a year in Réverie.

I wonder if they miss their lives here before a crown interrupted everything.

I wonder why Mom never visits California anymore.

As our SUV glides through neighborhoods lined with towering palm trees and spidery elms, I thumb through old photos of Mom on my phone. Nothing from online—the palace forced her to delete any social media accounts not linked to them. Nana sent these to me.

My mom, sitting poolside with neon-framed sunglasses and chunky '80s-style gold earrings. Laughing with friends at parties. Playing Helena in *A Midsummer Night's Dream*.

I don't know what it's like to enjoy a camera lens. To live so carefree.

"Your Highness?"

I lift my head. "Yes?"

Next to me in the roomy backseat, Samuel swipes the screen of one of his many smart devices. "Did you hear what I said?"

"Real quick"—I slide my phone into the inside pocket of my blazer—"can we cut back on the formalities? We're not in the palace. Or even in public. When it's just us, call me Jadon."

Samuel nods toward the passenger seat.

"Ajani doesn't count." I roll my eyes. "She's family."

I ignore her sigh of protest. She's at my side nearly twenty-four seven. I see her more than my parents. That's family.

"If you insist, Your High—I mean, *Jadon*," Samuel corrects after I flex an eyebrow. "Do you agree with what I said?"

"Of course." I straighten my tie. "But for refresher purposes, *what* were we discussing?"

Samuel looks two seconds from frowning, but refrains. "Building a community with your peers at Willow Wood?"

Oh, that. *Again.* I don't answer him.

Since the *People* article came out, even more attention is on me. At least two of Samuel's devices vibrate every other minute. I had to mute my alerts this morning.

What's even more annoying is the smile he gives me when he posits, "It will be great for what you're trying to accomplish here."

Great for them, he means.

Willow Wood is California's most exclusive prep school. Yearly, they graduate more future political figures and influencers and entrepreneurs than anywhere else. Having a prince on their roster certainly makes them more appealing to parents.

But there's something in this for me too.

In the history of Réverie's royal lineage, education after secondary school hasn't been an option. As an only child, Papa's commitments to the throne prevented him from going to university. It's been the same for every heir before him. But Annika's next in line, not me.

My life doesn't have to be meetings and handshakes and speeches. I can attend university. Willow Wood keeps me on track for that.

"Jadon?" Samuel attempts. "Do you agree?"

I ball my hands in my lap. What's the point of bonding with classmates? Putting in the effort to get to know anyone? I tried that once—with Kofi. No matter what, it always ends the same for me: alone.

I'm a royal. Friendship isn't a luxury I'm allowed to want.

Exhaling, I say, "Is it really necessary?"

"Absolutely." Samuel sips from his travel mug of chai. "You're great with new people!"

"Have you met me?"

"That was the old Jadon. *New Jadon* likes his peers. He makes a concerted effort to be friendly—"

Ajani covers a snort by clearing her throat.

I thump the back of my skull against the leather headrest. A stress zit is forming on my left cheek. Just what I needed: puberty and socializing.

"Trust me, it'll help," Samuel says, switching devices. His

confidence is nauseating. "It's only the first day. Try being cordial."

"It's too early for that," I grunt.

"How about *pleasant?*"

I suck in my cheeks. "Sounds exhausting."

The SUV slows to a stop. Outside the tinted windows, shops with umbrellaed patios, sun-washed exteriors, and chalkboard signs line the street. There's an emptiness behind all the cozy gloss. Like this neighborhood was built for aesthetics, not community.

It's nothing like Réverie's marketplace.

Something catches my eye: a corner coffee shop. The Hopper. Lush vines crawl up the pink exterior. A short green-and-peach awning shades the pavement where an older Black man is sweeping. On one of the windows, someone's painted an espresso bean with white bunny ears.

I muffle a laugh with my fist. It's so charming. Right out of the photos of Mom on my phone. I want to hide inside. But I can't.

The light finally changes. We turn left, leaving that one moment behind.

"Jadon?" Samuel prompts again.

I watch scenery blur past the window. Resigned, I say, "I'll try."

Samuel smiles widely until I add, "But I can't promise there won't be at least one *small* chemical fire by Friday."

"Bien sûr," Samuel sighs, no doubt wanting to throw himself into traffic.

Willow Wood Academy is a mini metropolis. The buildings are done in Mission Revival style—cream stucco walls, red tile roofs, open-air hallways. Pristine lawns slice through stone walkways. On the way to the headmaster's office, we pass a courtyard dotted with succulents. Hung over the main hall's foyer is a vinyl banner of a beautiful brunette girl smiling perkily.

OUR STUDENT PRESIDENT WELCOMES ALL!

Perfect.

Much of my education has been through private tutors. On jets thousands of miles above sea. In lavish hotel suites. Sometimes, when I'm lucky, in the palace gardens with the sunshine on my cheeks and ocean air in my lungs. I've attended actual school—Académie des Jeunes Dirigeants—before, but nothing quite like this.

The floors are so shiny, I can see every detail of my disinterested posture in a lilac, yellow, and gray uniform. I inhale deeply, fixing my expression into the one I use for photographers. Bright eyes, big grin, plastic charm.

"We're so happy you're here!"

Headmaster Parker looks young. Thick, deep brown curls piled on her head. Rosy cheeks and light freckles across her pale skin. The online article I skimmed before arriving said she graduated from Willow Wood in the nineties. I'm almost certain the collection of bobblehead figurines on her desk are from a popular Chinese drama.

Ajani and I sit in a pair of plush chairs across from her.

"Actual *royalty* on campus!" she gushes. "Should the faculty address you as Your Highness or—"

"Just Jadon," I interrupt, then quickly add, "*please*. Nothing formal."

Nothing to draw unnecessary attention to me.

"Well, Jadon," she says, tapping away at her computer, "At Willow Wood, we encourage our students to reimagine the impossible as possible."

I narrow my eyes at her direct quote from the school's web page.

"The academic year just started for us, which means it's everyone's first day," she continues, "so you shouldn't stick out too much."

"I'd prefer not at all," I say dryly.

Her shoulders tense at my forwardness. "Of course! It shouldn't be *that* weird for you."

"Why"—in my periphery, Ajani's head shakes slightly, a warning about my tone that forces me to raise the level of my smile before I finish—"would it be weird?"

Headmaster Parker waves her hands around. "Everything about high school is . . . awkward." She bites her lip, as if reliving her own teen years. "But you'll fit in nicely!"

My grin tightens as I nod.

"While you're in class, we have private waiting spaces for your . . ." She studies Ajani. "Secret service?"

Nostrils flaring, Ajani says, "I'm His Royal Highness Prince Jadon's Royal Protection Guard."

I jump in. "Thank you so much, Headmaster Parker. Should I get to class now?"

She hands me a locker assignment and course schedule.

"I've assigned you a tour guide," she notes enthusiastically. "One of our best students."

Hopefully, it's not the girl from the banner. I could live without that much bubbliness this early in the morning.

"Thank you," I repeat, hastily following Ajani out the door.

I immediately scrub off the fake Jadon for my usual resting prince face, glaring at my new list of classes.

"Oof," comes an unexpected voice. "Did someone kick your puppy?"

I raise my narrowed eyes.

My tour guide, Morgan, according to the name tag she wears with her pronouns underneath, clearly has no regard for uniform policies. Her lilac ascot is being used as a headband to keep big, loose black curls off her face. She's objectively cute, with a warm tawny complexion and cherub cheeks. The rest of her clothes are standard—yellow and gray plaid vest, matching pleated skirt. The top two buttons of her Oxford are undone, revealing a thin silver chain.

She smirks at Ajani. "Nice fade."

Then, she turns back to me. "Your Highness."

"Just Jadon is fine," I exhale, already bored.

"Okay, Just Jadon . . ." Morgan's a head shorter than me, but her zero-fucks-given-since-birth presence makes up for it. "Ready for the tour?"

I glance at my schedule again. I'm used to Académie's simple format—one room where most courses are taught with the same instructor, same faces. Willow Wood's classes are all over the place.

"I'm not waiting!"

When I look again, Morgan's halfway down the hall. Reluctantly, I double-time to catch up.

We're excused from first hour. Morgan shows off the two-story library. On the north side of campus is a visual arts center, an independent research facility, and the aquatic center. Computer, science, and drama labs are on the west side.

We pause at an alarmingly large stadium dedicated to their American football team. "Is that necessary?" I ask.

"In case you couldn't tell," Morgan says, "outside of academics, *this* is where most of the school budget goes."

"Are they any good?"

"Worst win-loss record in LA County!" She fakes a grin. "Donors are hyper-focused on producing the next Chad-Ben-Tom-whatever Super Bowl champion. As if Willow Wood hasn't birthed countless senators, scientists, and entertainers."

Her eyes scan over my physique. "My bad. Are you the sporty type?"

On weekends, while Réverie's marketplace is thrumming with patrons and sellers, I'd sneak away to the long stretch of grass tucked away from sight. There, I could always find kids playing football. The *real* football. After hours of running around, I'd bribe everyone with crème glacée to swear they never saw me.

I don't tell Morgan any of this. She seems as uninterested in me as I am in this tour. Instead, I say, "As much as anyone else is."

A bell rings. In the distance, students pour into the halls.

Without another word, Morgan escorts me and Ajani back to the main building.

After ditching my blazer—Southern California in September is too warm for layers—in my locker, I ask, stiffly, "Do I go to class now?"

Morgan scans my schedule. "Hmm. AP Lit and Composition. Okay, genius." She walks me to the classroom. "Pro tip: mythology is Professor Bayron's jam. Always highlight those sections for quizzes."

I force myself not to roll my eyes. "Noted."

Two hours later, Morgan's waiting for me outside the dining hall. It's not enough that I had to sit through uninvited stares from classmates and these prehistoric courses Americans call "education." Now, I'm being subjected to obligatory social time, also known as lunch.

"You look exhausted," she comments.

Jutting my chin, I huff, "Not even."

"Are you sure? We have a quiet room. A designated outdoor meditation space," she lists off. "Oh, and a coffee bar."

Of course they do. "I'm fine."

She spins away. "Come on, Just Jadon. Time for intros."

The quad is an exaggerated space. Wooden benches planted beneath the shade of thick laurel trees. Stone tables where kids eat or soak up sun from the cloudless sky. Conversations chase each other over hip-hop music from someone's phone. The air's spiced with fresh-cut grass and heady ocean breeze and too much body spray.

While we walk, more students pause to stare at me. Not as

many as I expected. Most are too busy on their phones. No one approaches us, though. Maybe it's the instinctive scowl I keep having to wipe off my face.

I hear Samuel's voice in the back of my head: *New Jadon likes his peers.*

"And over there . . ."

Morgan points toward a fountain. A second passes before I realize she's not talking about the marble dolphin sprouting from the center of the water. It's the two students sitting on the fountain's edge, looking like every popular clique from the teen dramas I secretly stream during boring press conferences and long flights. They have this charged air of untouchableness. The same energy me and Kofi had.

"Those are my friends," Morgan finishes. "Nathan Lim and Grace Miller."

Nathan is striking. Light brown eyes, round cheeks that contrast nicely with his sharp jaw. He pushes long, dark bangs off his face, laughing at something Grace says. His tie is undone, shirt untucked. Under his snowy-white Air Force 1s is a skateboard.

Grace is the girl from the welcome banner. Sharp green eyes. Shiny auburn hair chopped just under her chin. She sits like she *knows* people are supposed to pay attention. Her uniform's altered to show off every inch of her toned body.

"Nate's parents are pharmaceutical researchers," Morgan says. "Big donors. As in the Lim Science Building."

I nod as if I'm impressed, even though I'm not.

"And Princess Grace—not my nickname for her," Morgan clarifies, "is the daughter of a senator and '80s pop singer. Willow Wood's sweetheart."

She waves at Grace, leading me over to the fountain.

"So, the rumors are true." Grace stands, then nails an effortless curtsy. "Welcome, Prince Jadon. Grace Miller, student body president."

"And yearbook prez. Student gov prez. Cheer captain," Nathan lists off, amused. "Editor of the lit mag—"

"Thanks, Nate," Grace says with a slight edge.

He's unfazed. With an electric grin, he extends his fist toward me. "Nate."

"Boring, basic, skater-bro," Morgan narrates, flopping down next to him.

"You left off podcaster, second chair violinist in the orchestra," Nathan teases after I reluctantly bump his fist, "and drop-dead gorgeous."

"Or you could just drop dead," Morgan says with little heat.

He clutches his chest in mock pain. "Morg, babe. Seriously? Weren't we supposed to Hulu and chill Friday night?"

"God, Lim, no." It's the first time I notice a smile nudging at Morgan's cheeks. "I'm into girls, remember?"

"And I'm only into guys on the weekends." Nathan rests his head on her shoulder. "Why's that stopping us?"

"You're disturbed."

Nathan laughs huskily. "Does that turn you on?"

"So," Grace says, side-eyeing what's happening to her right. She scoots over to make room for me. "Your Highness—"

"Jadon is fine," I say for the thousandth time today, but with a prim smile.

"Jadon," she repeats, smirking. "Enjoying Willow Wood?"

"It's—" Again, Samuel's comments from earlier disrupt my urge to unload about how pretentious and overdone this school is. "Beautiful," I finish.

She cocks her head. "First time to LA?"

"No."

"Of course not," Grace says as if she was simply testing my own knowledge on . . . myself. "Your mom's from around here, right? Palisades?"

I square my shoulders. "Long Beach, actually."

"Sick vibes out there," Nathan comments. On his other side, Morgan crunches on a bag of Takis she must've pulled from her backpack.

"And single, too?" Grace arches a dark eyebrow. "Mutual or messy breakup?"

My jaw tightens. I haven't shared the details about what happened with Léon to anyone. But here's Willow Wood's class president, someone I've barely known five minutes, staring at me expectantly like I'm going to word vomit my entire relationship history. A familiar itching fire starts in my chest. I've officially gone from annoyed to *why the fuck am I still here* territory.

I don't let old Jadon take over. Not completely. I flash her an enormous grin, all teeth, no warmth, and repeat what every good royal says when faced with a topic nobody needs to know about: "No comment."

A beat. Grace's smile doesn't falter, but her eyes gleam.

"*Chill*, Gracie," Nathan says, and Grace's head immediately snaps in his direction, like she hates that nickname. "You can go all investigative journalist on my boy Jadon at this boujee-ass party we're throwing him Friday night."

"Sorry." I blink. "At the . . . what?"

"A small gathering," Grace insists, lips curling almost con-spiratorially. "A Welcome to America kickback. At Nate's house."

"Folks are up in Palo Alto for a conference," Nathan elabo-rates. "It's gonna be fire."

I stare at him like he's speaking an alien language.

"You don't have to come," Morgan starts.

"He wants to!" Grace cheers. "Ooh, let's do a TikTok. Intro you to all the fans."

Words try to scratch up my throat, but I'm too late. Everything happens so swiftly. Grace passes Nathan her phone. He gets into position while she tosses an arm around my rigid shoulders. All I can do is unclench my ass cheeks enough to smile at the lens, praying no one notices how hor-rified my eyes are.

A shadow falls over us, disrupting the shot. My gaze flicks to the source.

From behind one of those fancy Canon cameras, a boy smiles. It's hard to tell from my position, but he looks al-most my height. Medium fawn skin with near-black eyes. His hair is short, tiny waves at the top. It's also dyed a vi-brant pink.

In a smooth voice, he says, "Sorry, you're blocking my

shot." He motions his lens toward the fountain. "I need it for my—"

"That's nice," Grace interrupts in a tone that's equally sugary and terse. "Everyone knows this is *our* spot."

Pink Boy doesn't flinch. "Actually," he says, "it's *Willow Wood's* property. Specifically, Sébastien Tremblay, the actor. He's an alumnus. Donated the fountain ten years ago after winning a Tony." His grin is crooked. Endearing. Not that I really notice. "And if we're getting into more details, this land belonged to—"

"We get it." Grace sighs. "We're still not moving."

"Cool." Pink Boy adjusts his camera angle. "I'll shoot around you."

I bite my lip, feeling every muscle in my face aching to smile.

Who is this guy?

Grace's expression resets. Softer, politer. "Sorry, um," she prompts.

"Reiss," Pink Boy volunteers.

"Reiss," Grace says flatly. "We're almost done. Recording a quick TikTok with our newest student . . ." She waves her hand in front of me like he should already know who I am.

Reiss studies me, curiously.

My cheeks blister. It's way too hot out here.

"If you could just wait over there." Grace signals to a nearby recycling bin. "Thanks for your patience."

I wait for Reiss's reaction. He doesn't stomp away. Cry on the spot at Grace's dismissal. Instead, he points that crooked smile right at me. He bows dramatically like some aristocrat in a regency film, before disappearing.

For a moment, my brain is on a loop of *what the fuck just happened?* that Grace clearly doesn't notice.

She says, "So, you'll be there Friday night. At Nate's. For the party."

After the bell rings, it hits me—Grace wasn't making a request.

3

"Are we sure a *party* is a good idea?" is the first thing Annika says when I stroll into our Palisades living room.

I pause at the gilded framed mirror on the wall, inspecting my appearance. Curls tight, cheeks still glowing from a hot shower. Thanks to my rigorous skincare routine, the stress zit is gone. I straighten my Boss Henley. The turquoise brings out the gold undertones in my complexion, and it matches my mystic green Air Jordan 1 Mids.

I'm going for *I'm a friendly, approachable prince,* but also *please don't talk to me.*

"Jade."

I spin around, almost forgetting Annika's question. She's sipping boba on the beige love seat. My face wrinkles. "Is this what you did all week? While I worked my ass off trying to fit in at a new school?"

She grins shamelessly. "It's rose milk tea! We really need a bubble tea shop back home."

"That's not helping."

"Don't change the subject," she chastises lightly. "Is this the best idea? Considering what happened at the last party you attended."

"That was different."

"How?"

Well, for one, my best friend won't be there to sell me out, I almost say. It's crossed my mind. That attending another un-supervised gathering isn't the right move. But Grace said it'd be small. I can handle that, right?

Samuel answers for me: "C'est fantastique!" He glides into the room, clapping. "The prince needs to be seen making friends with his peers. Having fun! *Not* drinking."

When his back is turned, I roll my eyes.

He scrolls through his phone. "It doesn't hurt that he's a *hit* with Miss Miller's followers."

I fiddle with the buttons of my Henley. It was one TikTok. A brief hello, then Grace forcing me to do a silly dance. Nothing exciting. But, somehow, it's ended up all over the news.

"This party's the prime occasion to push our New Jadon narrative to new heights," Samuel is saying.

"New. Heights," I parrot.

"I don't want his new 'friends'"—Annika air quotes aggressively—"to turn out like the last one."

I fight off a grimace. Annika's the one who found me sulking in a Beverly Hills hotel suite when they first arrived in LA. Days after Kofi abandoned me. After he shoved shots in my hand, goading me into talking about Barnard, letting some random girl film it. Kofi, who I'd known since I started at Académie des Jeunes Dirigeants.

I spin around, grinning. "Aww. You care?"

"Shut up." Her lips flinch into a smile.

We're back. Memory forgotten.

"If you mess this up," she warns, "I'll never get to take that trip to New York."

Luc, who's also inexcusably slurping boba, says, "You're never winning that bet."

She ignores his cool smile. "They'll kick us out of America. Permanently."

"That's a bad thing?" When she starts chewing her lip, I add, "Anni, it's a party. Nothing to worry about."

"I'm always worried with you."

I flash a sarcastic grin. "Which is why you're getting premature gray hairs."

Annika gasps, her free hand patting her curls as Ajani steps into the room.

"The car is here."

"I'll be home by 2:00 a.m.," I say, checking my reflection one last time.

"Get your royal ass home by midnight!" Annika demands, and I bark out a laugh, shadowing Ajani to the front door.

Grace is a filthy liar.

The small, intimate party she promised has been swallowed whole by a bass-thumping rave. The Lims' mansion is in Brentwood, a ten-minute drive from Pacific Palisades. Lining the narrow street are countless cars: Mercedes-Benz, Tesla, Range Rover, Bentley, BMW, more Range Rovers, a stray neon-green Lamborghini. The long driveway is full too. Spilling out the front door are vaguely familiar faces from school and an unhealthy amount of pop music.

From the SUV's passenger seat, Ajani asks, "Are you sure you want me to wait out here?"

A second later, some freshman-looking student dry heaves into a potted plant by the door. Standing nearby, arms crossed and hip cocked, is Morgan. She's staring me down.

"Yeah," I exhale, already opening the door, "I'm good."

"It's not you I'm worried about," Ajani mumbles.

I salute her before strolling in Morgan's direction. "Were you waiting on me?"

"I have better things to do than babysit you," she says with that same dryness she's given me all week.

"That wasn't a no," I say.

"Have you always been this full of yourself, or is it part of your royal training?"

I shrug. "Comes with the scepter and ring, actually."

The corners of her mouth give the barest twitch. It's something, I guess. Not that I'm invested in whether she likes me or my jokes.

"Is this what you Americans consider a 'small gathering'?" I ask.

"Scared of a little rager?" she taunts.

I scoff. "You've never been around me and my best—" I catch myself, quickly resetting my expression. "This is nothing."

Inside, something shatters. I jump.

Morgan pats my shoulder. "Whatever you say, Just Jadon."

The interior is a masterclass in polished indulgence. Two stories of fine art and wood panels and open spaces with minimalistic furniture. Long stretches of muted colors occasionally interrupted by pops of red or green. It's big, yet simultaneously tiny with all the bodies coming and going.

"Chillest spot is the sofas outside," Morgan says over the synth-heavy music. "Best bathrooms are upstairs. Don't mess with the hot tub's temp. Nate's dad will know. And please don't be one of those uncivilized assholes who pees in the pool—"

"I can handle myself," I cut in.

Compared to the parties and clubs and dark, smelly, after-hours places Kofi snuck us into since we were fourteen, LA is harmless.

Morgan sizes me up. "Sure."

She easily dances through the crowd of bobbing heads toward the kitchen.

After a beat, I reluctantly follow.

Grace is the heart of the party. The luminous light all the other Willow Wood moths swarm toward. She's perched on the black marble kitchen island, chatting with various girls but never really *talking* to anyone. It's mildly impressive.

Behind her, Nathan is shirtless, pool water flinging off the ends of his cheek-length bangs as he mixes drinks in a metal shaker.

Leaning next to Grace is a white boy with copper-blond curls, deep blue eyes, and a long, well-toned frame. He's double-fisting White Claws. Annika would say he has "extreme bro vibes."

"Who's that?" I ask Morgan, far enough away that no one hears us.

She sighs. "Kaden. Graduated last year. Grace's ex or current fling. I don't know."

Judging by the concurrent flush in her cheeks and curl of her lips when Kaden whispers in her ear, Grace hasn't decided either.

When we reach them, Grace drops air-kisses to both my cheeks. She smells like rosewater and a hint of chlorine, even though her clothes are completely dry. "You're late to your own party."

"I wasn't expecting so many people," I say.

She bats innocent lashes. "Everyone wants to meet a prince IRL."

I strain out a smile.

"What do you think?" Grace waves her arms around like a game show host presenting a prize.

I finally take everything in. Red-and-white-striped plastic cups. Patriotic balloons. The WELCOME TO AMERICA banner taped along the kitchen's black cabinets. Even their outfits are themed: Grace in a star-spangled tank top, Nathan's stars-and-blues trunks, Kaden's MADE IN THE USA T-shirt, and Morgan's bare minimum effort of a patriotic scrunchie around her wrist to match her denim cut-off shorts.

I attempt to keep my face neutral. "Thank you?"

Grace shouts, "Welcome to America, Jadon!"

The crowd mimics, "Welcome to America, Jadon!" over the noise of a blender. When it cuts off, Nathan yells, "Frosé all day!"

"Frosé all day!"

I blink, stunned. Morgan shrugs it off, as if this is common party law. She joins Grace on the island, tugging out her phone.

"So, this is the famous prince." Kaden bumps my shoulder with his.

My eyes immediately narrow.

"Welcome to LA, Your Highness. What can my guy Nate get you?"

Nathan beams. "I make a *sick* blue martini."

"Sick as in you'll be hospitalized after one sip," Morgan comments without lifting her eyes. Nathan sticks his tongue out at her.

"I don't drink," I say.

"Oh, *riiight.*" Kaden tosses an unwanted arm around my shoulders. "Not since the vid, yeah? That shit was hilarious. I watched it like ten times."

"Kaden," Grace hisses when a handful of girls around us snicker.

"What, babe?" Kaden downs the rest of his drink before adding, "We've all seen it. Are we just gonna ignore the giant elephant in the room?"

He grins at me in an almost challenging way. I know his type. The spoiled, self-absorbed boy who hates having the attention on anything but him. He's expecting me to crumble. Slip into the shadows like a wounded dog so he can have the spotlight back.

Unfortunately for him, I'm used to playing—and winning—this game.

"Actually." My mouth pulls into a silky smile. "I avoid drinking because, somehow, I end up hanging around rich, needy toddlers who use getting wasted as an excuse to be the true assholes they've always been."

We're almost the same height, but I still look down at him.

"But that's not you," I say, "is it?"

The music's still playing, but there's this beat of silence around us. No one moves.

Finally, Nathan says, "Wow, roasted!"

The nearby girls snort-giggle. Someone coughs, "*damn bro*" from behind us. Grace leans back, amused.

Kaden stares at me for a second. Then, he says, "It's official. I like you, dude."

Soon, I'm immersed in the group's activities. I grudgingly participate in drinking games with glasses of water. Pose for selfies with whoever Grace introduces me to. Wave at someone's mom over Snapchat. Answer dozens of questions like: *How many countries have you visited? Can you solve climate change? HAVE YOU MET BEYONCÉ?*

"Holy fuck," Morgan says out of nowhere, raising her phone. "You guys know that SEC quarterback? The one who turned his back during the national anthem?"

Nathan leans his elbows on the island. "Kenzie Malcolm? Wasn't he wearing an I LOVE A COUNTRY WHO DOESN'T LOVE ME BACK shirt?"

Morgan snaps her fingers. "Yes!"

"What about him?" Kaden asks, annoyed.

"He's being benched for at least five games," Morgan says. "There's talk of NFL teams blackballing him for the draft."

Nathan's face twists up. "Over a *shirt?*"

"Good." Kaden opens another beer, squeezing between Grace and Morgan. "What an idiot move."

"His best friend was wrongfully murdered by cops," Morgan says, exasperated. She hops off the island, shaking her head. "He was making a statement."

Kaden rolls his eyes. "There are other ways of doing that *without* ruining your fucking future. Vote. Make a TikTok. Sign a petition or whatever."

"Dude, don't be an ass," Nathan says, laughing.

"I'm serious," Kaden groans. "What did he accomplish?"

Morgan shoves her phone screen in his face. "Got people's attention. Everyone's talking about it. There's even a hashtag."

"A *hashtag?*" Kaden gasps dramatically, his hand reaching up to clutch invisible pearls. "OMG, that'll save so many lives."

"You're a dick."

"And you're unrealistic." He chugs his beer, sliding an arm around Grace's shoulders. She shrugs it off, but doesn't add anything to the discussion.

Kaden turns his eyes to me. "What d'you think, Prince?"

I stiffen. Nathan's brows are lifted curiously. Grace tilts her

41

head, while Morgan crosses her arms. People whose names I still can't remember are staring.

A crackling heat flickers behind my ribs.

All my life, I've watched Papa answer questions like this. Réverie isn't like other countries. We live by different rules. *Survive* by staying as far from others' conflicts as possible. I know what I'm supposed to say.

But the fire in my chest sparks hotter when I think about the points Morgan made. What Kaden said. It's just like the day I overheard the prime minister. That night with Kofi.

I can't, I remind myself.

Carefully, I say, "Is it fair to have an opinion on something that doesn't affect me?"

It's too quiet for a beat. Nathan's face scrunches up like he's either contemplating my words or swallowed a bad piece of fruit. Something flashes across Morgan's eyes, then disappears when Kaden shouts, "Exactly! This guy gets it!"

Grace raises her cup. Others join, nodding. Faces blur together until I lose Morgan to the crowd.

After the music switches to a K-pop song everyone knows, I say, "Need some fresh air," not that anyone notices.

The night breeze is refreshing. My nerves are still buzzing, but my chest's cooling. I bypass the pool, waving to anyone who calls my name. I don't stop, though. I'm not in the mood to mingle anymore.

I need time alone to regroup.

As Morgan promised, at a far corner of the lawn, plushy furniture sits empty. In the center, a fire pit spits orangey light. I flop onto a deep blue sofa. Over the glass partition is a glittery view of Los Angeles. I wiggle my phone free from my back pocket to snap a photo.

Instinctively, I open my messages. Sitting at the top of my inbox is my thread with Kofi. It's where I'd always go after a shitty headline. A fight with my ex. Whenever the feeling in my chest got too hot.

But we're not like that anymore.

He didn't even look at me when the video was released. Just packed his bags and left while I was showering, after my call with Papa. No explanations. Now, he won't answer any calls. The remains of our friendship are nothing more than a series of unanswered blue message bubbles.

"Asshole."

I almost drop my phone when someone collapses next to me.

Pink Boy. *Reiss*.

He wipes his phone screen across his chest. "Nobody appreciates the sacred art of short filmmaking anymore." He glares in the direction of the pool.

The lights at the bottom of the water give everyone a fluorescent blue hue. Someone yells, "Marco!" The other swimmers squeal, "Polo!"

While he's not looking, I *casually* skim my eyes over his body. Water spots darken his pale green shorts. His frond-print button-up is also damp. The fire's glow highlights his round jaw. He absently licks his lips.

"Luckily, they didn't damage the equipment." He holds up his iPhone. It's not the latest model like every other student around campus carries. But there's no cracks either. The black

43

case says, in capitalized white letters, I LIKE FILMMAKING AND MAYBE 3 PEOPLE.

A surprised snort escapes my nose.

Reiss smiles.

This close, I notice the little details I missed the first time. His long fingers drumming on his knee. Tiny wrinkles in his forehead, like he's always thinking about something. The helix piercings in both his ears with twin hoop earrings. How his eyes are a rich, dark brown like a forest cast in shadow.

He clears his throat. I've been staring too long, too hard. I try to think of something nonchalant to say.

"Nice . . . shorts." *Okay, not that.* Now he probably thinks I was checking out his crotch. I straighten my shoulders. "Nice *night*. Great party."

Wonderful. Years of conversational training and that's the best I have.

Reiss doesn't seem to care. "I shouldn't even be here," he says. "My best friend dragged me. This is *his* crowd. Only cause his family's loaded." He makes a face at that last comment. "Not that he's not dope on his own. He totally is. I'd fight a hippo for him and—"

"Sorry, you'd do what?"

A blush spreads over his cheeks. "Fight a hippo? Wow. I really said that."

"You did," I confirm.

"Anyway, Karan's awesome," he says. "I tag along to these things so my parents don't think I'm lonely. Or tragic. Or desperate."

"Are you?"

"Sorry, you're a stranger and that's confidential information. Can't show off my emo to just anyone."

My lips have this need to grin. So, he's kind of funny. A little interesting too.

"You should be careful," he warns.

I furrow my brow. "Why?"

"No one told you?" He leans in, whispering, "I'm a scholarship kid. Instant social outcast status."

Fine. He's *really* funny. "Who said you were cool enough for social outcast status?"

"Ouch!" His laugh is scratchy, low. He eases back into his former relaxed position. "You got jokes."

I shrug, convinced my proximity to the fire pit is the reason for how hot my skin is.

"Reiss Hayes." He doesn't offer me a handshake or fist bump, or bow like some of my teachers have. Just that crooked smile. "In case you need to know who to avoid on Monday."

He watches me, waiting for a reaction. As if I'll confirm I'm like everyone else at this party—above him. Like I can't wait to get away. Which is how I felt ten minutes ago, under the spotlight of Morgan's friends. But not now.

I kick a foot up on the fire pit's ledge. Get comfortable. I'm *staying*.

"I'm Jad—"

"I know who you are," Reiss cuts in. When my eyes narrow, he stammers, "Not in a stalkerish way. I'm not into gossip or anything either. It's just—"

I interrupt this time. "My reputation arrives a whole time zone before me?"

Another laugh. "People talk. I don't listen. Unless they give me a reason to."

"Is that so?"

"Guess you'll have to get to know me to find out."

Something coy and shy crawls into his eyes. He's blushing again. Like he has zero confidence in what he's doing.

I bite down on my lower lip, steadying my expression. I've been in LA for almost two weeks, and this is the most *me* I've felt around someone new.

We go quiet. My head absently nods along to a dreamy melody coming from a wireless speaker. Tangerine from the fire and blues from his phone screen dance across Reiss's face. Smoke and chlorine fill my lungs. Underneath that, there's a faint, earthy scent clinging to him that I want to ask about.

He speaks first. "Is your first Willow Wood rager everything you expected?"

For a beat, I get lost in the traces of silver moonlight in his pink waves.

"It's . . . okay."

"Okay?" He snorts. "Not as interesting as the other parties you're invited to?"

I pause. His eyes are still on his phone, which is lifted just enough that the lens is pointed at me. Like that night at GOLDRUSH with Kofi.

Is he trying to get me to shit-talk the people here?

A familiar flame sizzles in my chest. Without thinking, I say, "Are you recording this?"

Of course he is. Why wouldn't he? Another amateur with a

camera selling me out to the media. Fuck. Five minutes talking to a cute boy, and I let my guard down.

I gave one more person permission to ruin my life.

Reiss blinks. "What? No, I'm—"

I don't let him finish. "I'm not interested in being in another shitty video for . . . *whatever* it is you're doing."

Something cold creeps into his eyes. It matches the iciness of his tone. "Are you serious right now?"

I glare at him, jaw stiff. "You tell me."

He shakes his head. When I notice the hurt tugging at his lips, I'm too late to say anything else.

"It's a good thing you're nothing like the guy people say you are." Reiss stands, pocketing his phone. "Being that much of an asshole would be exhausting."

"Wait," I attempt.

"Enjoy the party, Your Highness," he whispers, walking away.

I breathe deeply for a moment. Let my chest cool down. Refocus on my priorities. I don't care what Reiss said. It doesn't sting because no one here matters.

I'm leaving soon. Just like I should've left this party the second I walked in.

4

> **10 FUN FACTS ABOUT EVERYONE'S FAV REBEL ROYAL!**
>
> We love a bad boy (especially one with dimples!) as much as the next future royal-suitor-in-the-making. Here's a list of must-have facts about Prince Jadon, one of the world's youngest, broodiest, most eligible royals!
>
>

"So, Jadon, tell us what music you're listening to."

I fight off a yawn. It's 4:00 p.m., but I'm still exhausted from the party last night. From the two hours I spent in bed, staring at the ugly ceiling fixture, replaying Reiss's words in my head.

It's a good thing you're nothing like the guy people say you are.

"Your Highness," Samuel whispers from off-set.

I startle, then grimace at Khalia, the *TeenBuzz* interviewer. She's a young Black woman with short twists and a beautiful smile. Her head tilts as she waits for my answer. She's been patient all afternoon. When the photoshoot ran long because one of the four puppies they brought in—"People love dogs and we want them to love you!" Samuel enthusiastically explained—decided to pee on my shoes, delaying our start time by an hour, she didn't complain.

We're at a studio in the Arts District of Downtown Los Angeles. Samuel scheduled today's meeting to help boost Shiny New Jadon's fun side. I briefly stare off into the LED lights surrounding us, considering Khalia's earlier question.

So far, the interview has been easy, if not basic. Topics I could talk about in my sleep. If I got any, that is. But I'm feeling weirdly nervous. Like I'm being interrogated by Papa instead of someone who looks fresh out of university.

Every answer needs to be flawless, or I'll never get back to Rêverie.

"You can look at your playlist," Khalia offers, as if she can sense my anxiousness.

I let out a small laugh. "No, no. It's fine. Lately, I've been into a bunch of underground hip-hop. Some indie R&B artists. A little pop. House music."

"A man of taste," Khalia comments, impressed. "Any specifics?"

I think for a moment. "Moonglow."

Her eyes brighten. "Interesting. Do you have a fav?"

I wiggle around in my chair. A realization lights up in my brain like a giant neon sign: I only know one of their songs. The one that was playing while I was sitting outside with Reiss.

"Not really," I answer.

"Are you sure?" She sits forward in her own chair, beaming. "The dimples are out."

Reflexively, I reach up to touch my cheeks, then drop my hand. "It's nothing."

"Does their music remind you of someone?"

Maybe. "Not at all," I lie.

"A lot of their songs have a romantic vibe," Khalia notes. "Is it the kind of music you'd play for a crush? Potential boyfriend?"

My eyes cheat to Samuel. His face is growing increasingly concerned. Behind Khalia, the cameras feel closer than they were before. I rub my sweaty palms on the designer jeans selected for me. Typically, these questions are given to me in advance, but I didn't request them this time.

This was supposed to be a simple, *fun* interview.

What would Annika say?

I clear my throat. "That's a very unoriginal way to tell someone how you feel."

Well, she definitely wouldn't say *that*.

Somewhere, behind the lights, I hear Samuel facepalming.

Khalia's brow wrinkles. "All right," she starts slowly, "well, for any of our lucky readers here in the US who *might* be interested—how could they get your attention?"

"Be genuine? Friendly? Funny?" I offer.

Samuel, coming into focus now, gives me two ecstatic thumbs up.

But then my mind zooms back to Nathan's backyard. The splash of the pool. Cool night air. A pink-haired boy. The phone in his hand.

"Also, don't be a jerk pretending to like me for clout," I finish.

"Mon Dieu," Samuel mutters.

Khalia laughs. "Is that a joke?"

When I don't blink, she straightens her spine, trying to hold on to a smile that's quickly fading. "Noted. Let's move on to TV shows, I guess," Khalia says, like she can't wait for this interview to end.

She's not the only one.

Every morning before the first bell, Grace insists we spend time in Willow Wood's courtyard as a group.

"For good energy," she claims.

I'd rather spend that extra time in bed. Or anywhere other than with people I won't remember in a few months. But after my disastrous *TeenBuzz* interview, it's not optional.

I need to step up my game or I'm stuck here.

The courtyard is the first area students walk through each day. Grace always chooses the wooden benches closest to the front arch. She's next to me, intensely studying SAT flashcards—I'm *crushed* that I'll never know the joys of American standardized tests—while I scroll my phone.

"What about Top Ten horror movies?"

Opposite us, Nathan's tormenting Morgan with a list of ideas for his next podcast.

"You're scared of your own shadow," she says disinterestedly.

"So true." When I look up, Nathan's thoughtfully rubbing his chin. His eyes light up. "How about Top Ten Pixar movies?"

"Didn't you just do a Top Ten episode?" Morgan asks.

A sly grin melts across his face. "So, you listened? Tell me, Morgan Alexander, are you one of my eight hundred faithful subscribers?"

"You wish."

"I wish you and I would—"

Morgan smacks a hand over his mouth. "Finish that sentence and I'll end you, Lim." Then, she yelps, dragging her hand away. "Did you just lick my palm?"

Nathan winks.

"Could we *please* chill with all the nonsense," Grace requests, face pinched. She waves her multicolored index cards around. "Princeton isn't accepting me with a 1350 SAT score."

"Not with that attitude," Nathan claims, chomping into his breakfast burrito.

"Grace, come on," Morgan says, crossing her legs. Today, she's added orange, white, and rose suspenders to her uniform. "Princeton *knows* who your dad is."

"Just like Berkeley knows your stepdad," Grace says, ignoring the way Morgan's eyes narrow. "I don't want to get in because of . . . favoritism."

Morgan shrugs, staring down at her manicure. I'm so distracted by how easily she shuts off Grace's tone that I don't notice Nathan pivoting in my direction.

"Sup, Prince J?" He grins, collar popped, skin sun-kissed. "Got any suggestions for a fresh, new episode of *Nate Debates*?"

I frown. "That's the name? You can't be serious?"

"He is," Morgan and Grace say in unison.

"I'm listening," Nathan singsongs.

I hold in a sigh. As much as I want to walk away from this silly conversation, that's not what Annika would do. What a *respectable* prince would do. I study Nathan: hair pulled into a sloppy topknot, small acne breakout on his chin, his uniform slacks one size too big. Resting under his scuffed Vans is a brand-new skateboard.

"Isn't there a skatepark nearby?"

I saw it in a handful of Mom's old photos.

"Venice," Nathan volunteers, smirking like he can already see where I'm going.

"What about an episode focused on its history?" I suggest. "How it's changed. Interview some of the nonwhite skaters. Get their takes."

Nathan whoops and Grace's cards go flying. I almost laugh. "Genius, Prince J," he crows, stretching to offer me another fist bump.

With the face of a boy who's betraying generations of royal decorum, I reciprocate.

"Now that that's settled . . ." Grace snaps her fingers.

A random sophomore appears out of nowhere. She swiftly gathers Grace's fallen cards like a cartoon minion desperate for praise.

Grace doesn't give it to her, instead turning to Morgan with a sweet smile, as if nothing happened two minutes ago. "Babes, can you help me with my Honors English paper later?"

My face twists up. Morgan's considering it.

Nathan says, "Yo, why don't you just buy a paper off—"

"Some of us want to *earn* our grades," Grace says, turning back to Morgan. "We can go shopping for our Sunset Ball gowns after. Which reminds me—my dad says you're giving a speech at the ball, Jadon?"

I almost forgot about that. I didn't plan on being here that long.

"Yes," I say casually.

"Do you have a date yet?" Grace asks.

"No." I scratch the back of my neck. "Is that required?"

"Of course! You're a guest of honor." She trades her index cards for her phone. "I'll help. Are you on any dating apps?"

"I'm a *prince*," I deadpan. "And seventeen."

She rolls her eyes as if those aren't real barriers. "No worries. Are you into college guys? Actors? I know this one pop singer, total twink—"

"Are you allowed to use that word?" Nathan says, head cocked.

Grace waves him off. "Anyone at the party catch your eye?" One of her dark brows curves up. "You disappeared for a hot min."

"Ooh!" Nathan coos before I can deflect. "Smashing at your own welcome party? Sweet."

My nose wrinkles.

"Who was it?" Nathan eagerly asks. "Alex? Wilhelm, the exchange student? Wait—was it Eddie?"

"It wasn't—" I stand, shaking my head. "*Nothing* happened."

I didn't hide in a corner. Talk to a beautiful boy. Get dragged by said beautiful boy for accusing him of selling me out to the highest-paying news outlet.

Also, when did Reiss go from cute to *beautiful*?

On cue, I hear a familiar laugh. My eyes are drawn to the

noise. It's Reiss, hand on the shoulder of a lanky boy with terra-cotta skin and swoopy black hair. He's relaxed, cracking up. So different from the party.

Meanwhile, I'm breathing hard like I just ran a marathon. Reiss doesn't notice. But someone else does.

Morgan smiles wickedly, mouthing, *Really?*

I snatch my messenger bag from the ground, puffing my chest out. "Forgot something in my . . . locker," I say with only a small stammer. "So. See you!"

Problem is, I can't get to whatever imaginary item I don't need. Because my locker is jammed. I try the combination three times. Kick the door. Slam my shoulder against it until there's a dull throb moving through my muscles.

Still, nothing.

The warning bell rings. No one stops to help me. I have no friends here. Shiny New Prince Jadon is having zero effect since I'm still the scowly, silent, chin-high Jadon I was before coming to Willow Wood. I'm two seconds from calling Ajani to leave school early, when someone steps in.

The heat hits me first—his long frame fitting into the sliver of space between me and the locker. Next, an earthy, almost smoky scent. The burst of pink waves. It's him again, shoulder pressed firmly to the steel door while his long fingers jiggle the handle. He's all practiced motions and not pathetic, petulant whining over defective craftsmanship.

As he works, the wings of his shoulder blades brush my chest. I inhale sharply. Should I move? Give him more room?

55

Why is my body so content being this close to Reiss?

The door pops open. "Lift, then nudge," he advises coldly.

I finally step back, awed. "How did you—"

My words die in my throat. Reiss is already walking away.

He didn't wait for me to finish. Didn't give me thirty seconds to explain my reaction from the other night. Three words is all I get.

That and a clear view of his backside—which I'm pointedly not staring at—as he strides down the hall.

My face flushes. Anger flickers in my chest. Climbs past my tonsils. Who is he to ignore me? Swoop in like some pink-haired, fairy-tale hero and not even let me thank him?

I yell, "I could've handled it on my own!"

I didn't need him. I almost had the damn locker open.

Reiss barely pauses to shout, "Whatever you say, Your Royal Arrogance!"

Headmaster Parker's head pops out of the main offices, searching for where the disturbance is coming from.

I wave sheepishly, pasting on a camera-ready smile.

And Reiss is . . . gone. Not another word. Disappearing like whatever hopes I had of making this plan to win the world over work.

"Have you been to the pier yet?"

On my phone screen, Mom's tightening her favorite purple-and-emerald silk scarf over her graying curls. I feel bad for video calling her so late. It's a little after 4:00 p.m. here, which means it's closer to midnight in Réverie.

I just—I needed to see her. Despite how we left things after Papa banned me, hearing her voice and staring into her deep brown eyes loosens the corkscrew coiled in my chest.

"Not yet," I reply.

"You should," Mom says.

Judging by the pale indigo walls and pieces of gilded-accented furniture in the background, Mom's in her private sitting room. The low lighting can't hide the exhaustion in her shoulders. Or the laughter lines I know are from years and years ago, when life was less complicated.

When everything she or Annika or I did wasn't scrutinized down to the shoes we wore.

"I always wanted to take you," she laments, a faraway look on her face as if she's imagining it. "To Santa Monica Pier."

I can't remember much about California back then. Not my first trip to the beach. The cool rush of Pacific water splashing my ankles. Sitting under soaring palm trees with Mom. I see it in photos, of course, the press obsessively trailing us to get new snaps of Princess Ava and her two children, but there's one memory that sticks out: standing barefoot on my grandparents' deck, watching everyone else enjoy the sun and water, but not us.

"We can't be like them," Mom said.

It's still that way. Me, far from everything, unable to be like them. Like anyone, really.

My mom's voice pulls me out of my head. "I bet the beach is beautiful right now."

"Mom," I half-snort, "the beach is always beautiful."

"It is."

"But it's not Réverie," I whisper.

Silence hangs over us like a ghost. It wasn't like that before. Since I was strong enough to crawl into her lap, Mom's always had a story to share. A way to feed my hunger for life outside of Centauri's walls. When she had more time for me.

I kick off my sneakers—a pair of Kobe 5 Lakers that complement the yellow in my uniform—before stretching out on a bed that still doesn't feel like mine. I angle my phone until I'm back in focus.

"How are things there?"

Mom hums softly. She's going through her nightly skincare routine, which is almost as aggressive as mine. Being royalty doesn't exclude me, a seventeen-year-old, from acne or blocked pores.

"The usual. Meetings and such." A wry smile tugs at her lips. "Oprah invited me to another women's summit. Keynote speaker."

"Opening?"

"Closing," she says with fake outrage. "I'm nobody's opening act, Canelé."

Absently, I grin. *Canelé.* Mom's nickname for me.

A range of languages are spoken on Réverie, French and English being the most prominent. Despite being married to Papa for over two decades, Mom's French is still fairly bad. She knows her pastries, though. As a toddler, she claims I'd sneak handfuls of canelés—a warm rum-and-vanilla-flavored bread with a caramelized crust—from her plate. Eventually, she begged the chefs to create a liquor-less version just for me.

"Good for you, Mom," I say, smiling weakly. Another trip. Another moment when she'll be unavailable.

She returns to moisturizing her skin. Her image glitches for a second. Frozen pixels. A reminder of how far I am from her, from the comforts of home.

My chest aches. "What if I—" I pause, the last two words lodged in my throat.

Her brow wrinkles. "What if you what?"

I stare up at the ceiling. The ugly light fixture glares back at me. This isn't my bedroom. This isn't where I want to be. "What if I came home?" I finish.

More silence. I chance a look at my screen. Mom's not frozen again. Instead, she's staring blankly at me, confused. Then, her expression sharpens.

"Are you ready to explain yourself?" she asks. "Tell me and your papa why you decided to openly trash our country's prime minister instead of—what do the kids say? Keep it in the drafts? Save it for the group chats?"

"Mom," I groan, embarrassed. But she's not laughing.

"Are you going to apologize to him?"

I clench my teeth, chewing hard on the "no" ready to burst out. She doesn't understand what she's asking for. My mom's strong, the very definition of resilient, but I can't repeat what Barnard said that day.

Look at what we've become. No one respects our monarch. Because of her. She's an outsider. Toxic. And now her influence is corrupting the crown princess and that boy. They don't belong here. She's not one of us. Never will be!

I can't hurt her like that.

"Jadon," she says with a heavy, tired breath. "Where is this coming from? Why are you constantly acting out? Is it stress? Is about what happened with Lé—"

"It's *not* him," I say hastily, pinching the bridge of my nose.

"Then what?"

I drop my hand. On the other side of the screen, the exhausted lines around Mom's face have turned hard. She's frustrated. So am I. Anger bubbles inside my chest like those exploding candies dropped into a bottle of soda.

"What if I just came home?" I say, desperate. "What if I just got on a plane and—"

"You can't."

"What if I did it anyway?" I laugh roughly. "What's Papa going to do if I just show up?"

Mom doesn't smile. "He'll cut off your royal funds," she says, cool and even. "Revoke your title. Until you're twenty-one. Maybe longer." She rubs her temple. "If you come home before proving to us you're the prince we raised you to be, he'll assign you to the Royal Council of State. You'll work side-by-side with the prime minister. You'll be so busy inside the palace, we'll never have to worry about the Jadon you choose to show everyone else."

"Is that"—I swallow hard—"what he said?"

She sighs. "I can't change his mind on this one."

I blink, an unwanted sting behind my eyelashes. My lungs are tight, my free hand shaking on the bed. It's never been this extreme with Papa. Never this . . . *final*. But I have to know one more thing.

After another swallow, I ask, "Is that how *you* feel?"

It's not uncommon for Papa to be so strict. The moment he was confirmed as Réverie's new king, he took his position seriously. Follows every rule, never missteps. Sometimes, I think Annika's just like him. But Mom's different, like me.

At least, I thought she was.

Her stare is a mix of sadness and resolve. "Take advantage of this opportunity, Canelé," she advises. "It'll be good for you."

It's not the answer I wanted.

"This is your chance to grow up," she continues. "Are you always going to solve your problems by ignoring them? Running away? Making a scene?"

I bite on the edge of my tongue to stop anything from spilling out of my eyes. To keep my attention off the flickering flame in my heart. To prevent myself from saying something I'll regret.

"Prove yourself," she says. "Or don't. The decision is yours."

5

After ending my call with Mom, I find Annika poolside, stretched across one of the lounge chairs with a paperback in hand. California's picturesque skies have nothing on the colorful design of her luxury beach dress. Not too far away, Luc has earbuds in, watching something on a tablet.

I angrily throw myself into the empty chair next to Annika.

There's a decorative pillow digging into my spine. I toss it into the pool.

She lowers her copy of *Royal Holiday*, then her sunglasses. "I'm not paying for that," she says firmly.

"No, I am," I growl. "Just like I'm paying for one ridiculous video by being exiled to this trashfire of a country."

"Okay." Annika turns to face me. "Mom or Papa?"

"What?"

"You always get like this"—she waves a hand at my wrinkled nose, the elbows on my knees, my posture slouched over like I'm Quasimodo's long-lost son—"whenever it involves either Mom or Papa. So, which is it?"

I sigh. "Both."

"Yeah, that tracks."

Annika doesn't add anything else. She's great at leaving space for me to process situations. Waiting until I've finally unpacked all the clutter in my head before I tell her what's on my mind.

After recapping the conversation with Mom, Annika says, "You know she only wants what's best for you."

"She wants what's best for the throne," I argue. "What'll look good to our people."

"Same thing." Annika shrugs. "When she married Papa, she made a promise. To the throne. Our government. Our country."

I roll my eyes. "Well, I didn't."

"Aww, poor Jadon." She offers me a mocking frown. "Forced to live in a palace. Fly on private jets. He can have anything he wants. Two closets full of the latest and rarest sneakers, and all he has to do is not be a dick twenty-four seven."

"That's a pretty big demand."

My response is met with a pillow to the head. "You can do this, Jade," she insists. "You just have to get out of your own way."

"Again, that's a lot to ask."

Annika puts her book down before pulling her legs under herself. Sunlight kisses her soft cheeks. She looks younger out here. Refreshed. I've missed seeing this side of my sister.

"Hear me out." She waits until I look her in the eye. "What if being in America wasn't *all* about being un-banished?"

"Is that a word?"

"It is now. I'm the crown princess. I have the final say." Before I can protest, she holds up a finger. "Think about it. While we're here, you have a chance to be a teenager. Wasn't that one of the goals? Being normal?"

Her words remind me of what Mom said:

Take advantage of this opportunity, Canelé.

I cross my arms. "What does normal even mean for us?"

"You're always looking at those old photos of Mom," she points out, like she knows what I was just thinking. "This is where she's from. Explore more. Go do the things she did. Mom was in a bunch of school clubs, right?"

I shrug one shoulder. "I guess."

She holds out her hand, palm up. "Give me your phone."

I unlock the screen, checking if I have any incognito tabs left open before passing it over. She swipes around, then raises an eyebrow. My neck starts to sweat—*fuck, what was my last search?*—but Annika quickly moves on.

"Boom!" She flips the screen around. "This is perfect."

It's Willow Wood's newest Instagram post. Auditions for the upcoming fall theater production.

I read the first line of the caption out loud: "*'Willow Wood Academy proudly presents . . . CLUE!'* Ew, are you serious?"

That's her genius idea? A *play*? How will that solve my problems?

"Absolutely!" Annika is practically glowing. "Rehearsals. Costumes. *Peer bonding*. You can get to know more people."

As if spending every morning with Morgan and company isn't enough.

"Plus," Annika adds, "your mediocre acting skills need work."

"I'm not mediocre," I say, offended.

She purses her lips, unconvinced.

I flip her off. "I'm a *thespian*. Idris Elba has nothing on me. Those Willow Wood amateurs would be lucky to share a stage with—"

"Great," Annika interrupts, rereading the post. "Auditions are Thursday afternoon. We can run lines tomorrow."

I choke. It's not the auditioning part that trips me up. I pretend at almost every moment in my life. Memorizing a monologue is easy. It's committing to one more thing that might not change how anyone feels about me. Something that won't impress my parents or get me home any sooner.

"Wait," I try. "I didn't—"

"You're doing it, Jade. Crown princess, remember?" She

points at herself, ignoring my screwed-up face to swipe over my phone screen. "Now that that's settled, let's talk about *this*."

Annika has exited Willow Wood's account and opened my last Instagram search—the profile of one @TheReelReiss.

There's a small chance I got bored in Physics today. Spent half of class figuring out how to spell Reiss's name correctly: like the British football player, not the peanut butter–filled candy. Browsed his grid—careful not to accidentally like any of his photos—during lunch. It's nothing. I was simply gathering intel on the enemy.

"He's cute," Annika says.

"Not my type," I immediately announce.

"I like his hair. Nice smile too."

"It's horrible. There should be laws against . . . looking like that."

She rolls her eyes. "Is he into filmmaking?"

"Something like that." The second my tone softens, Annika's lips curl up in that triumphant way I truly hate. Flustered, I say, "I mean, I don't know. I don't care either. It's not like we've had conversations or whatever."

"See. Mediocre acting skills." Annika laughs. "What happened to American boys not being worth your time?"

"They're *not*." I snatch my phone back. "None of them."

"Is this about Léon?"

I wince. Why does everyone keep bringing him up? Why does hearing his name still feel like a wooden splinter buried so deep beneath my skin I'd rather cut off a finger than wait for the ache to stop?

"I'm good," I assert. "Reiss is . . . just someone at school. Nobody."

This time, she cackles. "You're so bad at this. They probably won't even give you a speaking part in the play."

Great, now I'll be next in line for the throne, because I'm clearly going to drown my sister in the pool. It's a shame. She had a promising future.

Before I can begin my ascension to crown prince status, Luc gasps, "Oh! No, no, no," throwing a hand over his mouth.

I startle to my feet. "Is it a security threat? Did someone die?"

Luc tugs out his earbuds, lowering the tablet. "Unfortunately, no." He sags defeatedly. "They eliminated Jennie from the villa."

"I'm sorry"—I blink multiple times—"*who*?"

Annika flops into her former position on the lounge chair. "He's obsessed with *Paradise or Purgatory*."

"The reality dating series?" I almost scream, incredulous.

Luc's nose wrinkles like I just said something unforgivable about his family. "It's a brilliant examination of greed, betrayal, and the promise of love. A masterpiece."

Annika shakes her head. "You're a sad human," she says, returning to her book.

When school ends on Thursday, I walk over to Gratton Hall. It houses the three-hundred-seat auditorium where auditions are being held. The main floor is buzzing. Small groups of students partnering up to rehearse lines. A red-faced girl stares into the void while, opposite her, a boy does loud breathing exercises.

Some of the conversations drop out as I pass. Two students glare, as if I'm stepping on their territory. I smile without acknowledging them.

Good. They know I'm a threat.

For the last forty-eight hours, I've been practicing my monologue with Annika. It's the butler Wadsworth's over-the-top retelling of how the murders happened. I'd never heard of *Clue*, but a handful of YouTube clips informed me it's a murder-mystery comedy. I can be funny. Stage acting can't be *that hard.*

Inside the auditorium, people are scattered among the red velour seats, either on their phones or chatting softly. The upper deck is blocked off. So are the first ten rows closest to the stage. I find a center seat in an empty row near the back. Ajani sits behind me.

I drum my hands on my thighs while waiting. I'm not nervous. Bored, really. Ajani's not a woman of many words. Whenever I'm trapped doing royal activities, she's usually reading books on her phone.

Horror is her favorite. I only know that from sneaking looks at her screen. She'd never volunteer that kind of information.

I sigh, staring at the stage.

"It's so you get that Broadway experience of auditioning under the spotlight," a voice says to my left. Someone drops down next to me. A lanky boy with swoopy dark hair and fair reddish-brown skin. "Doc Garza Villa is very professional about auditions. No competition front and center, trying to throw you off your game. They want the best version of you up there."

I study him. His face is all striking angles. I've seen him before. Did we meet at the party? One of my classes?

As if reading my mind, he says, "Karan Sharma. No relation."

"No relation to who?"

"The actor. Or the *other* actor. The cricket dude. Actually . . . I think there's two cricket guys. Can't keep track." He shrugs. "Anyway, you're the prince, right?"

I nod slowly.

"Figured," Karan says. "You're the only one sitting with a bodyguard, so." He inclines his head, lowering his voice. "No offense, but she could step on me, and I wouldn't complain."

My brows pinch together. "What the f—"

Applause cuts off my last word. On stage, Dr. Garza Villa, the drama instructor, is flanked by another faculty adviser along with Dustin, the student director advertised online. Dustin's cute in a shy way, fidgeting with his clipboard, stage lights shining on his black curls.

Dr. Garza Villa gives a breakdown of the process. Students can audition using whatever character they choose. But no roles are guaranteed. Every spot is up for grabs, no matter the script's gender specification.

Halfway through the explanation, Karan whispers, "Nervous?"

I wait for a beat. "No."

"Me neither. Which role are you after?"

I sit up, eyes forward. "Shouldn't we be listening?"

"Nah. It's the same every year." He clearly doesn't get the hint that I'm uninterested in chatting, because he keeps going. "I'm aiming for Wadsworth. The *real* Mr. Boddy. I'm ready to headline a show." He spreads his hands over his head like he's unveiling a glowing marquee.

CLUE! . . . Starring Karan Whatshislastnameagain?

In a deep, nervy voice, Dustin calls the first student to the stage.

"Thing is, I'm a little bit of a triple threat," Karan says in a voice more on the self-deprecating side than egotistical. "I can act, sing, and dance."

I raise both eyebrows.

"I know how it looks. This brown boy who's all bones and sick hair can move better than Shakira?" He does a small shimmy in his seat. "These hips don't lie, bro."

"Good for you?"

"Last spring, we did *A Midsummer Night's Dream*," Karan says, slouching. "I rocked Theseus. Standing ovation material."

"I'm . . . sure," I say quietly.

"I wanted Puck. The true star," Karan continues. "My parents dream of me being an engineer. Like them. But I swear, if they see me headlining a show, they'll finally believe *this* is what I'm meant to do." His eyes brighten. "This is my year."

I mimic his posture in my own seat. He did *Midsummer*, like Mom. And he seems genuine, unlike half the other people I've met so far.

"I'm going for Wadsworth too," I admit.

"That's dope." Even his smile is sincere. "Imagine one of the two melanin boys here snatching the lead role from all these Chris Pratt and Margot Robbie wannabes. Hollywood's shaking right now."

I laugh, hard enough to earn a *do you mind* glare from Dr. Garza Villa in the front row. I shrink lower. Dustin calls the next student up.

"Huh." Karan adjusts his T-shirt collar. VERSACE is printed in large block letters across his chest, reminding everyone he comes from money too. "My bestie was wrong about you."

My face scrunches, confused.

"That was low-key my fault, though," Karan clarifies. "I kept texting him while you two were talking the other night."

I inhale too sharply. *Fuck my life.* That's where I remember him from. He's the boy Reiss was laughing with in the courtyard the other day. The best friend Reiss mentioned at the party.

"So . . ." Karan grins. "Are you interested?"

I startle. "Interested in what?"

"Rei—"

I cut him off. "I'm not interested in *anything* that has to do with him."

"He's not that bad." When I stare skeptically at him, Karan adds, "He pretends to have this total emo, 'I make films for all the sad boys' energy. That he'd rather eat glass than socialize with anyone here. To be fair, have you met our classmates?"

I fight off another laugh, waiting for him to go on.

"The *real* Reiss is a quintessential softboy. In all the best ways." Karan's warm smile returns. "Smart. Funny. Exceptional taste in movies *and* friends."

I purse my lips, unconvinced.

"He said he really liked you," Karan casually adds. "Before the whole, you know."

I don't need him to finish. What happened lives rent-free in my head. The party. In the hallway after he opened my locker. All of it.

Hold on. I squeak out, "He likes me?"

Karan sparkles like this is the role he's been dreaming of all his life: *wingman*. He checks his phone. Then his eyes dart to the aisle. "Perfect timing. Ask him yourself."

Before I can turn my head, I hear: "Karan, you asshole. Hell no."

"Be quiet," Karan hisses, dragging Reiss by the elbow. They bicker softly until Karan shoves Reiss down. Into the seat next to me.

"Get me out of here *now*," I whisper over my shoulder to Ajani.

"Sorry, my prince. I can't." She doesn't even lift her eyes. "Not until you finish your audition. Strict orders from the crown princess."

"What?!"

Dr. Garza Villa whips around again. I sink so low I might as well be on the floor. Which would be much better than breathing in a now-familiar smoky, earthy scent. Staring up at a sharp jaw. Watching Reiss's cheeks turn scorched red.

"Bro, you promised you'd record my audition," Karan whispers.

"I lied," Reiss grits out.

Karan leans past him to look at me. "Prince, help me out. Tell my bestie it's a *dick move* to promise to support the biggest moment of my future career and then back out."

"I wouldn't dare," I argue.

"Like I'd listen to him," Reiss says flatly.

"Karan?" Dustin calls. "Karan Sharma?"

"Here!" Karan screeches. At the end of our row, two giggling girls fall into the last seats, blocking his exit. That doesn't stop him. "On the way, D! One sec!"

And just like that, he uses his long legs to effortlessly climb over the seats in front of us. He jogs up to the stage. Leaving me alone with Reiss.

This is a nightmare.

After a minute, Reiss begrudgingly opens the camera app on his phone. He directs the lens toward the stage. In all the movement, his shoulder brushes mine. He leans the other way. I don't care.

It's not as if I was secretly trying to figure out what bodywash he uses. Nope. Never happened.

Onstage, charisma pours off Karan. He wasn't bragging before. He's talented.

"He's right," I find myself whispering. "It's rude to lie about helping a friend."

"Like it's rude to be an asshole to someone who, just so we're clear"—he half-turns his head to glare at me—"wasn't recording you without consent."

He doesn't leave me room to comment.

"This is LA," he continues, voice low. "I see celebs all the time. Cate Blanchett *literally* had tea next to me this morning. Some of us don't give a shit about who you are."

I swallow, cheeks hot. "Point taken."

"I was texting Karan that night. About you."

He's not looking at me anymore, but his face has softened to a pale pink. Like he's embarrassed about admitting that.

"Good things?" I ask, conversationally. Curiously.

"Doesn't matter now."

My brain tries to work around what to say next. How to rewind, start over. Make this a little less uncomfortable. But no amount of royal training, lessons on diplomacy, comes to me. I'm stuck in a war of silence, just like I'm stuck in California.

Reiss seems content ignoring me. He kicks a foot up on the empty seat in front of him. My eyes widen. He's wearing red-and-white Jordan 1 Retro High OGs. I have the same pair back in Réverie.

Surprising myself, I say, "Great shoes."

Another surge of blush pours down his cheeks. "Sneakerhead?"

"I dabble," I reply, then grimace. *I dabble? Who the hell says that?*

But the corners of Reiss's mouth twitch. "Me too."

Huh. We have something in common. Other than happily avoiding each other.

"I'll have to show you my collection sometime," I say, immediately regretting it. "On my phone. Not like. I wasn't inviting you to my *bedroom*. I'm not some pervy—"

"I didn't think you were," Reiss says, mercifully ending my stammering. Another almost-smile brushes his lips. "I'm good at not assuming things about people."

My whole face is on fire.

Before I can say anything, Karan climbs back over the seats. *"Phew."* He fakes wiping his brow. "Not to brag, but I should probably start composing my acceptance speech for the Tonys. I slayed up there."

Reiss lowers his phone. "True. Your ego deserves at least Best Newcomer."

"That's not a category, bro." Karan nudges me. "You're up."

That's when I realize Dustin's saying, "Prince Jadon? Er, Your Highness? Your Majesty? Help, anyone?"

I jolt to my feet. "Jadon's fine," I say flatly when all eyes fall on me.

"Whenever you're ready."

I nod once.

Instead of squeezing by Reiss—and risking that awkward moment where either my ass or crotch will be eye-level with his face—to ask the girls at the end to let me out, I mimic Karan's earlier exit. But I'm not as coordinated. My foot gets caught between two seats. I pretend not to hear choked laughter as I stumble free. Is Reiss *grinning* at me almost face-planting in front of everyone?

"Relax those ass cheeks," Karan instructs. "Melanin dominance, remember?"

I collect myself, then nod again.

When I'm onstage, Dr. Garza Villa asks what part I'm reading for, making a note before telling me to start. The auditorium is cast in heavy shadows. But I know Reiss is watching.

I smile.

For all four minutes my audition takes, I think about what

Annika suggested. About not being prince of Îles de la Réverie. The boy all over the news. The problem his parents are tired of fixing. I'm just a semi-normal boy going after something that won't define or destroy him.

And it's . . . nice.

A feeling I want more of.

6

THE FALL OF JALE

Ever since Réverie's Prince Jadon and model/political son Léon Barnard split, fans of #JALE have been in mourning. Speculation behind the cause of their sudden breakup has been rampant. Here & Queer sat down with three prominent gossip bloggers to discuss their theories, the prince's viral meltdown, and why his trip to America is a cry for help.

"My prince," Ajani says, her tone just barely even, "are you sure this is the way?"

I bite a corner of my lip, looking down. My phone's GPS claims we're close. The place I'm searching for is two minutes away. But we've been walking for almost thirty. I can read the annoyed edge in Ajani's eyes.

"Yup." I nod. "Just around that corner."

And another block. Maybe. I don't usually travel by foot.

On cue, Ajani says, "Remind me again why we're hiking instead of taking a car? Or a *helicopter*?"

"I don't want to draw any attention," I reply. Ajani lifts an eyebrow as I turn around in a circle, trying to follow the uncooperative arrow on my screen. My face wrinkles. "Any *extra* attention. If we show up in a bulletproof Rolls-Royce, what will people think?"

Ajani waves toward the hot pink Porsche zipping by us. "That we have class?"

"I don't want to be noticed, okay?"

"Fine." Ajani exhales. "Next time I'll wear proper shoes."

I grimace at her boots. "Sorry."

It's a nice day in Santa Monica. Buildings reflect golden arcs of sunlight onto the streets. Thick trees sprout through the sidewalks, providing ample shade. Most of the people are flooding in one direction: Third Street Promenade, a three-block shopping district nearby. We fight the tide the opposite way.

Since Annika wasn't *completely* wrong about the play audition, I've decided to follow another one of her suggestions: exploring places Mom loved when she lived here. First stop is Pacific Harmony, a vintage music store. At least five of Nana's photos featured Mom sitting on the shop's floor, big headphones on, browsing through vinyls.

"Turn left," the GPS instructs.

The area is semi-busy. Tourists wandering around, locals stopping at their favorite restaurants and cafés. We pass a shirtless guy with a guitar. Someone dressed in Sailor Moon cosplay. A pack of all-black-wearing goth kids, their faces painted like skulls.

LA is full of overachievers desperate to be noticed. I don't want to be one of them.

In a shop's window, I see my reflection. Face shiny with sweat, flat curls, my expression somewhere between annoyed and murderous. I'm the actual poop emoji minus the smile.

The crosswalk's electronic voice repeats, "Walk! Walk!"

"Almost there," I tell Ajani.

"I'm so excited," she deadpans.

I'm unbothered. There's this anticipation vibrating through my bones. At seeing the record store. Being in a place my mom loved so much.

But the air is sucked from my lungs when I stand in front of Pacific Harmony.

Correction: the *former* Pacific Harmony.

The storefront is still there, but the inside is dark. The guts ripped out. Construction equipment is scattered all over the floor where Mom used to sit. On the door, a bubblegum-pink sign with blue lettering reads:

COMING SOON . . . YOGA & YOGURT!

"I don't understand," I say, throat tight. I recheck the address I found online. "It's supposed to be right here."

"The music shop?" An older Black woman in a cowboy hat pauses next to me. "Closed a month ago. Probably haven't updated their business profile. The owners retired. Lovely couple. This neighborhood's gonna miss 'em."

Then she drifts away with the crowd.

I close my eyes, thumping my head against the glass door. "*Ow*. Fuck."

While I sulk, Ajani stays silent. It's one of my favorite things about her. When I need to pout or scream or break things, she never intervenes. Even though she could. Papa probably thinks she *should*.

She knows I need to get whatever out of my system first.

After a moment, she says, "Would you like to go somewhere else?"

No, I want to say. I planned my entire Sunday around this. A day without Samuel advising new ways to improve my "likability stats." Without Annika being everyone's favorite for doing nothing but being photographed sipping boba. A day without overthinking what next week at Willow Wood is going to be like.

And now, when I look out at Santa Monica, all I see is a city where I still can't escape this Shiny New Prince Jadon I'm expected to be.

All I see is . . .

A pair of bunny ears painted on a coffee bean. A green-and-peach awning. The shop from my first morning before school.

"My prince," Ajani says, weary, "I don't trust that face you're making."

I turn to her, grinning. "Caffeine break?"

The Hopper's interior doesn't disappoint. It's like picking up your favorite book: the worn pages soft under your fingertips, the scent something no one can ever properly replicate.

Small circular tables frame the perimeter. Cozy armchairs fill out the center. All-white walls except for the one behind the espresso bar. It's pastel pink with WELCOME HOME painted in large black letters. Other than the soft strains of music playing overhead, the café is quiet and mostly empty.

Perfect. Caffeine and anonymity.

"New customer!"

At the front counter, a boy who can't be older than ten grins broadly. His sponge-twisted curls are almost as tall as he is. Up close, I spot the mini-step stool he's standing on to reach the digital register. There's something familiar about his dark eyes, his light brown skin. Pinned to his black apron is a name tag: DOMINIC!

"Wow," he gasps, blinking at Ajani. "Are you from a comic book?"

Ajani's lips quirk the tiniest amount. I lean forward, whispering, "It's a secret. Promise not to tell?"

Dominic nods eagerly. "Do you wanna order?"

"What do you recommend?"

His face brightens like the fairy lights strung around the letterboard menus. "The Dominic Special. Caramel iced coffee. Lots of cream. More caramel. Whipped cream and—"

"Let me guess," I say, amused, "even more caramel?"

"Extra, extra caramel drizzle." He strikes a pose like a boy band member—arms crossed, chin on his knuckles, smoldering eyes and lips puckered.

I can't hold in my laugh. It dies quickly when the door leading to the café's back room swings open and out walks Reiss. I freeze like if I don't make any sudden movements, he won't notice me.

He does.

His eyes narrow. Then, he yells over his shoulder, "Ma!

Dom's at the register again. We're breaking, like, at least a dozen child labor laws."

A woman's voice from the back shouts, "Dominic Ezra Hayes!"

"You're such a narc," Dominic complains, hopping down from his stool.

Reiss's eyes grow cartoonishly wide. "Who taught you that word?"

"Megan."

"Megan's a terrible influence," Reiss says.

Dominic sucks air through his teeth, stomping away. "You're a terrible brother!"

"That's my job," Reiss calls to the swinging employee door before turning to me. "Were you really gonna order the Dom Special?"

I shrug. "Sounded interesting."

"It'll give you diarrhea." Something flashes in his eyes. "Actually, you look like you need a good stomach cleanse."

My face prickles. But I'm not angry. Not when his lips curve upward as he watches me from behind the counter. He's wearing the same black apron as Dominic. I guess his family owns the shop.

"Fine." I cross my arms. "What do *you* recommend?"

You can tell a lot about someone by their coffee shop order. I want to know what he thinks of me. When he looks at me, what does he see?

Reiss doesn't falter under my gaze. "I'll surprise you," he says.

"Shouldn't you ask if I have any allergies?" I inquire. "Dairy issues?"

He sighs. "Do you?"

"Nope," I say, satisfied at the way his brows furrow in annoyance.

Then, I see it. The little crinkle in the bridge of his nose. Like he's fighting a smile that never appears.

He up-nods at Ajani. "For you? Ajani, right?"

She looks marginally impressed. "Tea. Black."

"Got it."

When Reiss walks away from the register, never typing in our orders or telling us a price, I say anxiously, "Wait! I can pay."

"Your money's no good here," he says, already behind the espresso bar, filling a metal pitcher. "Find a table. Let me do my job in peace."

My next protest evaporates in my throat. I'm too distracted watching him.

Reiss's movements are effortless. The flexed cords of muscles in his forearms as he steams the milk before he glides over to a tea station. He bobs his head to the café music, in a zone. Once again, I'm nobody to him. I don't pout or skulk over to a corner table, wanting his attention on me for a little longer.

I'm being silly. Reiss is at *work*. It's not like there's anything going on between us either. We had one moment at the party. Then, the thing at my locker. A five-second connection over shoes during the auditions. That doesn't mean anything, right?

I don't *want* it to mean anything, right?

"Careful." Out of nowhere, a plate and a mug are placed in front of me. "It's hot."

Without prompting, Reiss eases into the chair opposite me. One table over, Ajani's already sipping her tea.

I blink at the cinnamon roll drizzled in icing he brought. Then, the steaming mug. The drink's perfectly silky brown surface is broken up by white latte art.

"Is that . . ." I examine it closely. "An alien?"

"A *panda*. Don't judge me." His cheeks are glowing. "I'm no good under pressure."

"Performance anxiety?" I find myself saying in a teasing voice.

He rolls his eyes, but the blush doesn't fade. He's not wearing his apron anymore. His pink waves look good against the yellow and blue of his striped T-shirt. When he relaxes in the chair, his ankle accidentally brushes mine. "Just try it."

I raise an eyebrow. "Are you always this bossy?"

"If the occasion calls for it." Another streak of rose tints his nose.

"Hmm." I skim my ankle against his. "Sounds fun."

He coughs, eyes bulging.

I carefully take a sip. The shock of flavor is instant. It's a hot chocolate, as good as the ones made by the chefs inside the palace, but different. Creamier, with pops of spice. Cinnamon and nutmeg and—

"Ginger," Reiss says, smirking at my stunned expression. "The Reiss Special."

"Why is this *so good*?" I slurp more.

"It goes really well with"—he points to the plate—"that."

I've had cinnamon rolls before. Centauri's pastry chefs are some of the finest in the world. But this is . . .

"I think I'm dying," I moan, shivering. It's incredible. Tangy cream cheese icing. Buttery soft texture. The dough peels apart easily, revealing layer after layer of sugary cinnamon. "Who made this? Do you have personal chefs in the back?"

"Do we *what*?" Reiss's eyes crinkle when he laughs. "It's just a cinnamon roll."

"How dare you," I say, mouth full. "This is a gift from the gods."

"We buy them from a local baker."

I wave off his nonchalance, sipping from my mug. He was right. The hot chocolate's spiciness with the roll's sweetness is unbearably good. I keep my ankle pressed to his. He doesn't shift away.

"I'm honored our little shop meets royalty standards," Reiss comments.

"It was . . . okay," I say, trying not to lick sugar off my fingers.

He stares at me weirdly. A wave of self-consciousness seizes me. Then, he's leaning forward. "You've got icing right—"

His fingers hover near the corner of my mouth. I don't breathe.

He jerks back. "Sorry, um—"

"It's fine," I say. I track the way he watches me, face reddening, while I glide my tongue over my mouth, licking away the stray icing. "Better?"

"Oh, fuck," he whispers, then nods. "Sure. Great."

The squeak in his voice is cute. Wordlessly, Ajani shifts to a different corner of the café. Not without shooting me a judging stare, first.

"Are you on break?" I ask Reiss.

"They made me take one." He signals toward an older woman behind the register, rearranging coffee bags, and a tall, brawny man wiping down the espresso machine. His parents, I deduce. Both share little features I can see in Reiss. "Guess I'm making it hard to beat those social outcast allegations."

I shrug. "Better than a pretentious prince."

"*Arrogant,*" he corrects, biting on what I hope is the start of a smile. "And the jury's still out on you."

We go quiet. Like at the party, music settles between us. I'm not used to this. Wanting to fill the spaces with words. Worrying that my silence will be the reason someone walks away.

Loneliness and I are soulmates. The closest people to me, outside of my family, are the palace's staff. Every interaction I had at Académie des Jeunes Dirigeants felt cursory. I was the prince to them, nothing more. No one wanted to put in the effort of getting to know the other sides of me.

Kofi was the exception, but even he walked away.

Sometimes, with Léon, I wondered if he stuck around out of obligation. Because of the connection our papas share. Not because he loved the *real* me.

Too many seconds pass before I realize I'm too far in my own head.

"So, His Royal Arrogance has a sweet tooth," Reiss finally says. He stares at me, considering. "What else?"

I blurt out, "*The Way He Looks.*"

Deep, confused wrinkles form in his forehead.

"That's my . . ." I pause, trying to sound a little less unhinged. "That's my favorite film."

He nods without saying anything else. I take that as a cue to continue.

"I watched it years ago. On a jet somewhere," I say.

It popped up in my *Recommended For You* list on YouTube. I remember curling up in a soft leather seat. Earbuds in. Eyes glued to the screen as a sweet love story between a blind boy and the new student in his class bloomed.

"I don't know." I shrug. "I wanted that. To fall in love with someone who'll walk me home. Who makes me dance. Who holds my hand when the world is mocking us."

My face instantly heats. *Why did I tell him all that?*

Reiss's lips slowly lift.

"There's one scene," I continue, smiling sheepishly. "The boys sneak out. To watch the eclipse. On the way home, Gabriel, the new boy, gives Leonardo a ride on the back of his bike. It's this moment—" My breath catches. "Leonardo smiles. He *trusts* Gabriel. Nothing bad will happen as long as he's with him. It's . . ."

I trail off, barely able to swallow. I'm almost scared to look at Reiss.

But I do.

He's grinning. "I've seen it," he admits. "A prince with solid taste in films? Damn. Didn't expect that."

Something squeezes my chest. Pride? Happiness? I could never convince Léon to watch *The Way He Looks*. To get him to see what it meant to me.

But something in Reiss's expression tells me he understands.

I clear my throat. "What about you? I saw all those movie posters on your Instagram—"

The moment it's out, I cringe hard. *Well, shit.*

I ignore Reiss's sly grin to finish: "What's your favorite film?"

He doesn't hesitate. *"God's Own Country."*

"I don't know it."

Reiss groans like I've offended generations of queer film-makers. Within seconds, he launches into his favorite parts. The gorgeous imagery. Moments where the cinematography left him speechless. The way the movie speaks with very little dialogue.

"And the wall scene!"

He's all animated hand gestures, wild expressions. It's fas-cinating. A little funny, too.

"It's the reason I got into directing," he says, his voice soft-ening. His ankle shifts away. Mine instinctively follows.

"Go on," I request.

"I'm applying to USC's School of Cinematic Arts." He drums his fingers on the table's edge. "I worked so hard to earn my scholarship to Willow Wood. It's gonna look great on my college app. Going to USC is my dream."

"Wait." I jolt. "USC? My mom graduated from there."

"I know," he admits with a guilty smile. "I *might've* googled you. Low-level shit only. No wiki pages."

I flex an eyebrow. "Uh-huh. Tell me, Reiss Hayes, are you secretly writing fanfic about me? What's your AO3 username?"

His mouth opens, another admission so close to his lips. He stops, shaking his head. "You're a certified asshole."

"I prefer Your Royal Asshole, thank you."

He snorts. For a moment, I stare at his mouth. The way his

teeth pull on his lower lip, leaving it redder and fuller.

Eventually, he says, "What do you dream about?"

Home almost crosses my tongue. I swallow it back. Telling him that could ruin everything I'm working for.

Truth is, I don't have another answer. Royals don't get to dream. It's the crown, first. Duty and service to your people above everything. Just because I *want* to go to university, spend four years discovering myself like Mom did, doesn't mean it'll happen.

What would I even study?

And I can't have what two movie characters had. Or what Papa and Mom had either—falling in love over macarons during a one-week holiday. Look at my history. It didn't work with Léon, and we live in the same country. What normal boy wants to suffer through all the drama of dating a royal?

"Hey"—Reiss nudges my ankle—"what's with that expression?"

Reflexively, I reach up to touch my cheeks and brow. *Oh.*

"My sister calls it RPF," I say, self-conscious. "Resting prince face."

Reiss chokes on a laugh. "Wow. That's . . . awful."

I kick his shin.

"*Ow*. Fine." He edges his chair back. "I don't care what you dream about."

My shoulders relax, relieved he's letting it go. But then he stands, picking up the plate. We reach for the mug at the same time, fingers brushing. His knuckles are soft. I steady his hand when he almost drops everything.

His stare is like a wildfire under my skin.

"Uh," he stammers, "my break's over."

Before he's too far away, I ask, "Does this mean we're . . . okay? I can stop avoiding you?" My lips tick up. "For status purposes, of course."

His mouth twists into that crooked grin. "No. We're not okay."

My expression falters. "Why not?"

"You still haven't apologized," is all he says, adjusting the dishes in his hand. He starts to leave, then pauses. "But at least I know you're not the monster everyone says you are."

"That's a start!" I insist.

"Watch that movie, Your Royal Arrogance, or I'll tell everyone you can't open your own locker!" he half-yells with absolutely no conviction in his voice.

A full minute passes before I turn to look outside. My reflection in The Hopper's main window is absurd. Unforgivable.

Who the hell does Reiss Hayes think he is, making me smile this hard?

7

@LacesAndPlaces started following @TheReelReiss
@TheReelReiss started following @LacesAndPlaces

It's not until after liking five of Reiss's posts in a row that I realize I *might* be coming on a little strong.

My finsta is mainly for finding memes, searching for new recipe videos, and occasionally browsing thirst traps. It's not for creeping on a film-obsessed, maybe-beautiful, pink-haired boy's profile. But here I am at 7:22 a.m., debating on whether to unlike at least three of those posts, terrified he's already seen the notifications.

My @LacesAndPlaces account started off as a way to separate myself from the verified prince of Îles de la Réverie account. I don't control my official social media. Some palace staffer does. That account is nothing but boring photos and videos of meeting forgettable dignitaries, goodwill trips, and "candids" that were carefully staged. At least this is fully mine.

My grid consists of views and shoes. Snapshots of places I've visited paired with a sneaker from my closet. A glowing Eiffel Tower at night with metallic gold Air Jordan 1s. The Ionian Sea's clear water near Lefkada with pale blue Jordan Melo M13 XII Energy kicks. Louis Vuitton x Nike Air Force 1 Reds to match a phone box in London.

No one's traced @LacesAndPlaces back to me. I only have 102 followers.

One hundred and one. Kofi dropped me like Rose ditched Jack's frozen corpse in *Titanic.*

As of 10:11 p.m. last night, I gained a new follower: @TheReelReiss.

My cheeks ache from smiling at my screen. Thankfully, it goes unnoticed. It's too early to discuss my suspicious online activity.

We're in the courtyard again. Me and Grace on one bench.

Morgan and Nathan on the other. I'm sticking to this routine because, while some of the headlines about me are changing, there still isn't enough forward motion in the Team Jadon camp. I'm *trying* to do better.

"What about a hot zombie?" Grace suggests.

"Nah," Nathan says. "I'm going as a sexy mummy."

"No one wants to see that," Morgan says.

I'm still looking at my phone, but I can hear the sleaze in Nathan's voice: "Are you saying you don't want to help cover all my important parts with toilet paper?"

"There are no important parts on you, Nate."

"Morg, you wound me!"

I lift my eyes just in time to witness Morgan playfully punching Nathan's bicep. "Sorry," I say, confused, "what's this about?"

"Grace's Halloween bash," Morgan monotones.

"*Annual* Halloween bash," Grace corrects. Today, she's swapped SAT cards for a copy of *Pride and Prejudice*. Somehow, I've discovered this group takes their grades very seriously. Even Nathan. "An early birthday gift. My dad throws a party every year."

"She gives off ultimate Scorpio energy, doesn't she?" Nathan says to me.

"Um, I guess."

"You're coming, right?" Grace requests. It's an invite, unlike last time.

I hesitate. The last party wasn't very productive. But can I afford to say no? How is sitting in that hollow Palisades house, the one that keeps reminding me I'm *not* in the palace, going to help me get home? Being antisocial isn't going to prove I'm the prince anyone deserves.

Maybe Reiss will show up again? Because of Karan. Not because he wants to see me or anything.

"Jadon?" Grace scrutinizes me.

"Yes," I manage, throat dry. "I'll be there."

She beams. Her shiny lip gloss matches the pink bows keeping blunt bangs off her forehead. "I'll add you to the VIP list."

After unlocking her phone, Grace frowns.

"Kaden?" Morgan says.

Grace doesn't answer. She eyes the screen for a minute. Then, she blinks away whatever she was just thinking, smiling again. "We should plan a shopping trip. That way none of us wear the same costume."

While Grace and Nathan trade ideas, I study the courtyard. It's early October, and the sky's a sharp blue. Students are slowly trickling in. A boy from my Human Development class—Seb?—strolls by in a leather jacket instead of his cardigan. Behind him, someone's wearing a yellow beret and dramatic lilac cape.

I spin to Morgan, various pins scattered over her plaid vest. "What's with the uniforms?"

She barely lifts her eyes from her phone. She's always texting. I wonder who it is? Her mom or a sibling? I never ask.

"It's all Headmaster Parker." She locks her screen. "Back in her day, Willow Wood was very . . . *conservative*. Strict rules and expectations. She hated it. Said it made a lot of kids fail in a place where they were supposed to succeed."

My eyebrows furrow.

"So, when she was put in charge, she changed the rules," Morgan goes on.

"Within reason," Nathan adds, rolling his eyes.

"To appease the old, boring donors who have hard-ons for *tradition*," Morgan reasons, "we're required to wear at least one piece of uniform the standard way. The rest is up for interpretation."

I snort when Nathan stands, modelling a pair of gray slacks he's chopped into shorts.

"She's been good for the school," Grace concedes. "Even if people disagree."

For a moment, I think about that. How stifling tradition can be. How sticking to the same rules doesn't bring steadiness. Sometimes, it brings failure. Sometimes, just one step outside of the lines is . . . *freeing*.

My eyes do another sweep of the area. At the courtyard's edge, I catch a pair of yellow-and-black Air Jordan 1s. I slide my gaze up the legs, the torso, over the now-familiar shoulders of the sneakers' owner.

Reiss.

A fuzziness creeps into my cheeks. I don't know why the skin on the inside of my ankle heats up, like I can still feel his pressed right there. Why my heart's volleying around my chest like a Wimbledon championship game. Why I'm suddenly noticing the fading dye in his hair leaves it sunrise pink. Why my fingers curl to fists in my lap when I see that he's talking to a tall, freckle-faced boy.

They're whispering. Phones out. Shoulders almost touching.

The boy's head turns. His face so close to Reiss's ear and—

"Earth to PJ." Nathan waves a hand in front of my eyes.

I almost fall off the bench.

After recovering, I stammer, "What did you say?"

He laughs. "We're headed inside." Morgan and Grace are already hovering with weird expressions. Nathan kicks up his skateboard. "Need to get my morning constitutional in before Shakespeare class."

"TMI," Morgan groans.

"That's the same thing Miss Gong said!"

"Costume shopping after school?" Grace prompts.

I avoid looking in Reiss's direction. Instead, I tug my buzzing phone from my pocket. A reminder pops up.

My face wrinkles. "Can't. I have a meeting with Headmaster Parker."

She shrugs, hooking arms with Morgan. "Your loss."

But it's not.

Don't get me wrong, Headmaster Parker's proposition to spend my afternoon recording an advertisement for Willow Wood sounds tedious. The kind of publicity stunt deeply beneath an heir to the throne. But I go along with it because she's so earnest about the potential.

"Imagine how many kids will want to come here," she says, eyes glittery, "when they see a prince like *you* in our promotional video."

I go along with it because of what Grace said earlier:

She's been good for this school. Even if people disagree.

I go along with it because the moment I walk into the hallway where we're shooting the advertisement, my pulse quickens at who is behind the camera.

Crooked grin. Crinkled dark eyes. Sunrise-pink hair.

"*Oh*." Headmaster Parker starts. "You two already know each other?"

Did my helpless smile give it away?

"Yup," Reiss answers, stepping closer. "I'm a big fan."

I snort, then clear my throat. "Nice to see you again."

"So formal," Reiss whispers. "Thanks for doing this. It'll earn me extra credit in my Video Art I class."

"Anything for y—for the arts."

Headmaster Parker claps, satisfied. "Wonderful! Reiss is one of our brightest rising film students. I trust him. You're in great hands."

My gaze drifts downward. Long fingers, soft knuckles. Absently, I lick my lips. Reiss's cheeks pinken. Headmaster Parker is oblivious to the exchange.

"I'll leave you two to it." Then, she's gone.

Reiss swallows. "Shall we?"

Other than the Canon and tripod, I don't know the names of the equipment being used. Reiss spends a few minutes testing each one. Adjusting the lighting. Using headphones to check the audio. From behind the camera, he tries to direct me into position near a row of lockers, but I'm either too far to the right or too left or out of focus.

Sighing, he steps over and around equipment until we're face-to-face. His hands raise, fingers gripping my shoulders.

"Move . . . right . . . here."

"Is this just an excuse for you to touch me?"

He pauses abruptly. "What? N-no. You weren't following my directions."

"They weren't clear."

His hands fall away. I force myself not to sulk. His grip was firm, confident, tingles-up-my-spine inducing.

"How about this?" He backs away, exasperated. "Don't move. Stand here, smile big, and look pretty until we're done."

As he stomps away, I say, "So you think I'm pretty?"

"And don't talk until I tell you to," he yells instead of answering my question.

"Bossy," I mumble.

He resettles behind the camera, yanking his headphones on. After we record the short intro script Headmaster Parker composed, Reiss explains, "She wants this next part to be organic. Candid. Just talk about the school. What you like. Why you came here."

"Okay."

"Do you need a minute? Think about what you want to say?"

I shake my head. "Sounds simple. I can handle it."

Except, the second he signals me to start, my body goes rigid. I stare blankly into the lens. Being a prince isn't just a title. It's something you're *taught* to be. Decorum, how to handle situations, when and what to say.

It's also something I've always resented. I'm not a robot. I act on impulse. The second I'm uncomfortable, every little method I've learned goes out the window. Filter off, defensiveness on.

Annika's so much better at playing the part. She's polite

and magnetic. Never met a question she couldn't answer diplomatically. The kind of face Willow Wood would love welcoming new students to their prestigious establishment.

I'm not bitter toward her. I just wish I could be myself.

In moments like this, I wish being myself was enough for everyone else.

Maybe Kip Davies is right. I'm nothing but a rebel. The wrong kind of prince.

"Any time you're ready," Reiss singsongs.

I flinch. "I—so, like. Tell you what I love?"

"About the school." There's a hint of frustration behind his voice. "Why you came here."

"I love . . ." I swallow. Stare into the lens again. "The weather. And architecture."

Reiss's head pops up. "Six whole words," he says dryly. "I like it. Raw. Minimalistic. To the point."

"I'm *trying,*" I grit out.

"I can tell," he shoots back.

When I glower, he raises his hands. "My bad. You're obviously not a fan of cameras."

"Obviously," I repeat tersely.

"Pretend it's not here." He waves a hand in front of the camera like a magician attempting to disappear a rabbit. "Pretend you're staring at someone special. Someone you care about. A boyfriend, maybe."

My eyes narrow even more. "Considering my last relationship didn't end well, I'll pass."

Reiss winces. "That was an awful suggestion. I've never had a boyfriend. Or been on a real date. Unless you count bowling with Paxton Shen, which I don't." He rakes a hand down his face. "Why do people even say that? 'Stare into the camera like it's your lover.' No thanks. I'd rather look at a chicken taco that way."

As he rambles, I tilt my head. It's not the no-previous-boyfriends admission that amuses me, though my brain immediately saves that information for later. It's his unfiltered openness. The self-deprecating voice. That embarrassed wrinkle in the middle of his nose.

All of it smooths a smile across my lips.

"*Ah*, there they are," Reiss says almost fondly. "The dimples."

My brow rises again.

"Don't act like you don't know their power," he accuses.

"I have no idea what you're talking about," I say, smiling harder.

"Whatever." He flips me off. "New idea, Your Royal Arrogance—"

"Shouldn't it be Your Royal Dimple-ness?"

He ignores my baiting. "We need a change of scenery."

After securing Headmaster Parker's permission, Reiss switches locations: Willow Wood's Olympic-level outdoor swimming pool. Ajani accompanies us, sitting in the spectator stands. Reiss resets the equipment. He only brought the essentials. The camera setup, headphones, other small tools I still can't identify.

"Shooting outdoors is better," he tells me.

"Is it?"

"Natural light looks good on you . . . I mean, *on camera*."

I grin smugly. "Are you going to show me where to stand?"

He does. Unfortunately, without the touching this time. He uses something called spike tape to mark a spot on the concrete, near the pool's ledge.

"This is more in your element," he says as I get into position. "Being closer to the water. It'll help."

He's right. There's something about the cloudless sky. Sunlight glittering off the pool's surface as golden hour approaches.

I picture Réverie. The soft, sun-warm sand along the shores. Swaying branches on the fig trees in the palace garden. Clothes perfumed in fresh vanilla and spicy cloves after spending hours in the kitchens. Mom's laughter as I force her to learn a new online dance or Papa quietly telling me stories about our country.

Somewhere between the memories, I start talking. The things I like about Willow Wood. Instead of my practiced, fake grin, a real smile settles in. My eyes never leave the camera. Never leave Reiss.

It only takes a handful of takes, some angle changes. A brief pause when the wind picks up. Before I realize it, we're finished.

"It'll need some editing," Reiss says as he sidles up to me to play back all the best parts, "but not bad for a prince."

I snort. "I'm not sure you got my prettiest side."

"Shut up," he groans.

"No, seriously. You can barely see my dimples—"

"Glad His Royal Arrogance survived one afternoon with me." He lowers the camera. "It must've been so hard."

It wasn't. What's difficult is not getting lost in his dark eyes.

The way one side of his grin is higher than the other.

I'm so close to thanking him for helping me get past my insecurities today, when a screeching voice shouts, "We did it!"

I whip around as Karan comes jogging into the pool area.

He stops in front of us, flashing his phone. "Watch out, Hollywood!"

I lean in. Stare at the screen. It's a graphic on Willow Wood Theater's web page. A casting announcement. For some reason, I forgot Dr. Garza Villa mentioned the list would be out this week. But there it is:

Karan Sharma as Wadsworth.

"Bro." Reiss shakes him. "That's you! Holy shit. We love a murder king."

Karan tips his head into the sun, beaming.

Genuine happiness fills my chest. I don't know him that well—at all, really—but it's obvious how much he wanted this. How much he *deserved* it.

"Congratulations," I say. "You were incredible."

"*We* were." He's still pointing at his phone. Farther down the list—

Prince Jadon as Mr. Green.

I almost grimace at seeing my title in front of my name until it hits me. *That's my name on the casting sheet.* My heart leaps up my throat. I'm going to be in the play. Overwhelming joy spreads under my skin.

It never occurred to me, through the practices with Annika and the audition process, that I would actually *want* this. That I'd get it.

A now-familiar hand squeezes my shoulder.

"I knew you'd get it," Reiss says. Before either of us can comment on how sincere his voice is, he adds, "Mr. Green is a great character. Much more respectable than the butler."

"Hey!" Karan says, mock insulted. "Don't be rude on my big day."

He playfully shoves Reiss, who's too busy laughing to maintain his balance. He knocks into me. Which is fine, except it's not. Because I'm so distracted by how nice it is—our bodies pressed together—that I don't pay attention to where I'm standing. My left foot slides back . . . into nothing.

Nothing but air until I crash into the pool.

I'm still drying my curls when there's a knock against metal.

After pulling myself out of the water, disregarding Reiss and Karan's panicked offers to help, I stomped back into the school. Shoes squishing the whole way. Headmaster Parker ushered me to the nearby gym locker room. It smells like sweat and cheap soap and chocolate body spray. I'm ready to leave.

"Yes?" I call with an edge to my voice.

Ajani steps around the corner. "My prince. *This one* wanted to see you."

Reiss waves shyly from around her.

I lower the towel around my shoulders, face caught between a frown and mild annoyance. I'm not angry with him. I just don't want him to see me like this. Drippy, hair wrecked, someone else's athletic socks pooled around my ankles.

"Should I dispose of him?" Ajani offers.

Reiss's eyes go comically big.

"It's fine," I sigh out. "I'm not in the mood to get blood all over my new clothes."

I wave a hand at the Willow Wood Phys Ed uniform Headmaster Parker gave me. The gray T-shirt is itchy, and I'm still wearing my damp boxers. There's no way I was going commando in these cotton shorts.

"You can murder him next time," I compromise.

Ajani nods once, shooting Reiss a lethal glare before exiting the locker room.

"She's hella frightening," he says.

"Her scare tactics are very effective." I lean against one of the lockers, arms folded over my chest.

He mirrors my posture, but keeps his arms at his side. He's clutching something. A shirt or jacket?

"You're a great swimmer."

"Lots of practice," I say. "You know, ocean and all."

When he laughs, I do too. It's this contagious noise. Or maybe it's because he looks so embarrassed, like he didn't expect his day to go like this. Me either. But I'm not disappointed with what's currently happening.

The way we're staring at each other, mouths curled into smiles, chests rising and falling at the same rhythm.

"Karan's really sorry about the"—his eyes trail over me—"pool thing. I am too."

My eyebrow arches. "Is that an apology? From the great @TheReelReiss?"

"At least I know how to apologize," he counters.

Heat spreads into my cheeks. "I'm sorry. For what I said at the party."

"Anything else?"

"Nope." I smirk. "Just that."

"Fine. *Here.*" He shoves whatever he's gripping into my chest. "I didn't know if you'd have anything warm to change into. Gets a little cool this time of day."

I hold it up. A cotton hoodie. Soft, thin, and bright yellow like the golden-weaver birds around Réverie.

"Thank you," I whisper, still a little awed at the thoughtful gesture.

He shrugs. "Can't have Willow Wood's second-biggest star catching pneumonia before rehearsals start."

Oh, right. The casting announcements. Even though I spent most of my time reading Wadsworth's lines, I saw a lot of Mr. Green's name throughout the script. I'm nowhere near as anxious as he is, but he's funny. Plus, he plays a major part in the ending.

I slide the hoodie over my head. It's a tight fit. It smells of earth and smoke, scents I now recognize from The Hopper. As I struggle, my T-shirt rides up my abdomen. Even with the hoodie's collar caught around my nose, I can still see Reiss.

His eyes have zeroed in on my flash of brown skin. The definition in my stomach. *Thank you for the years of swimming lessons, Atlantic.*

I slow my motions. Give him an extra five seconds to look. When he twists his bottom lip between his teeth, eyes darker, I clear my throat, lowering my arms.

He startles back into the lockers.

"I should go," I say, almost failing to conceal my pleased smile. "See you around?"

"Uh, yeah, sure," he stammers.

"*Oh*." I pause by the entranceway. "Don't forget to highlight my dimples when you edit that video. Hate to disappoint my fans."

"You're way too cocky."

"It's not cockiness," I tell him. "Simply facts."

His lopsided grin returns. "Goodbye, Jadon."

I mock-bow, then leave with my chin high, shoulders elegantly drawn back. It's not until I'm halfway to the waiting car that it hits me. He didn't say *Your Royal Arrogance*.

Reiss called me Jadon.

○

The oven timer dings as Samuel spreads a pile of magazines across the kitchen island.

"We have a problem."

"Obviously." I pull a tray from the double oven. "How many trees were murdered for those? You know you can read that stuff *online* now, right?"

I inspect my pâte sucrée. Centauri's pastry chefs taught me the art of creating the perfect thin, golden crust. A buttery sweet scent wafts in the air as I sweep aside the magazines for a place to rest the tray.

Samuel's dramatic sigh begs for attention.

"Quoi?" I say.

He aggressively points to the hand-selected magazine pile. Each glossy cover features a different celebrity or political figure. Marriages, scandals, breakups, more scandals. Inlaid on a different corner of every front page is a photo of me with a new headline:

Rebel Royal Does America!

His Royal Finest: A Guide to Prince Jadon's Best LA Looks

CRUSH ALERT! Why Everyone's Falling for the Brokenhearted Prince!

Wild, Wild Westeros: How Prince Jadon Is Playing a Game of Thrones In the USA

"I have no idea what any of this means," I sigh.

"It means," Samuel says, incredulous, "the tabloids are in love with you."

"Where's the problem?" I tilt my head, confused. "I thought we *wanted* better headlines? For everyone to stop focusing on the video?"

For people to fall in love with the New Prince Jadon—the one I didn't feel like on the inside, I think, but don't say.

"Yes!" Samuel says, even more frantic.

"Sorry." I pause, blinking. "Are we speaking the same language?"

"Non." Samuel gathers the magazines into a neat stack. "We want everyone to love you. But we need *Réverie* to respect you, too. Right now, they don't."

"They . . . still don't?"

"I've spoken with some trusted sources," Samuel admits, already frowning like he knows what he says next is going to sting. "Our people *see* the new Jadon. Your likability numbers are up."

I exhale hard. Is that what I am now? A number? A stat based on opinions? Whether I can go home or not hinges on margins calculated by people who don't even fucking know me.

"But," Samuel continues, "they want more from you."

"More than smiling and being friendly and not causing international incidents?" I say, exasperated.

"Yes?"

I almost knock over the tray with my cooling crust. "What, then?"

Samuel hesitates. One of the glass doors leading to the main lawn is open. Sunlight dances on the pool's surface like a blanket of diamonds. The Palisades are quiet, but nothing like the tranquil air around the palace. The home I'm desperately missing.

It was never this hard in Réverie. Whenever one of my "incidents" happened, there was a swarm of chamberlains to contain the situation. I could hide in my room or in Centauri's gardens until it went away. But this is different. I've never publicly said anything negative against another Réverian before. I've never had to stare at the aftermath of my anger and figure out how to repair things on my own. To figure out why I'm so angry in the first place.

Calmly, I repeat, "What, then?"

"An apology," Samuel says. "To Prime Minister Barnard."

"Absolutely not."

"Your Highness—"

"I said no." I drag a hand through my curls. They're longer than I'm used to. I need a haircut. I need all of this to get easier, but it doesn't. "I'm not doing it, Samuel."

He tugs at his tie. He's wearing a suit. *On a Saturday*. He takes his job seriously, never a day off, while I'm baking.

It's not fair to him. He's doing everything possible to get back home.

I am too, right?

"I'll try harder," I promise. "We'll think of something else. Another interview. We can fly Réverie's ambassador in DC out here for a dinner. Arrange a photo op."

"And your speech for the Sunset Ball?"

"Working on it," I lie.

"Of course, Your Highness."

"Jadon," I prompt. "Remember?"

The smile on Samuel's lips isn't very convincing. "I'll add it to your itinerary." He whips a tablet out of thin air. "Should I set up something soon?"

"Can we work it around my rehearsals?" I request.

According to Dr. Garza Villa's email, the play's opening night is after Willow Wood's holiday break. Well, their first one. Why do Americans celebrate so many holidays? We got our production calendar yesterday. Read-throughs start next week.

For reasons I don't completely understand, I still want to go through with this.

To have a little more time not being Prince Jadon.

Samuel's expression remains neutral, even if I can read the indifference in the corner of his eyes. "Noted. Perhaps the night you and the crown princess are having dinner with Senator Miller and his daughter?"

Another of Annika's suggestions. Except *she* wasn't the one who had to propose the idea to Grace.

"Sure," I say.

Samuel smiles apathetically. "I'll send out communications."

When he's out of sight, my shoulders sag. This is fine. I can convince Rêverie to love me. *Respect* me. There's still time to make this right.

"Grace," I say, smiling, cheeks stretched to the limit. "About your Halloween bash."

She squints against the high sun. It's lunch hour. A trio of girls wave, trying to snag her attention, but she merely fixes the buttons on her cardigan, head tilted at me.

"Yes?"

"Is there going to be any . . ." I tug on my earlobe. "Press? Photographers?"

Despite how many people were crammed into Nathan's house party, no major media outlet reported about me being there. Only local gossip bloggers picked it up. Even Kip Davies barely gave it a mention on his nightly show.

But this is bigger. It's a *politician's daughter's* party. A significant event at a premier LA location. It's bound to attract more attention.

The kind that Réverie will notice.

Grace hums. "A few. Last year, my dad demanded a step-and-repeat outside. For the memories. He's always too busy to attend."

"Dude." Nathan laughs. "No one wants your dad there."

Grace looks like she's considering shoving him into the fountain. She turns back to me. "Why? Scared to be seen hanging with us normies?"

"No," I quickly say.

"I'm kidding, Your Highness." She lightly smacks my shoulder. I try not to scowl. "Seriously, if you need a backdoor entrance, I can—"

"No," I repeat, resurrecting my smile. "Photos are fine."

They're perfect. Especially if someone on the inside gets a video of me mingling with classmates. Surviving a party without incident. It's a small step, but I need Réverie's people to see me being the congenial, charming, down-to-earth prince they *deserve* around important people like Grace.

"I was just checking," I say. "For security purposes."

Grace nods like she understands. "It'll be small."

Small like the last time, I think to say, but that won't help my cause.

"Lies," Morgan says for me, cackling.

"Are you bringing a plus-one?" Grace asks.

I don't answer right away. Instead, I roll my shirtsleeves to my elbows. I haven't completely conformed to everyone else's uniform protocol. Only tiny adjustments. I consider Grace's question.

A plus-one. Someone to pull me away from boring conversations. Who'll make me laugh or call me out when my resting prince face kicks in.

Would Reiss say yes if I asked?

"I don't know," I finally say.

On the other side of Grace, Morgan gives me a look. Pursed lips, accusing eyebrow. Like she knows exactly what I was thinking.

I ignore her. "Would it be okay if I did?"

Grace straightens her posture, crossing her legs. "Let me know. I want to make sure . . ." She trails off.

The bell rings in the quad.

As Nathan scoops up his skateboard and Morgan packs away her lunch, Grace says, "Just get my approval first."

It's not a command, but there's a hint of something in her voice. Concern? Distrust? I don't know her well enough to decipher it. I haven't *tried* to get to know her either.

"Of course," I say before she walks away.

I jog after Morgan, who's headed in the opposite direction. "Wait," I say, a little breathlessly, when I catch up. "What was that?"

Morgan doesn't slow down, but her forehead wrinkles. "What was what?"

"With Grace," I get out. For someone shorter than me, Morgan's fast. Was it like this when she gave me a tour of campus? "The plus-one thing."

A realization flashes in her eyes. "Grace is . . . uptight about certain things," she says.

"Certain things?" I repeat with a skeptical stare.

Morgan adjusts her backpack. "She doesn't trust everyone. Look at who she is." She sizes me up. "I'm sure you understand."

I make a face. "I'm not like—"

Her hard stare, pinched face, dares me to finish my sentence.

"Point taken," I relent.

"She has her reasons," Morgan adds without elaborating. "She likes to know who's going to be around her inner circle or whatever."

"Sounds controlling."

"You're no trip to Disneyland yourself, Just Jadon," Morgan comments. Again, I don't argue. I follow her around the corner. "Also, maybe don't bring a certain film student with pink hair to the party."

I stumble a little.

"I have no idea who you're referring to."

"You're a bad liar," she says impassively.

"Why not him?" I ask, voice tight.

"Reasons," is all she says, nodding to the end of the open-air hallway we've just walked into.

There's a thick, white column almost blocking him, but I know it's Reiss. His constantly moving hands give him away.

Standing a little too close to him is a short boy. He whispers in Reiss's ear. Shadows partially hide Reiss's expression, but not the other boy's smirk.

"This isn't the palace, Just Jadon," Morgan says. "People have their secrets around here."

I watch Reiss's hand brush the boy's as he takes his phone, types something, then returns it.

Logically, I know Reiss is allowed to talk to whoever he wants. We're not dating. We're not . . . anything. And I'm not mad. My knuckles aren't aching from how hard I'm squeezing my fists at my sides.

"I'm late for class," I say hoarsely, *not* stomping away like someone who's clearly bothered by what he just saw.

It just looks that way to anyone who sees me.

Rehearsals are a disaster.

Truthfully, *I'm* the disaster. We're on day four of read-throughs. Everyone's present—the cast, stage crews, techies—as I stumble through my lines. Dustin's face is alarmingly red, like he's made a huge mistake. Dr. Garza Villa spends half our allotted time correcting me. Either I'm too tense or too monotone. Speaking too fast or missing my cue.

By the end, Mr. June, the second faculty adviser, is tugging off his heels and shaking out his deep blond hair. He mutters, "I didn't leave Broadway *twice* for this," stomping offstage.

"Let's do some independent meditation and reflection before we call it a day," Dr. Garza Villa suggests.

Students huddle together onstage for the exercises. I flop

into one of the auditorium's front row seats. Head down, I roll and unroll my script. Try to clear my head. Focus on something other than what Morgan said.

People have their secrets around here.

Why did her words surprise me? It's not like I haven't encountered this before. Classmates at Académie des Jeunes Dirigeants smiling in my face, only to catch them making fun of me in the restrooms. Kofi ditching me in LA. Prime Minister Barnard insulting my mom behind closed doors.

Léon.

A sharp, unwanted pain cuts across my chest like a blade. The memories come in clear, vivid colors. Orange like a dying star when Léon stopped being around as much, blaming travel and modeling gigs for all the missed calls. Watercolor blues when he kissed me in Centauri's gardens, only to end our relationship the next morning with an "I'm—*we're* not happy. It's not the same anymore." Bloodred when he walked away from me as I tried to talk about what his papa said.

I know how this goes. How it always ends. It's why I keep my guard up. Maintain a distance from people. But Reiss—he feels different.

I *want* it to be different.

"Bro!"

I startle as Karan drops into the seat next to me. "Is this a method acting trick? Are you purposely fucking up because Mr. Green is an anxious, clumsy mess?"

My brows knit. "Yes?"

"Don't get me wrong—I appreciate the dedication. But it's not that serious."

"It's not?"

"Of course it is!" He clutches his chest in faux distress. "How am I going to make it to Hollywood, star in the ultimate badass movie franchise that finally overthrows that Fast and the Furious nonsense if you don't get your head in the game? Did you know Vin Diesel is my villain origin story?"

My lips quirk into a small smile. "No."

"Now you do." He stretches his legs out. "Wanna talk about it?"

"Not one bit."

"Perfect. Group psychologist is Lo's strength, not mine."

"Who?"

"Bestie number two. You haven't met them?" His face scrunches. "Makeup crew manager?"

To be honest, outside of Karan, I hadn't bothered to memorize the cast or crew list. The same way I haven't bothered learning most of my classmates' names. Half of my teachers too.

He shakes his head. "Don't worry. We'll fix that. Tomorrow night."

"What's tom—"

"I'm officially inviting you to hang with the squad," Karan interrupts, smile glowing brighter than the stage spotlights. "Movie night. It's a tradition."

"Movie night," I repeat, considering.

Samuel wants me to concentrate on finding new ways to win over Réverie's approval. Regain their trust. Which I'm working on. But I'm supposed to prove I'm capable of living a normal life too. That not everything I'm involved in is drama and scandal and *breaking-news*-worthy.

"Sounds fun," I say.

"Oh, it is." Karan's grin widens. "Great food. Stellar movie selection. Instant relief from whatever's making you look like this."

He mimics my expression. It's a very accurate impersonation of resting prince face. I choke out a surprised laugh.

"We usually have it at my villa," Karan explains, "but my parents are renovating. Mamma refuses to let the Warrens' kitchen outshine ours." He waves at a few cast members as they leave. No one makes eye contact with me. "We could probably do it at Lo's—"

"What about where I'm staying?" I offer.

Karan hums, most likely weighing his options.

"I have the space. And a screening room," I attempt. Karan's mouth puckers like that's the norm around here, so I add, "I'd love to host. Please."

"Are you sure? We can get pretty rowdy."

I snort. As if watching a movie could top anything I encountered at that Welcome to America bacchanal Grace put together.

"Positive," I confirm.

I *should* run all this by Samuel and Ajani first. Royal privacy, official paperwork, security measures. But it's just one night. A friendly hangout. Something I rarely had in Réverie outside of Kofi coming to the palace for video games or the times I snuck Léon into my private suite past midnight.

How difficult can it be?

"Sick." Karan yanks out his phone. "I'll let Lo know. Reiss, too." His eyebrows waggle in a way that makes my face uncomfortably warm. "He'll love it. Movie night at a prince's crib two days before his birthday—"

"His birthday?" I blink.

"Don't make it a big deal," Karan insists as he types. "His fam already goes overboard."

"Of course," I say, going for casual, even though my heart's drumming harder than the bass in a hip-hop song.

"Bet," he says. "Message me your addy."

I do. This is good. A nice, normal, real Friday night hangout with my peers. With people I *like*. With Reiss.

Morgan's words still cling to the corners of my skull like a poltergeist. But I'm not letting her warning ruin things. I need to know for myself if I can fully trust Reiss.

If this is something . . . more.

9

SPOTTED: REBEL ROYAL AND CROWN PRINCESS DO LA IN STYLE!

While their father, King Simon, is attending a climate conference in Norway, Crown Princess Annika and Prince Jadon were seen Saturday morning in Santa Monica's famed Third Street Promenade complex. Exclusive photos show the royal siblings, flanked by heavy security, emerging from Hugo Boss with multiple bags in hand. The fabulously dressed duo (see our coverage of HRH Princess Annika's best outfits!) also visited Nordstrom and Nike.

Later, HRH Prince Jadon was photo'd at Trader Joe's with his personal bodyguard. He left with an overflowing grocery cart. How long is this new, low-key royal planning to stay in America and avoid his problems back home?

I'm fine. Pacing around in the same circle for thirty minutes is fine. Repeatedly checking my phone, anticipating a cancellation text—because who would want to hang out with *me* on a Friday night?—is fine.

It's only a movie night. With a boy who's also *not just a boy*.

I pause long enough to check my reflection in the living room mirror. Slim-fit chinos rolled at the ankles. White V-neck T-shirt giving intentional glimpses of collarbone. Dewy skin from a recent face mask. Curls that still look natural despite my constant touching.

I look casual. Calm. Not the expression of someone panicking.

"You're panicking," Annika comments when she sweeps in wearing a Badgley Mischka wrap dress under an emerald blazer. She pauses behind me to fix her earrings. "It's cute. Very first date vibes."

"It's not a date," I correct her. "It's a group thing. With people I go to school with."

"*Friends*," she insists. "It's okay to use that word."

Is it?

One, I've never met Lo. Two, outside of rehearsals, Karan and I haven't had conversations. Three, Reiss and I are . . . I don't know. Does what we've done—talk at a party, his family's coffee shop, in a smelly locker room—count as a friendship? Is that enough?

When I'm quiet for too long, Annika raises inquisitive eyebrows. I lean into my favorite rule of being a royal: *deflect, always*.

"I want everything to be right," I say.

Organizing a get-together is new for me. It's a job usually handled by the palace chamberlains. Or Samuel, since we've been here. Even ordering the food was a tremendous effort. Another reason I long for the comforts of home.

Annika smiles in mock sympathy. "Poor Jade. Do you want to google 'how to make friends' together?"

I stick my tongue out at her just as Luc strides into the room. He's in an all-black suit. "Don't worry, Your Highness," he says. "The princess isn't good at social activities either. She almost broke out in hives making a dinner reservation."

"It was an allergic reaction to cheap sunscreen," Annika argues.

"Keep telling yourself that."

Luc smirks. Something indescribable sparks behind Annika's eyes. "Nerves are good," she tells me. "It means you *like* Re—"

"Aren't you going to be late?" I cut in.

She's attending *A Night at the Orchestra with Romeo + Juliet*, a music exploration of the Baz Luhrmann film. It's at the Los Angeles Philharmonic. My sister, the cultured one.

"He's right," Luc announces after confirming with the security team over the phone. "Traffic is already disgusting."

I smile. "Everyone must've heard the future queen is coming."

Annika smacks my shoulder. "Remember: no fires. Wait thirty minutes after eating before swimming. No escorting cute, pink-haired boys up to your bedroom—"

"Bye, Your Majesty!" I shout.

Annika's loud cackling echoes through the house long after she's gone.

When the doorbell rings, I'm too anxious to answer.

Samuel greets everyone with a polished smile. And a ready-to-sign NDA on his tablet. "For discretionary purposes," he says smoothly.

I want to die.

Thankfully, he was open to my Friday night plans. Though, I received a subtle amount of side-eye when I avoided his question about the progress of my speech for the Sunset Ball.

By his side, Ajani collects everyone's phones. Who starts off a movie night like this?

To their credit, no one balks or turns around to leave.

Instead, Karan whistles in the foyer. "Eff my parents' bank account. Dope crib, Jadon!"

"Welcome to my house," I announce, my voice way too loud. "Er, not *my house*. I don't own it. My family does have several vacation homes across the world. And the palace is much bigger—"

I cut off my rambling, skin prickling with embarrassment.

Karan laughs. "Jadon, meet Lo Jiménez."

Lo steps forward, wearing ripped black jeans and a shirt that reads, THEY/THEM > YOUR PRONOUNS. Their hair is dark green, almost black, cut in an asymmetrical bob. Sparkling gunmetal nail polish contrasts nicely with their pale beige skin.

"The best slice of our epic trio," Karan adds.

Lo smirks like they know something about me even I don't yet. "Nice to meet you."

They step aside, and I finally have a clear view of Reiss.

Pure-white low-top Nikes that match his shorts. A navy crewneck sweatshirt, the sleeves tugged over his knuckles.

Bedhead pink hair. So perfectly effortless, I can't take it.

He flashes that crooked grin. "What's up, HRA?"

I smile back.

"HRA?" Karan stage-whispers to Lo. "What's that?"

"His Royal—" Reiss starts.

Karan snaps his fingers. "His Royal Aristocrat!"

Lo shakes their head, hair swishing across round cheeks. "His Royal Attractiveness."

Reiss's face goes absurdly pink. "What? No. It's His Royal Arro—"

"I like His Royal Attractiveness," I insert, smirking. "Don't you?"

His skin turns a shade darker. He holds up two white bags with the distinct red-and-yellow In-N-Out logo on them. "We brought food," he deadpans, avoiding my question.

"Oh." I glance over my shoulder. "I ordered . . . things."

They follow my gaze to the kitchen. On the island is a massive spread of food I had delivered from all the best-reviewed restaurants nearby. Plus, sodas and cans of the bubbly water brand I've seen everyone at school drinking.

"I wanted to bake a peach galette too," I say, frowning, "but Trader Joe's only carried jarred slices. Nothing fresh."

Reiss cocks his head. "So, you're kind of an actor, a great swimmer, and you bake? What aren't you perfect at?"

I arch an eyebrow. "Nothing."

He chews on his lower lip, inhaling. I don't look away.

Not until Karan says, "Sorry, Animal Style fries, but you've got nothing on Pearl Dragon's crispy veggie spring rolls!"

He steps around us into the kitchen. Lo silently follows.

I linger with Reiss. His face is unreadable. But his eyes skim over me.

"Should we," he tries after another deep breath, "start the movie?"

I offer him one last teasing grin. "This way."

Inside the state-of-the-art cinema, Lo and Karan *conveniently* claim the reclining chairs on the ends of the row. Which leaves the plush love seat in the middle for Reiss and me.

"Which movie did you pick?" I ask as Karan dims the lights.

"*Clue*," Lo says with very little enthusiasm.

"An '80s classic," Karan explains. "Plus, it's bonus prep work."

"I'm only watching for costume ideas," Lo mentions.

I half-turn to Reiss. "You're okay with this?"

He's not in the play. And he's a movie enthusiast. I'm sure there are dozens of other films he'd prefer to watch.

But his eyes light up in the dark. "Are you joking? It's a cult classic. They don't make comedies like this anymore."

"Okay." I wiggle around until I'm comfortable. My knee brushes Reiss. He doesn't flinch away. Instead, he presses back, and a smile curls my lips. "Let's watch."

He's right. The movie is hilarious. I can't stop laughing into my food. Snorting at someone falling over or screaming. Every character catches my eye, even Yvette, despite her questionable French accent.

"They filmed at a mansion in Pasadena," Reiss narrates.

He does this every few minutes. Offers little anecdotes. Excitedly drops information about the director's shot choices. Describes how scenes come together. In the wash of blues and whites from the screen, his face glows like lightning, eyes crinkled, mouth stretched into a nerdy grin.

It's hard to look away.

"Ooh! And *that*." He points again. "All the secret passages connect to rooms exactly like in the board game. The attention to detail is—"

"Some of us," Karan says loudly, leaning forward, "didn't ask for the director's commentary version."

Reiss shrinks, cheeks flushed.

Lo giggles. "You know how bad he geeks out about this shit."

"I'm doing character study here," Karan grumbles, eyes forward like there's going to be a quiz after the credits roll.

I nudge Reiss's shoulder, voice low as I say, "What else?"

The flutter in my stomach when his crooked grin returns is intolerable.

"Well . . ." To avoid Karan's wrath, he scoots closer. Warm breath against my ear. "See their clothes? They're purposely wearing outfits that don't match their names."

It takes everything not to shiver. Since when has talking about wardrobe been so . . . attractive?

I clear my throat. "That's . . . interesting."

It's nice. His unguarded expression. His shoulder pressed to mine in the dark. The way we both laugh when Karan tosses nachos at us. Reiss's hands in constant motion as he talks, an anxious tic I've picked up on.

I can't help myself. The dopamine high is too strong. While he's going on about another one of the film's nuances, I reach out. Grab his hand. He stops midwhisper.

Panic freezes my muscles. Did I read this wrong? Was I too impulsive, like always, or should I have asked before—

He fits his fingers between mine. Squeezes gently with a timid smile.

I let out a soft breath.

We stay like that until the lights come up.

"So," I say, "I'm playing a queer-baiting character?"

"Wrong," Lo answers. "He didn't identify. Just because he has a wife doesn't mean he's not bi."

"Or pan." Karan munches on a spring roll. "Like me."

I scan the room. "Are all of you . . . ?"

"Queer?" Lo volunteers. "Fuck yeah. Is there any other way to be?"

A laugh tickles my throat.

"I'm demi, BTW," Lo puts in.

Reiss's gaze darts to where our hands were five minutes ago, tucked between our hips, fingers tangled. "Very, very gay," he manages.

Karan leans sideways. "Wait, there aren't any queer kids in Réverie?"

I fight off a frown. I'm not sure. There could've been some at my old school, but it wasn't visible. We had very strict uniform policies. It's not like anyone could walk around wearing a big SAPPHICS ONLY pin like Morgan did the other day.

Not like anyone offered that kind of information to me, despite how openly out I've been.

It always felt like Léon and I were the only ones. Kofi is painfully straight. I want to believe generations of elders were queer in secret, then publicly once the world changed.

But Rêverie doesn't host parades or gatherings during Pride month. Not like the ones I see on the internet.

Every year, it's a quiet celebration. Just me, alone, inside Centauri Palace.

"Not that I know of," I sadly admit.

Karan pats my shoulder. Not condescendingly. With a wide grin, he says, "Welcome to California! Everyone's either queer or not-so-secretly hating you for being queer."

"Isn't that all of America?" Lo proposes.

"The whole world, actually," Reiss sighs.

"Wow. That got dark," Karan says. "Anyway. Jadon, now that you're initiated, I've got one question: when do we get a tour of this epic mansion?"

Convincing Samuel to take Karan and Lo around the grounds takes a tremendous amount of smiling and big, pleading eyes. While he escorts them through the house, I walk out to the main lawn with Reiss.

We stand on one of the cement squares surrounding the pool. The air is cooler tonight. Beyond swaying palm trees, Los Angeles is a field of neon. Between the glittery city and the underwater lights, we're glowing in artificial blues. In the distance, Karan's surprised gasp seeps into our silence.

Reiss shakes his head. "He probably wanted to take Lo on a *private* tour."

I tip my head curiously.

"You can't tell?" He laughs. "Those two are the definition of that 'shut up and kiss already' meme." He dramatically puckers his lips, and I *don't* lean in. But the thought crosses my mind. "Lo's been soft on him since freshman year. After Karan came out, I could tell he was into them too. He wears his heart on his sleeve."

"And you . . . don't?"

"I'm a man of mystery."

We both snort. I wobble a little and Reiss is right there, hands on my hips, steadying me.

"Careful," he says, eyes crinkled. "I'm not explaining to Ajani how you almost drowned. Again."

My skin warms. "Then stop trying to push me in."

"It was an accident!" He groans. "Is it my fault you're clumsy?"

"I'm not clumsy."

"Well, you sure fall easy."

I don't, I almost say, but my tongue's too heavy. I'm hyper-aware of his fingers still on my waist. The darkness in his eyes. Cool breeze kissing my feverish cheeks. The tiny glimpse of pink tongue as he wets his dry lips.

His hands drop away. He turns to face the water. I mirror him, forcing disappointment out of my expression.

"Sorry if this was a boring way to spend the Friday before your birthday," I say.

"It wasn't." In my periphery, his smile is light, delicate. "My family is so extra about birthdays. It's a weeklong thing. Singing and cake and gifts—"

"What's bad about that?"

"You didn't let me get to the part where my mom sobs over me getting older. Or my dad and brother fighting to the death over the last cake slice." He looks mortified. "Did I mention the library of baby photos?"

"Not yet," I say, grinning.

"There. Are. So. Many."

I tip my head back, a breathless laugh catching on the wind.

"I just want to chill with friends," Reiss whispers.

A sad exhale slips through my lips. I miss moments like that. Birthdays where Papa bakes crèmes au caramels. When Mom would wake me at sunset for long, quiet walks along Centauri's private shore. Annika being *home*.

It's not like that anymore.

For my birthday in August, I got a box of macarons. A FaceTime call from Annika promising we'd party together soon. An apology note hand-delivered by Papa's *chamberlain* because another meeting with foreign ambassadors kept him and Mom away.

The crown above everything. Including turning seventeen, I guess.

Reiss's elbow nudges mine. "Is there a lot of singing around the palace on birthdays?"

I shake my head.

"I bet there's a lot of good desserts."

"Always," I confirm, genuinely smiling.

"Is your fam—"

Karan's voice from somewhere overhead cuts off Reiss's next question. "Holy shit! These views! Oprah *who*?"

"The footage you were trying to get at school and the party," I say, eager to get away from the subject of family. Of how much I wish things were different. "What's it for?"

His expression turns sheepish. "Oceanfront Film Fest."

He takes in my twisted, confused face.

"It's a teen festival for short films. Open to all LA County students. The winner earns a summer internship." He pauses, chest expanding. "And a scholarship to USC's film school. The deadline's December first."

"What's your movie about?" I ask.

He cringes, and I laugh until my face is warm again.

"It's about me, isn't it?" I barely get out. "You really do write coffee shop fanfic about me, don't you?"

The threat of kicking me in the pool darkens his face. "I'm not telling, okay?" He sighs. "I'm kind of superstitious."

"That's fair," I say, dipping my head for a polite nod. "But if you're making a film about my dimples, you can tell me. Promise I won't get mad. I'm flattered."

"God, shut up." But he's laughing now. "So fucking cocky."

"Confidence is attractive," I tell him.

"Not on you." His crooked grin and lingering stares say otherwise.

"Fine," I concede. "Keep all your movie secrets to yourself."

"I plan to."

I watch him rock on his heels, suspended in my own awe.

He keeps surprising me with all these little quirks. Quiet admissions. And I keep shocking myself by committing every detail to memory. Like I'll want to remember them. Remember *him* when I'm gone.

The point of everything I'm doing is to get home, but here's this boy sneaking inside the iron ribs I've fortified around my heart. He can't be there. Why am I letting him in?

Why has my "no boys" policy suddenly turned to dust?

I clear my throat. "So tonight was good, then? A decent birthday date?"

"It was good," Reiss agrees. "But it wasn't a date."

Wait. Did I—no. I said *date*.

"I mean—" I scramble to say, my voice way too high.

"Reiss," Karan calls, interrupting my semi-meltdown. "It's pumpkin time. Gotta get Lo home before curfew."

Lo smiles apologetically. "Mamá will murder me if I'm late again."

Reiss nods, half-turning toward me. He's not quite frowning. But his smile isn't as wide either.

"Let me walk you out," I offer.

Outside, Karan pulls his sleek gray BMW up the driveway. Lo launches themselves into the passenger seat. Reiss hovers by the back door. He gives me a soft, wondering look. I don't know how to respond.

A year of dating Léon, and suddenly I don't know how to say goodnight to another boy.

Impulse wins again. I blurt, "Would you like to go on a date?"

Reiss pauses, one hand on the door handle. The tinted windows are lowered. A Moonglow song pours from the speakers.

It's too ironic. Almost too perfect.

"Go on a date with me," I say with more sureness. "Tomorrow."

I ignore the way Lo and Karan are both grinning like their favorite ship just became canon.

Reiss stays motionless, gaping at me.

Karan croons, "Broooooo. It's a date with a prince! If you say no, I will—"

Lo smacks a hand over his mouth just as Reiss says, "Okay. Yes."

I let out a breath that was trapped in my lungs for way too long. "Tomorrow," I repeat before the door closes. Even as they drive off, I can hear Lo's squealing and Karan's whooping and Reiss's embarrassed laughter.

"How disturbing," Ajani says from behind me.

I ignore the dryness in her voice. I'm on a high. So far in the clouds, I can snatch the stars from the sky.

Suddenly, being stuck in America a little longer isn't that bad.

10

YOUNG, BLACK, AND . . . ROYALLY UNINTERESTED?

All eyes are on Prince Jadon. He's the brooding bad boy royal making headlines and crushing hearts globally. *TeenBuzz* sat down with him to learn everything about him. From his fav TV series to his love for pop band Moonglow to what an American boy must do (and what not to do) to win his heart!

"Are all your dates like this?"

I smile sheepishly at Reiss. We're standing on Ocean Avenue. Under the blue-and-yellow arch leading to Santa Monica Pier. It's the first place I thought of after last night. Where Mom always wanted to take me.

A perfect first date with Reiss.

Next to me, a throat clears. "I look ridiculous."

Correction: a perfect first date with Reiss *and* Ajani.

I twist to face her. "You look fine."

She's dressed in yoga pants, an "I ♥ Beach Life" T-shirt

under a blazer, designer sunglasses, and a bucket hat to hide her instantly recognizable hairstyle. On a late Saturday afternoon, the foot traffic around the pier is heavy. We need to blend in.

Reiss eyes me, smirking. "Sweet threads."

The fact that I'm wearing *his* yellow hoodie, the one he gave me after the pool incident, is a complete coincidence. It complements my joggers and retro Lakers Dunks, the purple rib-knit beanie covering my curls. No other reason.

I ignore the fire spreading up my neck. "I've always wanted to visit the pier."

Crinkly-eyed, he says, "Let me show you around."

He navigates us through the crowd, down a steep hill. The moment we step onto the pier's worn wooden surface, Santa Monica blooms around us. Cloudless azure sky. Cool air soaked in salt and a heady spicy-sweetness from all the food vendors. The afternoon's soundtrack is a mash of screams from the Pacific Park amusement rides, seagulls mewing, and waves crashing.

Golden sunbeams accentuate Reiss's smile. "You have to try this."

This: a freshly made tamale from a bright red food cart.

This: a cup of mango slices sprinkled with Tajín seasoning.

This: a Wagyu beef hot dog with seaweed, teriyaki sauce, and Japanese mayo. I shamelessly bite into it. Reiss's laugh when sauce drips from my chin is like a burst of dopamine.

"Sorry," I moan, still chewing. "It's incredible." Another bite. "I can't stop."

"I have good taste." His eyes linger on me.

I hide my smile behind a napkin. "What's next?"

He leads me over to the chipped blue railing overlooking the shore. We fit between friends taking selfies and an old man watching birds soar. The horizon stretches forever. Sunlight smears a gilded band across the teal water. My breath hitches.

"What?" Reiss asks.

The ache in my chest is loud. "It reminds me of Réverie."

We lean against the railing together. His elbow presses to mine, telling me to go on.

"How peaceful the sea is," I say. "Like walks with my mom. Or when my papa would tell me stories passed down from the elders."

"What's it like? In Réverie?"

"Breathtaking sunsets." I smile almost absently. "Mountains to the west. Never-ending beaches. The stars—do you know how the palace got its name?"

He shakes his head, self-conscious. "They don't teach us much outside of US history. A lot of European history too. But not yours."

"Of course not," I huff. "Centauri Palace was named after Omega Centauri. The constellation. When my people were at war for their freedom—when their struggle was nearly unbearable—the elders would say *Look to the stars*. Omega was the clearest constellation in the night sky." My heart thuds with pride, remembering how Papa would recite this story. "They promised that every generation would remember what they did. Just like we remember the stars."

Awe widens his eyes. As if he's hungry for more.

"When they designed the palace," I explain, "they wanted it to stand out like the constellation. A place my people look to for strength."

"Sounds amazing," he exhales.

It is, though I haven't thought about that story in so long. I walk the halls, pass all the art and statues. Our journey etched into the architecture. But I forgot what the palace means to Réverians. To our existence.

How much of that weight I've unconsciously carried with me here.

I study Reiss. I wonder what it'd be like to take him there. To my home. Show him around Centauri Palace and the sprawling marketplace, to the field where I play football. What would it be like to introduce him to my world? How would my parents feel about him?

It's a heavy thought. One I'm not ready to parse through.

"Réverie is incredible," I tell him instead, grinning. "So much life. Community."

He shifts closer. Our biceps touch, then our shoulders. A solid wall of warmth and support.

"I miss it." I lower my eyes. Another wave dampens Santa Monica's shore.

Reiss laughs quietly. "You talk like you're never going back."

When I tense, his gaze intensifies, like he's searching for the reason. My brain says not to tell him. As a royal, I've learned only to give what is necessary. Because the world will take so much from you. Expect so much of you.

I've been betrayed, hurt too many times to do this again.

But my heart—it *trusts* Reiss. He's been open, unguarded.

Forgiving when he could simply be cruel like everyone else has.

It's okay, I tell myself, *just this once*.

"I can't go home," I admit. "Not until I prove myself."

His eyebrows jump up, so I share the barest details. Papa's anger about the video. His demands. How I'm supposed to be the prince my people deserve. I leave out the parts about what the prime minister said and fill it in with how much I want my old life back.

"I'm sorry, that sucks. But I don't know." Reiss shrugs. "Maybe give this place a chance. While you're here, at least. Not all LA people are bad."

"I never said LA people were bad," I retort.

"Your RPF did." The corners of his mouth rise. "Some of us are worth getting to know more. Try it."

There it is again. Those amused crinkles around his eyes. The steadiness in his stare that I fall into.

I bump his shoulder. "I'm here with you, aren't I?"

"I'm so honored," he says wryly. "Come on. There's a lot more to do."

Playland Arcade is just in front of Pacific Park. A spill of noise greets us when we step in. Laughing children, the sharp clatter of air hockey tables, and the sad sound of characters dying. Ajani secures us rechargeable game cards. We leisurely walk around, scouting for what to play first.

I stop abruptly in front of a row of Skee-Ball machines parked opposite the bank of claw machines brimming with stuffed animals.

Reiss's face wrinkles. "I don't know. I'm not very good."

"Afraid I'll beat you?" I challenge.

His eyes narrow. "Fine. Let's go."

As he brushes against my arm, he says, "Be gentle with me," in a coy voice that leaves me frozen for five long seconds.

The newer machines with glow-in-the-dark inclines are occupied by kids half our size. Reiss strolls over to one of the classic versions at the end of the row. I quickly swipe my card. Cheesy music plays. A set of Masonite-covered balls releases into a slot on the side.

My first attempt is decent. The ball hops up the ramp, landing in the center hole. The digital scoreboard lights up: 30 points. I whoop. It's a short-lived victory, as my eight other balls land in lower-value slots.

"150 points," I announce, the machine spitting out a small strip of prize tickets.

Reiss gives me a slow, unenthusiastic clap.

"Don't worry," I say, skimming my fingertips across the back of his hand as I pass, "I can teach you."

"Can you?"

I rest my hand lightly on the small of his back. He's in a long-sleeved graphic tee and denim shorts today. I guide him forward, chin on his shoulder. With another card swipe, a new set of balls releases. I push the first one into his palm.

"It's all in the arm," I instruct. "And the hips."

"Any *other* tips?" he asks, amused.

My back stiffens. "Nope. Sorry. Um, proceed."

His first roll is wobbly. The game makes a pathetic noise as the score reads *0 points*.

"So close," I encourage.

After a couple of practice arm swings, he says, "Oh, that was just a warm-up."

My brow creases. "Just a warm—"

His next roll is smooth, fluid. The ball leaps gracefully from the incline's peak into the 40-point hole. The next lands in the 50. Another 50. His fifth and sixth balls swish into the tiny 100-point rims at the top corners.

The scoreboard climbs and climbs. Red flashing lights twirl, a siren wailing. Reiss ends at 480 points, a new high score.

I stare at the long ribbon of tickets he rips off. "You said you weren't very good."

"I'm not." That damn crooked grin. "Lo *crushes* me whenever we play."

Whatever frustration, embarrassment I have from losing, from him *scamming me*, quickly dissipates at the light in his eyes. The innocence in his pout. A laugh shudders through me.

Reiss Hayes is an anomaly. And I'm so into him.

He uses his winnings to buy Ajani a stuffed Charizard from Pokémon. He gestures in my direction, says, "For putting up with him."

She almost smiles, the traitor.

At the front of the arcade is a photo booth. "We have to," I tell him. "For the memories."

We don't exactly fit behind the closed curtains. We're both too broad-shouldered. I scoot left. He squirms right. Nothing works, so I suggest, "What if you sit on my lap?"

His eyebrow lifts, doubtful. "What if *you* sit on *my* lap?"

"Oh." My face burns. "Okay."

And there I am, prince of Îles de la Réverie, second in line to the throne, easing into the lap of a pink-haired Californian boy.

He swipes his card. The touchscreen lights up. Like last night, his breath dances over my ear as he picks a setting. Every motion pushes his chest into my back. I don't move, too afraid he'll notice I'm semi-hard in my joggers.

"This one?"

He's picked the classic design. I slowly turn my face. His teeth tug on his lower lip, leaving it red, a little swollen.

I rush out, "Sure. Definitely. That works."

"Cool."

His other hand squeezes my hip. Lightning strikes in my veins. I squeeze my thighs together, praying to whatever god that presides over this damn pier to keep my body in check.

"Smile!"

"Wha—"

The first shutter catches me off guard. Recovering, I prepare myself for the next one, watching the countdown on the screen. Reiss holds up his hand, his thumb pointed downward with his index finger curled forward. I snort, then mirror him. We grin widely as our fingers form a heart.

For the third photo, I make a joke, and the shutter goes off as Reiss's head tips back in laughter, my own head resting on his shoulder.

"Last one," he whispers.

I angle my head to look at him. His soft smile. The flecks of hickory in his dark eyes. His slow breaths. My hand slips up to cradle the back of his neck.

"Three . . . two . . . one."

We don't blink. Our eyes never leave each other. The shutter clicks.

"Here." Outside, Reiss passes me the photo strip. "You keep it."

The final shot at the bottom is hard to rip my gaze from. We're almost kissing.

A very, very close almost.

"Thank you." I slip the photos into the kangaroo pocket of my—*Reiss's*—hoodie. "Let's go see the park."

Reiss rejects getting on the Pacific Wheel, the solar-powered Ferris wheel. "I don't do heights," he says. Instead, we walk around the rides before he coaxes me to the end of the pier for carne asada tacos at Mariasol.

There, we eat and watch the sunset streak the sky a heavy pink from a patio overlooking the Pacific.

"What was it like"—I squeeze lime over my taco—"being raised here?"

His index finger raises in a "one moment" fashion. He's already halfway through his third taco. After swallowing, he launches into life in Santa Monica.

As a kid, he fell for the laid-back culture. He hates visiting his cousins in Seattle, because it never rains in Southern California like it does there. Growing up, his passions jumped from animals to surfing, then finally film.

"Dom came along when I was six," he says, crunching on nachos. He talks about adjusting to life as a big brother. The coffee shop came a little later, his hardworking parents quitting their respective jobs to open the business.

"It was their dream. Since college, I think."

I wonder if Mom's ever had thoughts like that. Abdicate her queenship. Return to her other passions. I'm too nervous to ask her. Too scared she'll say this is who we're supposed to be, period.

Reiss talks about primary school. Never having a real friend group until Karan and Lo. Getting into Willow Wood.

"At first, it sucked," he admits after stealing my last taco.

"You mean, life as a social outcast?"

He tosses a used lime at my chest. "No." A frown tightens his features. "Being one of the very few Black kids there."

I nod. It's one of the most painfully apparent things about Willow Wood. Other than the oversaturated, pretentious content. There's just enough visible melanin to check all the diversity boxes. I've never experienced that in Réverie.

We go quiet as we eat. At the table next to ours, two college-aged boys share enchiladas. One has tan skin and dark hair, wearing a Stanford sweatshirt and black-rimmed glasses. The other's wild curly hair stands out against his fair brown complexion. His T-shirt reads STAFF OF ONCE UPON A PAGE.

Without staring, I can tell they're in love.

It's in their smiles. Their easiness. The way the curly-haired boy feeds his boyfriend.

Something shifts in my belly as I turn my gaze back to Reiss.

Léon was never like this—so open. Vulnerable. We're sons of powerful figures. Our walls are built so high, sometimes we couldn't see the sun. Or each other.

He'd let me talk for hours about the things I hated, what I wished was different, but he rarely shared his own struggles.

He was great at deflecting. Maybe he was better at being a royal than me too.

Our waitress refills our water glasses, head tilted as she looks at me, then Reiss. Wordlessly, she slips back inside.

"Anyway." Reiss sighs. "Lo helped me dye my hair green. Then bright red. Now pink. I gave everyone at school another reason to stare. Other than my skin color." He smirks. "Also, fuck them. I look amazing."

"Now who's the confident one?"

"Can't help facts." He leans in. "Or maybe you're just rubbing off on me."

Silence again. I see the moment he realizes what he said. The big eyes, drooping mouth. I burst into laughter. Even Ajani chokes on her water.

"That's it." I snatch his Mexican Coke away from him. "No more. You're cut off."

Under the table, his ankle crosses over mine. He presses firmly. "What if I'm not ready to go home?"

That instant charge from the photo booth returns.

I clear my throat. "Then don't."

I don't know if I'm talking to him. Or myself.

Do I want to stay?

I never answer that question. Night creeps over the pier. Our time is winding down. Reiss's parents don't have a strict curfew, but they still want him home at a reasonable hour. We climb back toward Ocean Avenue with the same reluctant energy.

My phone pings. A message from Samuel. I ignore it, but my eyes catch on the date:

October 12. Tomorrow is Reiss's birthday.

"Shit," I hiss, reality sinking in. We stutter to a stop. My eyes scan around, Ajani shifting into position as if I've spotted a threat, ready to use her stuffed Pokémon as a weapon. But that's not it. I say to Reiss, "Can you wait right here? I forgot something."

He frowns.

"It'll be only a minute," I promise.

"Sure" is barely across his lips before I signal Ajani to follow me. We hastily move through the crowd. Back to the pier. There are even more bodies than earlier. I almost trip over a group taking selfies in front of the ROUTE 66 sign.

I don't know where I'm headed until I see a yellow shop with a blue and white awning and a neon sign: FUNNEL CAKES.

If Papa saw me here, buying a plate of greasy fried dough instead of *baking something,* he'd exile me to a place far worse than California. It's a poor substitute for a real cake. But I'm working with very little resources.

"Cake," I announce, breathless, when I reach Reiss again. "Kind of."

A beat. Reiss blinks at the golden dough buried under powdered sugar. Eventually, his lips tip into an intrigued smile.

"Is this for . . . my birthday?"

I nod. "A valid interpretation, right?"

He laughs. "It's the thought that counts."

We share the chewy lump. It's not as mouthwatering as anything Reiss has treated me to, so far. The weird mix of too much oil and even more sugar leaves my throat dry. But he doesn't complain. He beams, and I do too, absorbed in his world.

In *his* Santa Monica.

Nearby, outside Palisades Park, an amateur rapper/singer duo mashes up Nas's classic "If I Ruled the World" with that "Everybody Wants to Rule the World" song I hear everywhere. There's powdered sugar on Reiss's nose. On my hands too. I dust them off, then step forward.

We're under the arch. A cloud of silvery light pours on us.

"You've got a little—" I swipe my thumb over the tip of his nose. "Sugar."

Harsh pink floods his cheeks. "Is it bad?"

"No. But . . ." A wild spike of adrenaline flows in my blood. My fingers slip lower. Brush powder from the corner of his mouth. "There too."

It's like something out of a movie.

Ocean Avenue's traffic slows. Every noise muted by the sound of my heart. Reiss inhales sharply, anticipation burning in his eyes. Consent in his dilated pupils. But I don't want to read the signs wrong.

"Can I kiss you?"

My fingers are still hovering near his mouth. His gaze is steady. I wait for him. He doesn't take long. Swallowing, he says, "Yes."

I press my lips against his, closing my eyes.

Santa Monica fades. Nothing matters more, not a single car honking or breeze changing, than his fingers touching my jaw. My hand on the nape of his neck. His soft mouth opening. The tease of sour lime and powdered sugar and *him*.

His kiss tastes like everything wrong is finally going right.

"*My prince.*"

An urgent voice. I think it's Reiss. But it can't be. Our lips are still shifting, learning. It comes from somewhere else, but my brain is caught in the sparks exploding behind my eyelids as his hands grip my waist.

Wait, no. Those aren't sparks. They're *flashes.* Quick bursts of light followed by shutter noises louder than the ones from the photo booth. Voices yelling from all sides of me.

"Prince Jadon! Turn toward me!"

"Your Highness! Over here!"

"This way, Jadon! Look at the camera!"

11

I made a massive, unforgivable, rookie mistake.

The rules were laid out as soon as I was old enough to tie my own shoes:

Never smile too much in photos. Head high, posture straight. Keep all royal matters private. Any discussion with the media will be coordinated and approved of by the palace first. No politics. Greet everyone with a polite smile or wave. Refrain from all public displays of affection unless it bene-

fits narratives created by the palace. Never bring shame to the crown.

That last one is why I'm banished to America. Why I was supposed to be focusing on regaining my country's trust. Convincing everyone I'm someone different. A *respectable* prince. I was supposed to be avoiding bad headlines.

Four out of four unaccomplished goals. At least I'm consistent.

By 8:00 a.m., photos of the kiss are everywhere. Social media. Newsfeeds. Morning talk shows. A nonstop cycle.

No one's identified Reiss yet. Ajani stepped in at the last second to cover his face with her blazer. The grainy images are mostly focused on my surprised face. But there's no telling how long that'll last. The press is ruthless and smart and rich.

Samuel plunks four different smart devices and a mug of chai onto the kitchen island. "We need to strategize," he says. "Now."

I glance at him from over my phone. My current strategy? Obsessively checking my messages to Reiss. I waited until at least 8:05 a.m. before sending the first one. Well, the first since my apology DM last night.

HAPPY BIRTHDAY! 🎉🎂🎈

I'm incredibly sorry about
what happened.

I'll fix this.

I hope this doesn't ruin your
special day.

No response so far. No read receipts either. I suppose it's good he's gone dark. But it's the worst too. All I can think about are the seconds before the first flash—his hands on my hips, the softness of his mouth.

How perfect it was.

"It's so romantic," Annika gushes from the plush sofa in the entertainment room. "The glowing pier sign overhead. A prince and a civilian. The feral photographers screaming at my little brother while he makes out with a boy. So royal teen rom-com!"

"Not what I was going for, Anni!" I yell, head in my hands.

"It may very well be a death sentence for our plans," Samuel sighs out.

I lift my eyes, frowning. This kind of conversation would usually be happening behind the Rouge Room's closed doors. With chamberlains and specialists talking over each other. Emergency countermeasures being coordinated. Now, it's just me, my sister, our guards, and a frantically pacing Samuel.

What a team.

"The LA news agrees." Luc points toward the wall-mounted flatscreen, the sound muted.

The headline scrolling across the bottom of the screen:

REBEL ROYAL CAUGHT IN ANOTHER SCANDAL?

A scowl tightens my face. Is me kissing someone truly a *scandal*? Or is it because we're boys?

I don't have the energy to dissect everything that's wrong with the media.

"It's fine," Annika insists, her expression softening. "It happens."

"To *who*?" I almost shout. "Literally, who else does this happen to?"

"Whom," Annika corrects, unfazed by my tone. "At least you'll have lots of photos from your first kiss with Reiss. First date!" She turns to Ajani, grinning wildly. "Was he nervous?"

Ajani smiles. "Like a child on his first day of primary school."

"Can we focus on more important matters," I shout, my face on the verge of combusting from the heat.

"Yes, please." Samuel types away on a tablet, then his phone. His eyebrows knit. "We need to counter this. Fast."

"Counter what? Jadon having a boyfriend?" Annika asks.

"I don't have a—" I cut myself off.

I don't . . . do I?

I like Reiss. As far as first dates go, it was unforgettable, even better than the one I had with Léon. But I'm not in America for a relationship. I have something to prove, a home I'm trying to get back to. A boyfriend isn't included in that plan.

"It was just a date," I whisper to my phone, where there's still no answer from Reiss.

"Unfortunately, it wasn't the wisest choice either," Samuel says. "If we're trying to win back Réverie's favor, being romantically involved with Mr. Hayes might've done more damage."

Anger tightens my jaw. "Why? Because he's *American*?"

I hear Barnard in my head again. The Réverians like him, who don't like "outsiders." Who believe our country is fine the way it is, the way it's always been.

The ones who hate my mom.

Samuel startles at the bite in my voice. "No, Your Highness. Because they adored and admired you and Léon together. The perfect homegrown, noble romance."

I scoff. Perfect romances don't end out of nowhere. They don't crash and burn like we did after the breakup.

"But isn't Jadon courting"—when my eyes flash at Annika, she corrects—"*being seen in a possibly romantic way* good for his reputation too? It shows an approachable, kind side of him. Not surly and moody—"

"We get the point, Anni," I groan.

"Yes, Your Highness," Samuel agrees, "But we want *Réverie* to love and respect him again. To see him as the royal figure he is."

He clears his throat, clearly nervous about his next words. "Reiss isn't royalty. He's . . . just a boy."

"He isn't," I say through my teeth.

Samuel bows. "Deepest apologies, Your Highness. It's your decision on how to move forward. But if you choose to continue this romance publicly, then I fear we won't win the war we're fighting."

My fingers curl to fists on the island. It's *our* war, yet I'm the one on the front line. The one taking all the casualties.

I know it's not fair to think that way. They're all trying to help. But I'm exhausted. My entire life, someone's made decisions for me. Where I'm going, how long I stay, what to wear, and when to speak and when to listen.

Nothing is ever fully in my control. But I'm not giving them this.

This isn't just about me. It's about Reiss too.

"I need time to think," I tell them.

Samuel bows again. Annika hugs her knees to her chest, looking like the little girl I remember who hated wearing heels. Whose royal suite was always a mess, no matter how many times the staff cleaned it.

She gives me a small smile. "I'm here if you need me."

I mouth, *I know*, nodding. Then, I walk away.

I hide away in my bedroom the rest of the day. I lie in the bed that still doesn't feel like mine. I leave my phone untouched. The only notifications coming through are media alerts, probably more nonsense from Kip Davies and his lackies. I consider calling Mom, but I know where that conversation will lead, the questions she'll ask.

She'll be the queen when all I want is my mom.

You're a prince. It's not about what you want. *It's about what our country* needs.

That's what she'll say.

What Papa says when I fuck up. Which is constantly, apparently.

"It was one kiss," I whisper to the ugly ceiling fixture. But it's never just one, is it? Life is a row of dominos, one falling into the next, everything moving so rapidly, beyond your control, until every piece crashes to the ground.

The only glimmer of hope is that *you* get to decide what the pattern looks like when it's finished.

So that's what I do. I make the decision.

I snatch up my phone. For an hour, I research, then make a call, ignoring Ajani's suspicious stare when I ask about credit card information. After it's coordinated and paid for, the woman on the other end asks what name to sign the card with.

I grin. "His Royal Arrogance."

The first message lights up my phone at 7:22 p.m.

did you do this?!?!

The next message is a video attachment. The camera angle opens from behind The Hopper's front counter, panning over Dominic's giggling face before zooming in on the four people in old-school pin-striped vests and hats. Leave it to Reiss to turn this moment into a cinematic masterpiece.

Through my phone's speaker comes a tinny harmony. The singing quartet is serenading "Happy Birthday" to Reiss. It's a short clip that ends with a familiar laugh.

My heart races as I type.

Remember the singing telegram
part in the movie?

You laughed so hard.

I just wanted to make you smile.

His reply is instant.

ASJKLFDSJ! lol thank you!

sorry i was busy all day w fam . . .
bday activities

can we talk @ school tmrrw??

I'll see if I can make time for you 😚

After Monday's rehearsals, I cross through campus to Adler Studio. The halls and classrooms are all empty, except for the film and video lab. That's where I find Reiss working at the last desktop station near the windows, bathed in late afternoon sunlight. Ajani waits outside. I ease into the rolling chair next to him.

When he notices me, his lips twitch a little, but he doesn't fully smile. He swings his chair around to face me. Silence hangs between us for a beat. He fiddles with one of his helix piercings. I nervously bounce my left leg, stop, then start again.

This isn't awkward at all.

"So, about that first date—" he tries.

"I'm sorry. I know the press can be a lot," I blurt.

"—and that kiss," he's saying, but I'm too busy stammering, "No one knows it's you. In the photos."

Yet, I don't add.

We both pause. I can see him rewinding what I said as I piece through his words. Then, we're laughing, heads shaking.

He sighs, deep crinkles around his eyes. I slide my chair closer, our knees touching.

"You first," I offer, softly.

His fingers drum on his thigh. "I don't like attention. *That* kind of attention. It's why my friendship with Karan works. He loves a spotlight." His arm waves around the lab. "I like to be behind the scenes. Keep things just between me and whoever."

I nod, forcing my eyebrows not to fall. "I understand. I'm sorry the photographers ruined that." Carefully, I add, "But you knew who I was. I'm a prince."

"I know, I know," he groans, face pinched. "I didn't think about that before I said yes to our date. Before we kissed."

"Do you"—I swallow—"regret it?"

"No," he rushes out. "Not at all. I still like you."

I smile. "Is there an 'and' or 'but' coming?"

"*Buuut*," he says, nudging my knee, "I'm worried too. What if cameras show up at the coffee shop? What if they find out where I live?" He frowns. "Fuck, what if they start following Dom around? I don't want that."

"I don't either."

"But you can't control it, can you?"

I lift one shoulder. "In some ways."

By not seeing you anymore, I don't volunteer.

It feels like there's no other way. I hate this part. Dating as a royal is nearly impossible. There's no such thing as privacy and discretion, because the media wants to document every first kiss, first date, first "I love you," and every messy, scandalous fight thereafter.

Samuel was right about one thing: it *was* easier with Léon. At least he knew what to expect.

"I'm sorry," I repeat. "I can—"

"There's something else I haven't told you."

My stomach knots. I run my eyes over him. The way his fingers are drumming on his knees again. His somber eyes. Is this what Morgan was talking about?

People have their secrets around here.

I try to swallow, but my throat's too dry.

"Thing is . . ." Reiss cracks his knuckles. "Well, I kind of have a side hustle."

When I don't speak, he continues, "I write essays. Lit papers. Personal statements for college apps. Whatever Willow Wood's upper elite need and are willing to pay for to keep Mom and Dad off their asses."

I finally blink, surprised. "Sorry, what?"

"It's great money," he asserts, the tops of his ears turning red. "You'd be surprised how much someone will pay for a solid B in a class." He lets out a long breath. "But, um, yeah. That's what I do."

It all makes sense. His hushed discussions with other students between classes. Nathan's suggestion that Grace hire someone to write her paper. But I wasn't expecting this to be his secret. It's not even bad.

Unethical? Yes. But I've done far worse.

It's almost kind of sweet. His leg jiggling nervously. The

way his gaze barely stays on me, like he's waiting for me to shame him.

But I'm not going to. I ask, "What's the money for?"

"Half goes toward a college fund," he confesses. "The rest is for new fits. Better haircuts. Shoes,"—I clock the pair of recently released LeBrons he's wearing—"whatever helps me blend in around here."

"Blend in with people you don't like?" I say, confused.

A muscle jumps in his jaw. "Sometimes, I just want one less target on my back. Sometimes you have to play the game to survive."

It's like ice in my lungs. Hearing someone else say it. Knowing that's exactly what I've been doing at Willow Wood. Playing a game to get back home, at first. But now there's Reiss and I like him and . . .

I don't know what's next.

I recline deeper in my chair. "Your parents don't notice? The new clothes and shoes?"

Reiss nods toward his backpack on one of the desks. "Quick change before home or work. I'm good at hiding things too."

I snort. "Like how good you are at Skee-Ball?"

He shrugs listlessly. "Look, USC is hella expensive. Even if I win Oceanfront Film Fest, it's not a free ride," he explains. "I don't want my parents in debt forever because of me. Dom's only eleven. Not even in middle school. I can't afford to fuck any of this up."

"And dating me could ruin that," I offer, managing a neutral expression.

"Not you," he says. "The press. I can't have them following

me around all the time. Being seen with you might—"

"What if you weren't," I say without thinking. "Seen. With me, that is."

He tilts his head, confused.

I am too. A little. The smart, doesn't-want-to-ruin-his-chances-of-going-home-again Jadon would walk away from this. The Jadon who knows if Kip Davies gets one whiff of my situation, it's game over. Yet, I can't get Samuel's words out of my head:

If you choose to continue this romance publicly . . .

"What if we weren't seen together," I suggest. "*Publicly*. No going places together. No kissing. No touching—"

He groans, clutching his chest melodramatically.

"We keep it between us. Private," I say, serious.

He studies the wall behind me. My heart kicks against my ribs, threatening to shatter bone. It's a wild, risky idea that absolutely no one would agree to—

"I mean," he starts, his mouth creeping higher, "It was a solid first kiss."

I let myself smirk. "Worth keeping things low-key between us? Until we figure the rest out?"

He pretends to think. "I could possibly be convinced?"

My eyebrow arches. "How so?"

"You're the prince." He rests his cheek on his knuckles, smiling innocently. "Aren't you supposed to be charming and creative and—"

"Cute?" I flash my dimples.

"*Conceited*," he huffs. "I was definitely gonna say conceited."

I ignore him, standing. My heel sends the rolling chair

across the room, and I close the small gap between us. Hands gripping his chair's armrests, I bracket him in, towering over him. His head tips back to look into my eyes.

"It was a great first date," I whisper.

And I find my new favorite thing—watching how Reiss gets right before a kiss. The way he chews his lower lip. Hunger dilating his pupils until there's nothing but a thin brown ring around the blackness. His short, tight breaths. Fingers wiggling in his lap, eager to touch me but still unsure where.

That soft, little exhale he lets out in anticipation.

I don't keep him waiting long.

"Ready?" Samuel asks.

I'm not. You'd think I was sweating through my button-up shirt, deeply nauseated, because of another interview. Making an unplanned, emergency television appearance. Or giving a speech. Not from a blank laptop screen.

There's one more conversation that needs to happen today.

I wipe my damp palms on my pants. "Yes."

The video call connects instantly. On-screen, my mom sits on an ornate teal sofa in one of the smaller palace rooms. Hands in her lap, hair down, face almost bare. It's late in Réverie, and she stayed up for this. They both did.

Next to her, in a tailored navy suit, shoulders straight, chin held regally as if this were being broadcast worldwide, is King Simon.

My papa.

I haven't seen him since the morning the video was

released. He still looks the same as he did that day. Angry, disappointed. Heavy wrinkles in his forehead, stern lines around his eyes. His frown is outlined by a dark beard shot through with silver, like streaks of lightning, the same pattern in his low-cut hairstyle.

Samuel bows from his seat. "Your Majesty. Queen Ava."

They vaguely acknowledge him, then it's my turn. I clear my throat. "Bonsoir, Papa. Mom."

Papa gives a small nod. Nothing else. A great start.

Mom says to Samuel, "Thank you for arranging this," then to me, "I thought we agreed on staying *out* of the headlines unless it was for a good cause."

"To be fair, kissing a boy *is* a good cause," I offer, half-smiling. "I like him. He's American. Really nice."

"That's . . . nice," Mom says evenly. "But—"

"It's not that bad," I insist. "We just kissed. On a crowded street. And people saw. What's the big deal?"

Papa hisses, "Ça suffit!"

My mouth clicks shut. *That's enough.* Two words. A month and a half without any communication, not a single phone call from him, and that's the first thing he says to me. Heat fills my chest.

"Son," Mom attempts, softer, but still as serious. "The photos are everywhere. It's a distraction. No one thinks you're taking this seriously. You're a representative of the crown. Of our people."

"So what I did is a bad look for Réverie?" My jaw tightens. "Sorry being seventeen and gay and kissing a boy I like—"

"You're a *prince*," Papa interrupts. "Of royal blood. You're meant to represent our country at the highest level. Maintain a scandal-free reputation. That's what you said you'd be doing in America."

"I am," I attempt.

"Yet," Papa continues, "every time we turn around, there you are! Rebel Royal. Once again, the center of drama."

It's hard not to flinch when he says it. *Rebel Royal.* But the sting is so sharp. The cut, so deep. My eyes mist, and I bite down on the inside of my cheek to stop anything from falling.

"You're there for a reason, remember?" Papa asks.

I nod stiffly.

"Is this the kind of prince you want to be? Is this how you want Réverie to see you? As a joke?"

"I want—" My voice cracks. I try again. "I want to show them I'm better."

"Better than what?" Papa challenges.

Than Prime Minister Barnard, I think to say. *Than people like him who see my mom, my sister, me, as lesser. Unworthy. Better than the son you think I am. Better than who I think I am.*

"I'll work harder," I get out.

"Your chances are running out," Papa warns.

"Simon," Mom whispers, squeezing his forearm. Her eyes flick to me. "Son, we want the best for you. I'm happy you met someone, but—the press is going to be watching you even closer now. Him too."

"He won't be a problem," I say.

Mom's forehead creases, concerned. Samuel clears his

throat before she can ask me any questions. "Pardon me, Your Majesties, but I may have a solution."

My head snaps in his direction. What's he doing? I didn't tell him about my arrangement with Reiss, and we never discussed an alternate plan.

He smiles congenially. "Recently, I was contacted by a dear friend of the royal family. He can help redirect the media's focus. Show the world that, no matter what past difficulties have occurred, our prince is determined to maintain strong bonds with his people."

"He?" Mom says.

The front door chimes. I twist around, working through Samuel's words.

Who is he talking about?

Then, I hear a familiar voice speaking with Ajani in the foyer. A ghost I've been running from walks into the room. Tall, deep brown skin, perfectly square jaw and white teeth, a wide smile I know way too intimately.

"Your Majesties." After bowing, his sharp eyes fall on me. "Bonjour, mon beau."

Léon. Standing five feet from me in the living room. In fucking America.

12

THE HEARTBREAK HEARTTHROB

Posing in Armani ads, wearing Tom Ford on Parisian runways, or doing silly dances for millions of social media followers, chances are you've seen (and secretly crushed on) eighteen-year-old Léon Barnard. He's the son of a prime minister, an occasional model, and the ex-boyfriend of a certain rebel prince. Here's all the tea we have on the world's favorite new heartbroken heartthrob!

"How is he even here?" I shout.

Thankfully, this Palisades house is in a secluded neighborhood. We're on the main lawn. Me, Samuel, and a very smug Léon. I've considered shoving him in the pool more than once.

"Almost thirteen hours on a *commercial* airline, actually," he says. "I expected more from the monarchy."

Samuel facepalms, like Léon wasn't supposed to mention

that part. I tear my glare from my soon-to-be-ex-royal liaison, arms crossed as I wait for Léon to explain more.

"I tried to warn you." He adjusts the sleeves of his suit jacket. Of course, he'd show up unannounced looking like a GQ daydream. I hate him. "Do you ever check your DMs?"

"Not ones from demon ex-boyfriends," I retort.

"And how many of those do you have now?"

I stiffen. There's an unsubtle arch to one of Léon's eyebrows.

"Why are you *really* here?" I ask, avoiding his question. If he's not going to mention the photos, neither am I.

"Mon beau—"

"*Don't*," I snap, "call me that." It's infuriating, the goose-bumps freckling my forearms. How that one nickname undoes me.

"Fine. Your Highness." His grin doesn't slip. "I thought you needed me."

"I don't—"

"Let me finish," he asserts, holding up a finger. "I know the media's all over you. Especially after those . . . *photos* appeared."

Fuck. Now he said it.

"It hurt, Jadon." He sounds anything but. "Seeing that you moved on so quickly, so easily, so"—he pauses, pretending to wipe a tear from his eye, sniffing—"miserably."

"Annoyed the spotlight wasn't on you for once?"

Was that petty? Maybe. Gratifying when his fake-endearing expression slips, his nostrils flaring with agitation? Definitely.

It wasn't always like this. We've known each other since we

were ten. When Barnard was elected prime minister and then, soon after, Papa's coronation. Both of us shoved into a bigger spotlight before we were ready. We've seen each other's worst moments—his parents' divorce; my, well, *everything*—and our best—coming out to each other; our first kiss in the shadows of the palace gardens.

He was the one person I could lean on, other than Kofi. The only one who really knew me.

Now there's this Léon with the perpetually bored expression as he says, "I don't care about the photos. Or your new boytoy."

"He's not—"

He cuts me off. "I'm here to tour American universities. Maman says I can't coast by on my looks. I need to get a real education."

My face twists up. "Wait, *you*, who thinks the world of Réverie? Who constantly says we're better than the rest of the world—"

"Because we are."

He sounds so much like his dad, I want to scream. Or throw him off the cliffside. I refrain only because Samuel's still present.

"Maman says there are great schools here," Léon points out. His defiant grin resurfaces. "And, as I was saying earlier, me being here benefits you too."

"How?" I ask, dryly. "In what world does *you being in LA* benefit me?"

"Well," he begins, "a certain someone mentioned—"

My eyes cut to my left. I'm never going home. Because I'm going to murder Samuel.

"—you need assistance getting Réverie to adore you again," Léon continues. "What better way to accomplish that than being seen together. Proving their former power couple doesn't hate each other. There's no bad blood between you and my pa, because we're friends."

He holds his arms out wide, like he's thoroughly impressed by his own speech.

I'm not.

"*Now?*" My voice breaks. Not out of hurt. Or disbelief. Out of pure, face-heating anger. "You want to be friends now?"

I can barely look at him. It's as if he doesn't remember that day. A week after we broke up. After we agreed things changed and he wasn't happy, and I didn't know how to fix it. That moment when I wanted to talk to him about what I heard his papa say, when I said I needed a friend, and he walked away.

I can't be your friend. The last thing he said to me before the DMs started.

Léon shrugs. "For the media. For your sake, too."

"Your Highness," Samuel tries, "to be fair—"

"What about inviting my ex to America and divulging confidential royal information concerning my life is fair?" I bite out.

He bows. "My apologies. But time is short. You heard the king."

I grimace. When Léon unceremoniously showed up, I

rushed off the video call with my parents. Promised an explanation later. But Papa didn't let me end our discussion without one final warning about my time clock. About proving I'm a *deserving prince*.

"We need to try something different," Samuel advises.

"*This*"—I wave a wild hand at Léon, ignoring the disdain in his expression—"isn't something different."

It's what Barnard wants. Things to stay the same. For the power in Réverie to remain in the hands of its own. No outsiders. No one who dares to defy what we've always done, how we've always existed.

"Jadon." Léon drops a hand on my shoulder. He's unbothered when I flinch away. "A few photos. A dinner or two. Some smiles for the cameras. Just like the good old days."

But I don't want that. Our past is just that—*history*.

Problem is, I don't have another solution. Another way to win back my country's trust. I'm stuck, again.

"He can't stay here," I say to Samuel, exhausted.

Léon scoffs. "I didn't plan to."

I give him one final glare. "Don't make me regret this."

The last thing I hear as I walk back into the house is "What in the fresh hell is this?" from a wide-eyed Annika, frozen in the doorway, finally home from a gallery opening.

It's barely a second before Reiss appears on my phone screen, bleary-eyed and yawning out, "Did you mean to call me?"

"Um, yes?"

I don't mean for it to come out as a question. Truthfully, I didn't think this through. FaceTiming him at midnight. Waking him up. I needed someone to talk to, but Annika's currently ripping Samuel a new one, and Kofi's out of the picture, and my fingers moved quicker than my brain.

When I see his face, half-illuminated in ivory from his own screen, the other half smooshed into his pillow, I realize he *is* the one I want to talk to. About this. About . . . everything.

"Hey," he says, raspy. "What's wrong?"

I stare at my own video square. Wrecked curls, tense shoulders, a pixelated resting prince face. Today has been far too long, and all it takes is one question from Reiss to unleash the flood.

I tell him about Léon being in LA. About how weird and annoying and frustrating it is because—because I've moved on. From him. From the Jadon I was then.

Then, I backtrack to talk about the call with my parents. How no one back home believes I'm different. How Samuel proposed Léon's presence will change that. How pretending to be friends will suddenly reinstate Réverie's trust in me. That I agreed to go along with it not just for myself, but to keep the press off Reiss and his family too.

On the screen, Reiss's eyebrows are practically kissing his hairline.

My heart lurches. I said too much. I didn't explain things right—

"Wow." His eyes crinkle. "Who knew being a royal was so dramatic?"

"It's not funny."

"It isn't," he confirms. He shifts around, revealing a pillow crease on his cheek. "But you seem like you needed a laugh. And a hug."

I sigh. "A hug would be nice."

"So, your ex is gonna be around."

"Only platonically," I rush out. "For the media. He knows about you. There's nothing between me and him."

He snorts. "Obviously. Why would you go back to a six when you have an eleven?"

I squint at him, smirking. "Who's the confident one now?"

"Just stating facts." He yawns again. "If hanging with him means people will stop focusing on what happened the other night, then cool. More alone time for us, right?"

"Right." I toe off my Jordans, scooting onto the bed. Crash into the pillows with an embarrassingly big smile. "Just you and me."

He nods, eyes heavy. "I don't have to meet him, do I?"

"No."

"Good." He pauses. "Not that I'm worried. I don't get jealous."

"Allegedly," I say with a laugh.

He flips me off, but the corners of his mouth tease up.

Silence creeps in. I realize this is the first time we've ever FaceTimed. We haven't even talked on the phone before. I've never had to figure out how to say goodbye to him.

So, I don't.

We lie on our sides and eventually let sleep say it for us.

❖❖❖

"Okay. That's enough."

I almost knock over a full carafe of water when Léon reaches across the table to steal my phone away. I'd been studying the photos Samuel forwarded me from today's appearance: throwing the first pitch before a playoff game at Dodger Stadium. He'd scheduled it early in our operation. Back when this was supposed to be less complicated. Before we involved my ex.

Now, I'm hours away from a *People* exclusive of me and Léon sharing hot dogs in the stands. Perfect. While my sister's off greeting children at a youth development center, I'm fake-smiling for all the telephoto lenses aimed at me from across the street.

"Give me my phone," I say through my teeth.

"Non." He hides it under a cloth napkin. "We're supposed to look like we're having fun."

"I am," I lie.

We're on the outdoor patio of a chic LA restaurant. The area's been closed off for us. Léon's bodyguards—"Can you believe they only gave me *two*?" he whined earlier—wait by the door. Ajani is here too. The neighborhood's all palm trees and designer shops and a sea of valet-parked luxury cars.

"That's your fun face? Looks like your diarrhea face." Léon does a poor imitation of whatever's happening with my expression.

171

I smile, all teeth. "Go. To. Hell."

"I'm already there," he comments dryly. "The palace has me staying at the Waldorf in Beverly Hills."

I pick at my tacos. They're not as great as the ones from the pier. The ones I shared with Reiss. I should be with him. Not pretending to care that Léon isn't receiving the red-carpet treatment he's accustomed to.

"What has you so distracted?" He points his fork to my hidden phone. "Boytoy drama?"

If I stab him under the table, will the photographers notice?

I bypass my knife for a glass of water, just in case. "Wouldn't you like to know," I say after a sip.

"*Please.*" He laughs. "The American doesn't concern me. I'm here as a friend."

"Oh, is that what this is?" I say, head tilted endearingly when I sense the cameras focused on me.

"Yes," Léon replies tightly. "This can't be easy for you."

"This?"

He manages to sigh and maintain a glinting smile at the same time. "I still have sources on the inside. Gossip travels fast. Royal gossip travels faster. I know you're not here by choice."

I make a mental note to interrogate every single palace staffer when I get home. *If* I get home. Clearing my throat, I say, "It's complicated."

Another breathy laugh. I hate the way the sun makes his deep umber skin glow. How easy his smile comes, like lightning in a storm.

"Mon be—" He stops when I glare. Rolling his eyes, he says, "*Jadon*, we both know it's not. You did what you always do. Set the world on fire instead of using your words."

"I tried to tell—"

He cuts me off. "What I don't get is why you're so desperate to go home."

I pause, eyebrows scrunching. "What?"

"Come on." He forks around his salad. "You were literally Rapunzel stuck in the tower back on Réverie."

"I was happy."

"You were *miserable*," he counters. "Either annoyed or antisocial. Always so desperate to leave. How many times did you sneak out to see me?"

Too many, I almost say. Memories rush my brain: hiding in corners, running down hallways. Following heavy shadows until I hit the gardens, my lungs filled with night air and freedom.

I miss those moments.

"It's my home," I tell him. "I know it like the back of my hand. I was okay. Comfortable."

It's where I never had to deal with the ashes left behind after one of my incidents.

"Shouldn't you be more than 'okay' in a place you call home?" he asks, his smile a little too sympathetic. "Maybe it's time for you to get comfortable with being uncomfortable."

I squint. "What does that mean?"

He lifts one shoulder. Then, in true Léon fashion, he changes the subject. "You look different. It's the curls. They haven't been that long since . . ."

I wait for him to say *since we were fourteen*. When we came out. When he kissed me.

Instead, he says, "Get a trim."

"You first." I study him over my water glass. A tight 'fro of tiny curls. Clear complexion. He's been working out, his muscles filling out his rose blazer and Alexander McQueen T-shirt.

He leans back in his chair, sunlight cutting across his strong jaw. "What's really going on with you?"

I bite the inside of my cheek. Pick around my tacos. I could lie again. Or ignore the question. But this is Léon, and despite where we left things, he still knows me better than anyone who isn't family or Ajani.

After a deep breath, I say, "None of this feels like it's working. Like it's . . . me."

"How so?"

I tell him the things I've tried. Willow Wood, and the interview, and now a baseball game. All the little tricks that were supposed to make people like me. *Respect* me. But nothing is showing the Jadon I want them to see.

"Which is?" Léon asks.

My brows knit.

"How do you want them to see you?" he clarifies.

Over the occasional car driving by, I hear the *snapsnapsnap* from cameras. Quickly, I adjust my expression. Force out the biggest grin while considering Léon's question.

How *do* I want them to view me? Every second in America has been dedicated to countering the Jadon from the video. The prince I can't be known as. But I never thought about the one I want to show everyone. I haven't figured out who *I* want to see myself as.

"Oh, mon Dieu." Léon laughs. Not in a mean way. Surprised. "You don't know."

"I do!"

He eyes me skeptically. "Where's the pain-in-the-ass prince I've known forever? He had no problem telling me who I was."

"You're a dick."

"There he is." That sparkling smile again. "Remember how our papas really thought they were doing us a favor? Setting us up on a 'date.'" He air-quotes theatrically.

"In Madrid," I put in.

"Before that climate event. We'd already been making out for a month!"

"Six weeks," I correct, ignoring his little eyebrow raise.

"I didn't have the heart to tell them the truth."

I guffaw. "They were so proud."

"Bringing our country even closer together by uniting our two gay sons," he says, mocking his papa's voice.

I do my best not to flinch. Not to remember what else Prime Minister Barnard said. Or how Léon never stuck around long enough for me to tell him.

His hand touches mine on the table. I look up at his sincere smile.

Snapsnapsnap.

I almost forgot about the cameras. This is just acting. Right?

"They were clueless," he insists. "So are they."

With a practiced nonchalance, he shrugs a shoulder in the direction of the photographers.

"Instead of rushing home," he says, tapping my knuckles with his index finger, "maybe give yourself time to figure out who you are. LA's not Réverie. But it's decent."

A quiet laugh escapes my lips. "And then what?"

"Then . . ." He drags his hand away to lift his empty glass in a salute. "Pay for my lunch. A better hotel too. My services aren't free, Your Highness."

Cameras or not, there's definitely going to be some bloodshed between us before this is all over.

13

Holidays are sparse in Réverie. We celebrate New Year's with the rest of the world. Réverian Independence Day is in early August. Every year, the country commemorates the current monarch's birthday. Varied religious holidays are observed in different regions of the island too, vibrant, colorful festivals that wash over the streets for days.

But nothing compares to how the Hayes family does special occasions.

The Hopper is closed for the evening. All the lights are off, save for the track of bulbs over the bar. Situated on the café's tables and front counter are boxes labeled in heavy black Sharpie—DECORATIONS! NOT DOMINIC'S TOYS!

Tonight's mission: stringing Halloween lights.

"Orange ones next."

Reiss is balanced on a questionably safe folding stepladder. For an hour, he's been affixing countless bulbs to higher and higher surfaces. It's a wobbly dance that he seems comfortable doing while I gasp, swear under my breath, and try to slow my anxious heart down.

Somehow, I've been coerced—tricked—into being his assistant.

"Orange ones," he calls again.

I snort while rifling through a box. "Bossy."

"Is this," he says as I pass him the bulbs, "the most work you've ever done?"

"No," I huff.

From high above, he smiles incredulously.

I almost knock him off the ladder myself. "I work hard."

"Putting on a suit and tie," he says while clipping the lights, "then smiling for a bunch of cameras isn't hard work."

"You've obviously never been to a state banquet. Or a charitable ball."

"Nope."

On the counter, classic '90s music plays from his phone's speaker. I detangle a new string of lights. I'm faster than I was when I first arrived, but now I'm distracted.

Reiss has never been to a banquet. Or something like the Sunset Ball. Should I ask him? Whatever's happening between us is still new, nameless. The speech was supposed to be a last resort, but we're edging closer to November, and even with Léon around, the headlines aren't changing quick enough.

Do I want the Sunset Ball to be our goodbye?

"See," Reiss says, grinning crookedly. "You're not about that hard-work life."

"Just hang the lights," I say with no heat, offering him the new strand. Our fingers brush. He hums as he works, and my eyes linger on his ass in a pair of heather-gray joggers a second longer than I mean them to.

We haven't had much alone time recently. Between play rehearsals and his short film project—and Léon—these moments are rare. I'm starting to recognize the tightness in my chest when hours go by without even a text.

I miss him.

In the beginning, I never expected to meet a boy. To care about him this way. But here I am, smiling when he says, "Next box." Happily unraveling decorations for a holiday I never gave any thought to before.

I ask, "Why is this such a big thing for your family?"

Outside the lights, the other boxes are stuffed with decorations his parents plan to put up tomorrow.

"My fam *loves* holidays." He looks mortified. "They're single-handedly keeping Party City in business."

I laugh, even though I've never heard of the company.

"Fourth of July. Thanksgiving. Christmas." He loops more lights. "Valentine's Day is super extra."

"Why?"

"My dad proposed to Ma right here." He gesticulates wildly. I almost climb the ladder to steady him. "Before they bought this space."

Once he's back on solid ground, Reiss tells me about his parents meeting during university. Their nightly study sessions at the coffee shop led to dates. To his dad proposing on one knee with a ring in an empty mug.

"Someone posted a video of it on Facebook," he says, helping me work through the next box. "It got a lot of buzz. Doubled the café's sales for nearly two years. So, when the previous owner was ready to sell, he gave my parents a generous discount. For all the extra attention."

I smile, soft, unfiltered. It's a love story like Papa and Mom. One that I'm certain can't ever happen to someone like me.

"Do you like it?" I say after clearing my throat. "All the holiday stuff?"

He ducks his head, face twisting.

"Wait . . ." I dip to meet his eyes. "You do! You're so into it."

"I'm not!"

But he is. It's the pink spreading across his face. His proud eyes admiring what we've accomplished so far. It's another thing I like about him. How nerdy he is about movies and holidays.

How, unlike Léon, he keeps letting me into his world.

"What does it for you?" I rub my chin, barely holding it together. "Is it the decorations? Songs? The costumes? Do you secretly have dreams about dressing up as Santa—"

"Let me stop you right there," he says, climbing the ladder again.

This time, I reach out. My palm presses to the small of his back. My other hand hovers near his thigh. The coffee shop is cast in shadows. Too dark for anyone to see inside, but I hear my pulse grow louder at taking such a gamble.

"It's *fun*," he finally grumbles. "We have this tradition."

"Tell me it involves elf hats."

"I'm gonna kick you out," he threatens, but there's a grin in his voice. "Instead of trick-or-treating, my parents invite all Dom's friends here. Ma makes kettle corn with M&Ms. Dad whips up his specialty green milkshake. There's music and games and—I dunno. I like it."

I do too. Even if holidays aren't a major thing in Réverie, it'd be nice. To have that many memories with just my family, not the entire country.

Guiltily, I rub the back of my head, say, "I'm going to Grace's party. Léon is too."

With me, as a friend, I think to add, but Reiss doesn't need me to.

He says, "Figured." It comes out even, nonchalant. "That's not my scene."

We shift to another corner. He sets up the ladder. I unravel another string.

"Besides," he says, smirking, "The last party I went to, I met a real asshole."

"Are you sure? Maybe you read him wrong?"

"I didn't. He was an arrogant, royal pain in my—"

"That's enough of that," I say. As he works, my fingers tip-toe over the knobs of his spine. "Would you . . . want to help me pick out my costume?"

"No." Again, I can hear his smile.

"Should I go as James Bond?" I tease. "Ken from *Barbie*? A Victorian aristocrat? You could help me with my wig—"

"How about," Reiss interrupts, "a pretentious, entitled king?"

I make a face. "A bit basic."

"We'll get you a robe, a crown, and a big scept—" He stops abruptly, swallowing. His dark eyes trace down my chest, lower. "Um, never mind."

"No, no." I grin. "Please continue. Something about a big—"

Before I can get the word out, he blurts, "All done! Er, hit the lights for me?"

I let it go. For now. Because, with one flick, the entire Hopper is transformed.

I'm standing in a meadow made of stars. A freshly shaken snow globe, glitter falling from the ceiling. LEDs throw soft purples against the walls. Orange icicles wink in and out above the bar, the café's perimeter made of glowing candy corns—yellow at the base, tangerine at the tip. Strands of mini-jack-o'-lanterns outline the menu.

As Reiss climbs down, I steady him. One of his hands slips

around my neck, while the other grips my shoulder. I squeeze his waist. Fight a shiver when his fingers tease along the short hairs on the back of my head. We pause, frozen, his feet still not touching the ground.

"You're, uh." His Adam's apple dances. "Kind of strong."

I smirk. "It's all the waving I do. Hard work being a royal."

"I bet."

When I finally lower him, he doesn't speak. Instead, he tugs me through the swinging employee door. Into the half-dark back room. He nudges me against a supply shelf. Reiss plants his hands on either side of my head, leaning in, but never all the way.

I watch him hover, biting his lip. "Is this some form of new employee initiation?"

"You don't work here."

"Not yet." I drag my fingers up his sides. "Was considering it. You know, to prove myself."

He edges even closer. "Prove what?"

I shrug one shoulder. "That I'm more than just dimples and a great kisser."

"Who said you were a—"

I seal my lips over his. I wait until his muffled words turn into a soft exhale, then cup his cheek. Guide him. We're still new to this. *He's* still new. On campus, we hide in darkened classrooms or empty bathrooms for practice, for ten-second spurts of mouths fumbling and hands searching and things stopping way too soon.

Afterward, he always stares at me, breathing hard. Like he

wants more. Like he can't get the words out to tell me.

But I need him to say it. I don't want to get it wrong.

"Hey." I rest the back of my head against the shelf to look at him. "Before we continue—and *please*, continue—is this . . . are you . . . do you *want* something else?"

"Something else?"

I lift the hem of his T-shirt. Tap the waistband of his joggers. We're so close, he undoubtedly feels how hard I am.

"*Oh.*"

That one word—sound, really—bubbles a laugh from deep in my chest.

He grins too, red-faced. "Yes, but . . . thing is. I'm sort of, like, a virgin."

Oh, I think this time. I don't know why I didn't consider that. Why I thought he was like me. Why, suddenly, this means a lot more.

"I'm not. Léon and I, well."

"Thanks for telling me," he whispers, still chewing his lip in that unsure way, like his brain's firing off a million other questions.

"We don't have to," I quickly add. "*You* don't have to. Ever. If it's something you're ready for, talk about it with that person first. Consent is important. Communicate. Be clear."

Wow, I didn't mean to sound like one of those online guides Papa showed me when we had The Talk. But it's true. I want Reiss to feel safe with whoever.

He relaxes, one side of his mouth rising.

"Cool. I want that," he says. "Eventually. Not now."

I smile, then nod.

"Right now . . ." He's close again. Breath ghosting my lips. Hands smoothing from my hips to my back, lower. I gasp at his boldness. "I kind of want to make out before Ajani shows up to crash the party."

"We have an interesting history with parties," I say playfully.

"God, shut up. No one talks like that."

My retort dies when his mouth crashes onto mine. It's fine. Who cares about words, anyway?

Grace's party is at a rooftop club her dad rented out. As promised, a step-and-repeat awaits guests once they've cleared the bouncers crosschecking the invite list. Flashes pop across my vision. Photographers shout my name. I slip into prince mode—shoulders straight, back stiff, smiling and nodding regally.

As best as I can in my costume, that is. Despite Reiss's very . . . *convincing* outfit suggestion, I went simple: the original Black Panther suit from the Marvel films, minus the mask.

Warmth sidles up to my side. More shouting. Not my name, this time.

"Léon! Over here!"

"This way, Léon! Nice! Closer to the prince!"

Without hesitation, Léon follows directions. He tosses an arm around my shoulders. Flaunts a well-trained grin that's all fangs. For tonight, he's gone full *Twilight*—dark skinny jeans, red contact lenses, black V-neck T-shirt with I SUCK in a dripping blood font. The finishing touch: glitter smeared across his skin.

"I hate this," I say through my teeth, still smiling.

"Cheer up, Spare." He half-turns his head for another photo. "This is the easy part. The fun hasn't even started yet."

"The fu—"

I'm cut off by another photographer: "Prince Jadon! Are you and Léon friends again?"

I blink, throat gone dry, but Léon quickly steps in.

"The *best* of friends," he assures the crowd, making a show of grabbing my hand before tugging me farther down the carpet. "Shall we?"

Ajani and Léon's bodyguards lead us inside. It's all low lighting and velvet booths and glow-in-the-dark bars serving nonalcoholic drinks. Golden Medusa heads are carved into the walls. The DJ transitions from Zayn to K-pop. Sweat and body sprays and the salty ocean air from the open balcony doors waft around us.

From behind a roped-off section with green sofas, Grace spots us. She's dressed as an angel with a white silk minidress and LED light-up wings. Her smile is small and guarded.

"You look great," I say, by way of greeting.

"My hero," she says, winking.

On the walk here, I've accumulated history's worst wedgie. Still, I manage a grin, waving at the others.

Nathan's werewolf look is completed by yellow contacts and pointed ears, claw shreds along his T-shirt. Morgan's all goth: hair in a braided crown, black tulle lace dress, severed hand perched on her shoulder. On Grace's other side, Kaden hasn't put in any effort: he's wearing a TRICK OR TREAT shirt that has an arrow pointing from the "Treat" to his crotch.

Over the music, Léon clears his throat.

"Everyone," I say, "this is Léon."

He bows, kissing the back of Grace's hand. "Enchanté."

She raises an eyebrow. Asking her permission to bring Léon was a chore by itself. "Charming," she says, smirking. "Glad you could come."

"Wouldn't miss it."

"Whoa." Nathan nearly spills his glowing orange drink, tiny umbrella included, sidling up to Léon's side. "Immortal enemies at the same soirée? Fuck Edward and Jacob. We're hot."

Léon inspects him. I know that look. One second from saying something cold and rude.

I almost step in to spare Nathan, but Léon surprises me with a grin.

"I like you," he says.

The semi-dark club can't hide the brightness in Nathan's cheeks.

"Join us," Grace insists, and I find myself wedged between her and Morgan.

All around, phone cameras flash. Selfies and videos of weird, offbeat dancing to Halloween-themed songs. I pose for the occasional photo, shout lyrics along with Grace for her TikTok.

A sofa away, Léon is absorbed into multiple conversations. This is his element, thriving under the spotlight, instantly fitting in with strangers. He doesn't have to force it. Unlike me.

"Smile more," Morgan advises, bumping my knee. "You look miserable."

"Didn't we discuss this?" I say, nudging her back. "I don't need a babysitter."

She rolls her eyes, but there's a tiny grin at the corners of her mouth.

When Rihanna's "Disturbia" comes on, someone shouts, "Fuck yeah, this is my song!" The crowd erupts. I half-turn to Morgan.

"No date tonight?"

"As if I'd date anyone from our school," she says dryly. Her phone lights up. She checks it. "Willow Wood is fine, I guess. The people? Not so much."

"Present company excluded?"

She pointedly looks toward Kaden. "Included."

I shake my head, chuckling.

Her attention shifts to where Léon is laughing at something Nathan says. "Bringing your ex here? That's shocking."

I want to tell her it wasn't my choice. That, like everything these past two months, I'm doing it for a reason. A reason I'm questioning a lot lately. But we're not on that level. We're not even friends, despite the weird ache in my belly that wishes we were.

"In a good or bad way?" I ask.

"Undecided," she shouts, eyes on her phone again.

Kaden flops next to her, almost tipping over his mock-margarita. "What's with the face, Morg?" He tips his chin up. "Or are you just in character? Wednesday Addams, right?"

She exhales. "Go be basic somewhere else, Kaden."

He peeks at her phone. "Oh, fuck me. Again? Who reads *the news* at a party?"

"Me," she snaps. "Don't act like I haven't seen you checking ESPN at these things."

"That's different," Kaden moans. He sips, then sighs. "What's Anderson Maddow, Rachel Anderson, or whoever yelling about now?"

For a beat, Morgan stares, like she's considering leaving him without an answer. Or simply leaving. I am too.

Finally, she says, "You know Lio Heart?"

Kaden shrugs lazily. "The pop singer? Sure."

"Lio was supposed to headline the Gateway Music Festival in Tennessee," Morgan explains, lifting her phone. "But after they came out as nonbinary last month, the organizers backed out. Too much pressure from 'concerned' parents. It's bullshit. There are a bunch of petitions going around. Fans are upset."

"Is that all?" Kaden guffaws. "Who the fuck wants to go to Tennessee anyway?"

"Not the point," Morgan tries.

He waves her off. "Lio needs to perform somewhere queer-friendly—like here!"

"What about the fans there who deserve to see them live? Be exposed to people like them?"

"Move. Live somewhere else."

Morgan looks ready to throw her phone at his head. I feel it swelling before I recognize it. The fire behind my ribs. The want to step in. Speak up.

"They're *our age*," Morgan argues. "They can't just move. Not everyone has a trust fund waiting for them when they turn eighteen. This is all they have."

"It's a music festival," he asserts. "Not life or death."

"For some of them, it is!"

Kaden ignores her outburst, leaning over to pat my knee. "Help me out here, Prince. She's overreacting, right?"

I fight with the heat building inside me.

It's just us. Grace is pretending to care what some zombie cheerleader is happily yelling at her. Nathan and Léon are absorbed in their own chat. It still feels like a million eyes are on me. Like at any moment, someone will pop out of nowhere with their phone, recording whatever I say. Like that night with Kofi.

An old Kesha song comes on, but all I hear is Mom's voice: *I thought we agreed on staying out of the headlines unless it was for a good cause.*

Then Papa's: *Prove you're the kind of prince Réverie deserves.*

Réverie doesn't want a prince who involves himself in conflict. Who speaks out. Who's seen arguing and yelling and smacking that smug, toothy grin off Kaden's face.

But it's what *I* want.

Only, I can't afford to be that prince. So I say, "I think my opinion, either way, won't change the outcome," trying not to grimace when Morgan gives me an icy glare.

Kaden salutes me with his empty glass. "Very diplomatic."

"Bathroom break," Morgan grumbles to Grace, tugging her away without sparing me another look. Kaden leaves too.

I turn to Léon. "Can we talk?"

"About what?" Léon returns, only half acknowledging me as Nathan dances nearby.

The crowd's thicker, the noise overwhelming. I raise my voice to say, "Your papa. About what happened."

About what's happening inside me, I think to add. The continuous stirring in my chest. I need to get it out.

"My . . . papa?"

I nod, not that Léon's looking at me. He's cackling, mimicking Nathan's motions.

"I want to talk about—"

"Jadon, seriously." Léon lets out a heavy sigh. "I didn't come all the way to America to talk about him."

I clench my teeth. This is the Léon I've known forever. The one whose walls come up so swiftly when it comes to his parents.

"Then what did you come here for?"

"To . . ." He pauses, eyes finally on me. "To help you, of course."

"Talking about what happened *will* help."

"No, it won't." He taps my temple. "You're thinking too much."

Before I can argue, he shuffles over to Nathan, swallowed up by the sea of bodies.

It's just me, alone, like always. A fate I'm so accustomed to, I don't even allow myself two seconds to be angry or sad.

I march out onto the terrace, Ajani trailing behind.

For a moment, I watch the deep indigo skies from the railing. A line of red brake lights edges up Ocean Avenue. Palm tree fronds sway. Winking neon stars form Pacific Park. Santa Monica Pier is a constellation in the black sea.

I snap a photo. It's a good one. The clash of colors will pair beautifully with my Tokyo Bio Hack Jordans.

On an empty sofa, I scroll my phone. Haphazardly, I end up on @TheReelReiss's grid. I double tap his birthday post, a slideshow of pictures from age five to the latest of him with his family in front of the Hollywood sign, before clicking on his newest stories.

Pirate Dominic chased by Reiss dressed as Ghostface from the Scream films. His parents in Thing 1 and Thing 2 onesies. Dominic's friends getting brain freezes from lime-green milkshakes. Those same kids dancing with Reiss. Then, Dominic snoring on his brother's shoulder.

I'm surprised by my own soft smile. They're so . . . *normal*. A life I don't know. All my family vacations are shared with photographers. Birthdays celebrated with the palace staff instead of my parents.

This is the longest Annika and I have been around each other in three years.

"How appropriate," a voice says above me.

I tip my head back. It's Karan, dressed as the Phantom of the Opera.

"Creeping on my bestie's IG," he goes on before I can say anything, "when you were just holding hands with your new 'bestie.'"

His air quotes are as aggressive as his scowl.

My forehead wrinkles. "What are you—"

He cuts in. "I saw how he looks at you. It's the same way I

look at—" He stops short. The white half-mask doesn't hide his blush. "Are you sure you're *only* exes?"

"Karan, listen." I pinch the bridge of my nose. "You have no idea what you're talking about."

I pause, reminding myself that Reiss hasn't told his friends about us dating in secret. About why I'm hanging around Léon. He's respecting my situation, which I should do better about thanking him for.

Eyes start to flit to our corner. People casually observe us. I stand, hands raised in a universal *calm down* gesture.

"Maybe we should talk—"

"You need to be honest with my friend," he demands. "I'm used to people like you. They're everywhere at Willow Wood. But he deserves better."

"I agree, which is why—"

"Some prince you are."

It's like cold water to my face. His icy tone. The four words he spits. My lungs are overheating. I can't stop the way my teeth grind, the venom in my response.

"You don't know me. At all."

He laughs, a short, tinny noise that echoes. "Apparently."

"I'm not like *them*," I bite out.

I force myself not to point. To give any sign about who I'm referring to. But Karan's little eyebrow raise, his derisive sniff, says he's already aware.

"Fuck, I was wrong." He steps back. "You're one hell of an actor. Playing both sides. Pretending you're cool. One of us. Bravo, Jadon."

My shoulders droop. The anger recedes, and I gently say,

"Karan, I swear. I'm not a bad person. A bad—"

Prince, is what I want to say, but who am I kidding? I'm so far from the royal Papa wants me to be, I might as well abdicate now. Spare my family and country any more embarrassment.

Whatever Karan's going to say next is cut short.

"There you are." Léon approaches. "They're about to cut the cake."

Inside, I hear the dissonance of singing voices. It's not as loud as Karan's expression when Léon grabs my hand, threading our fingers together.

"Let's go, mon—"

"Don't," I hiss, "call me that."

Léon huffs. Then, his eyes turn to Karan. "Is there a problem?"

"Yes," Karan starts.

Léon immediately twists away from him. "We're supposed to be spending time together."

I blink hard. Why has his voice dropped into that deep, rich, sweet tone he only used when we were alone? Why is his thumb stroking the back of my hand?

Why the hell am I not pulling away?

Over his shoulder, Karan shakes his head. In my periphery, phones are focused on us.

Léon's voice startles me. "Jadon."

I barely register how close he is. His crimson gaze leveled with mine. Fangs peeking through his sly grin.

"Relax." He leans close, tipping my chin up before whispering, "Make it look good."

Make what *look good?*

I don't have time to answer my own question. Because Léon is kissing me. In front of Karan. For all the people watching. And one painful reality kicks me in the stomach:

I don't pull away until the last camera shutters.

14

LOVE CONQUERS ALL!

Prince Jadon and ex Léon Barnard were seen sharing a swoony rooftop kiss at an exclusive Halloween bash hosted by Jadon's classmate Grace Miller. Despite a messy summer breakup (and the prince's controversial statements about Léon's prime minister father), the pair looks stronger than ever. Who says there are no second chances in love? #JALE fans rejoice!

"Once more from the top!" Dr. Garza Villa calls, waving their script around. "Griffin, pretend you know where you are. Lydia, a little more Miss Scarlet, a lot less Scarlett Johansson. Jadon, for the love of Selena, at least *try* to be funny!"

I wince.

Rehearsal is a mess today. Forgotten lines and stage cues. Calvin, our Colonel Mustard, disappeared for thirty minutes because he decided sampling Taco Tuesday for lunch was a good idea. Someone—*me*—almost falling offstage. Twice.

Backstage, Dustin is on the verge of an aneurysm. And Karan—

Well, Karan looks like a tiger shark, and I'm the bloodied surfer who decided to take a dip in the Pacific.

He hasn't spoken to me since Grace's party. Each time I mess up, he exhales noisily, smacking his script against his forehead. Professor Garza Villa hasn't commented on the tension between us yet—too busy filling in for Calvin—but it's coming. Their twitching right eye demands it.

We almost make it to the end of scene three when I crash into Lydia on the way to check on a potentially poisoned Mrs. Peacock.

"Cut!" Dustin screeches, crouching to put his head between his knees.

When I get to my feet, Dr. Garza Villa says, exasperated, "That's it, people. We're done! Go home. Cry on your TikToks. Think about your life choices before tomorrow's rehearsal."

Their sharp glare lands on me. "Jadon, a moment of your time. Over here." They snap their fingers. "Ahora."

Reluctantly, I follow. Mr. June's sparkly heels clack as he leaves the stage. Behind the curtains, I catch Lo's sad smile before they follow the tech crew out. Dustin's gone too. Which means it's just me and Dr. Garza Villa.

"I promise I can do this," I blurt.

Lips a thin, deadly line, Dr. Garza Villa says, "When? When are you going to show me you can handle this?"

"Tomorrow," I swear.

"Mmhmm." Dr. Garza Villa raises a skeptical eyebrow, fixing the multicolored scarf keeping their cloud of dark hair off their forehead. "I saw your audition. Watched you in read-throughs. During blocking. You're no Leslie Odom Jr. up here, but you have potential."

My chest puffs with pride.

"Hold on," they immediately say. "You have talent, but I can't unlock it for you. Whatever's holding you back, it's time for *you* to let it go. Ditch that anchor, sweetie. Let yourself fly."

I laugh softly. I know I can act. All I do is put on a show—for the press, for dignitaries, for my peers. My life has always been a production. Problem is, I've never been the one directing it.

"I don't want to fail anyone," I confess.

"It's a high school play, not the monarchy," Dr. Garza Villa deadpans. "My advice: stop trying to be the Mr. Green you think everyone wants to see. Start being the Mr. Green you want us to see."

I crack a smile. Okay, Dr. Garza Villa. Subliminal message received.

After they exit stage left, two girls appear. Nadia, who plays Yvette, and Mia, the Singing Telegram Girl. But I recognize them outside of the play too. Nadia's in my Human Development class. Mia's locker is three doors from mine, and she's in the courtyard every morning, studying.

"We can run lines with you," Nadia offers.

"We weren't eavesdropping," Mia promises, shyly tucking curly hair behind her ear.

"We get it," Nadia says. "Last year, Mia didn't get her lines right until tech week."

After a quick elbow to Nadia's side, Mia says, "We just want to help."

I blink, surprised. Outside of interactions during rehearsals, we've never really talked. I go from the courtyard to classes to rehearsals. I've never gone out of my way to say anything to them. I haven't done that for anyone at Willow Wood.

But here they are, warm smiles and scripts in hand, ready to help.

I want to ask, *Why me?*

Instead, I choke out, "Th-thanks."

Nadia shrugs. "We're in this together. Wanna meet tomorrow morning?"

"Sorry," Mia says, frowning. "We'd start today, but I have music lessons."

Before I can answer, Karan strolls onstage. "I can help him today." His script has at least a dozen neon tabs between the pages. Perpetually prepared.

When I try to make eye contact, he pivots to Nadia and Mia. "In this together, right?"

They nod, then wave at me, disappearing down the stairs.

The second we're alone, Karan says, "I'm not doing this for you. Opening night is sold out. Word got around that His Majesty is performing in our little play."

"Actually, His Majesty is my pa—"

"My parents have front row seats," he continues as if I'm not even here. "This is my chance. I'm not letting you ruin it."

My face scrunches. "I don't plan on ruining anything."

Karan's jaw works like he wants to say something. I do too. About the party. What happened with Léon. The kiss I still haven't mentioned to Reiss, the one he hasn't brought up either.

In his best Dr. Garza Villa voice, Karan says, "Scene one. Page twelve. Action!"

We rehearse for an hour. I nail the words, but not the delivery. Every time, Karan makes me start over. It's frustrating. I want to storm out, give up, but when I finally stop thinking about the lines, stop trying to cage my annoyance, he pauses with the slightest impressed curl to his lips.

"It's about time the real Jadon showed up."

I exhale, relieved. *Elated*.

Until a voice echoes from the back of the auditorium: "There you are!"

It's Léon, once again showing up in my life uninvited.

He climbs onstage. "You haven't answered my calls. What are you doing at this primitive school that's so important?"

"We were rehearsing," I grit out.

"Rehearsing," he repeats, offended. His narrowed eyes fall on Karan. "It's you, again."

Karan's small wave transitions into a middle-fingered greeting. "Thought we had a zero-tolerance policy for trash here."

"They let you in," Léon bites back.

I step between them. "Léon, why are you here? I told you at the party—"

"Before or after you two kissed?" Karan puts in.

"Jealous?" Léon scoffs. "Is this the little American boytoy you've been fu—"

"Don't you dare finish that sentence," I warn him, standing

200

taller. "I'm the prince of Réverie. I will not tolerate you disrespecting anyone I care about. Understood?"

"What about *our people?* Do you still care about them? About being the prince they need?" He flails an arm around. "Or is everything about this nonsense?"

"I'm doing both," I say.

A beat. The irritation buried in his sloped eyebrows gives way to softness. All his sharp edges go tender as Léon grabs my hand. "Then, let's go. We were supposed to have dinner. Let's show Réverie how great we are together—"

"Jadon?"

For a second, I can't move. My blood goes ice-cold, while my skin is feverish. When my head finally turns, my eyes catching a splash of pink hair, I snatch my hand from Léon's.

Center stage, Reiss's eyes roam my face. Then, he stares at Léon.

"*Oh.*" Léon sniffs. "This is the replacement."

Karan growls, "You really don't know when to shut the fu—"

"What's he doing here?" Reiss asks me.

My mouth opens, but nothing comes out. I can't get past how stiff Reiss is. That flash across his eyes like he doesn't really want an answer—because he knows I'm going to lie.

"Don't worry, Frank Ocean," Léon says. "I'm not staying. Neither is Jadon."

"Be quiet," I snap.

Léon raises his hands innocently. "We're friends. He knows that, right? It's not like he saw the photos."

My stomach twists.

The fun hasn't even started yet. That's what he said the other night. Before we walked into Grace's party. Léon planned to kiss me the whole time. He just needed the right audience.

Rage crackles in my chest. It's like standing outside the Rouge Room again. Hearing Prime Minister Barnard.

"Word to the wise," Léon says to Reiss. "Don't get too attached. Dating a royal sucks. You'll never be first in their life."

"Tais-toi!" I growl. "I can't believe you—"

I never finish. My gaze jumps back to Reiss. His wide, glassy eyes. The irregular rise and fall of his chest. I know what's coming before his name leaves my lips.

He shakes his head, walking away.

"Wait! Please!"

I catch up to Reiss in the quad. After ordering Léon to leave. After trying to find words to apologize to Karan and coming up with nothing. I didn't have time. This . . . this is more important.

Reiss stutters to a halt when my fingers curl around his wrist.

"He's nothing," I say, breathless. "It was all for the press, and I made a big mistake. But I did it for you. Your family. To keep the attention off us. We agreed, remember?"

"Really?" He laughs humorlessly. "We agreed it was cool for you to *kiss* him?"

"No, no." I grimace. "He kissed me—"

"Fuck, when are you gonna stop playing the blame game? Take accountability for something?"

"I—" Heat burns my face.

"You what? Weren't gonna tell me?" He yanks his uniform tie loose. "No need to. *Everyone's* talking about it. At lunch. My bio lab partner. The whole school!"

The quad is empty. All the after-school clubs are gone for the day. It's a chilly evening, but that's not why I'm shaking.

I manage, "You said you're not jealous."

"I'm not," he says flatly.

"I'm sorry, Reiss," I whisper. "I'm just—I'm doing what I have to."

His expression is frighteningly lifeless when he says, "Do you even care if people like you? Is any of this for you? Or is it for someone else?"

I swallow, unable to answer him the way I want. Because I don't know anymore.

"You said we should lay low, right?" He tugs his blazer closed. "Cool. Don't call. Don't text. Don't come see me. At all. Is that low enough?"

He leaves me with no room to argue. Shaking his head, Reiss stomps out of the quad.

"Wow, he's spicy. The little puppy has some bite."

I jerk around, ignoring the irritating tears gathering behind my eyelashes, the ache settling in my gut. I glare at Léon.

"What the fuck are you still doing here?"

"Jadon, enough." He clucks his tongue. "Whatever you're trying to prove, stop. You were fine before all this."

I frown at the crimson-pink sky. "Was I?"

"Call your parents. Tell them you're coming home to apologize to my pa—"

I laugh hollowly. "You would think *I'm* the one who should

apologize." There's a large gap between us in the middle of the quad. An ocean's worth. "You still have no idea what he said."

He shrugs. "Would it matter?"

"Yes, Léon, it would!" The heat coming off me could melt Antarctica. "Why did you come here? Tell me the truth."

His lips purse. "Listen, Your Highness, none of these people understand what it's like."

We stare at each other. The same way we did when we were fourteen. When this life was too much and neither of us had anywhere to turn.

After a slow exhale, Léon says, "I do. We get very few choices in life. It's all decided for us."

I chew the inside of my cheek.

"But I *choose* to make the world respect me," he continues, jaw tight. "Sometimes, that means doing things people don't like. Being the bad guy. But that's how they always see me, isn't it?" He smiles bitterly. "I'm a Black boy with power. They're never going to love me."

But I did, I think. Because I thought no one else could see me like he did.

Maybe I never knew the real Léon.

A new wave of tears stings my eyes. I don't blink. Léon doesn't either. We stand quietly, and I don't know why I'm surprised by this turn of events. With him, with Reiss.

This is how it always ends for me—lonely. Letting someone walk away because it's too hard to keep them close.

"You never answered my question," I say, my voice neutral. "Why are you here?"

His face hardens. "I can't . . . say."

I nod. He can't say because it wasn't his choice. But this— this is *definitely* mine.

"Go back to Réverie," I tell him. His lips open to argue, so I add, "I can handle this on my own. I always do."

And *finally*, I'm the one who walks away first.

A cloud of smoke hangs over the kitchen.

I haven't burned macarons since I was nine and tried baking some for Papa's birthday. The pastry chef nearly had a heart attack when she found me. Now, there's a charred tray of raspberry macarons sitting on the marble island and tears clouding my eyes.

Scowling, Ajani fans a tea towel around. When the air clears, she trades looks between the tray and me.

"I'm fine," I tell her in a wobbly voice.

"My prince, I mean no disrespect," she says calmly, "but get out of the kitchen before you set us all on fire."

I drag the back of my hand across my wet eyes. Very prince-like. "But—" I try, sniffling.

"Now."

Ajani has been trained in at least twenty different styles of unarmed combat. And she's one motion away from a knife. Royal or not, I don't tempt her with a sarcastic retort.

I stumble outside, hoping the fresh air will clear my head. It doesn't. I flop onto one of the lounge chairs, head throbbing, and am contemplating jumping into the pool when I hear, "Whoa, you look like Caroline when Gabe voted her out of the villa."

I blink against the sunlight to see Luc stretched out on the next chair, wearing a T-shirt and swim trunks. He tugs out his earbuds, locking his phone.

My nose wrinkles. *"Paradise or Purgatory* again?"

"It's so good."

"Hard pass," I exhale. "Where's Anni?"

"On the phone with your nana." A small smile brushes his lips. "They talk once a week."

I didn't know that. Then again, I've lost track of what Annika's been up to while my life's falling apart. I should ask more. Stop checking Samuel's itinerary for her schedule and *talk* to my sister. But not now, with my runny nose and swollen eyes and empty ribcage.

It's been days since everything happened. I've managed to act mostly normal around school. But one batch of ruined macarons and I'm undone.

Luc swings his legs around, facing me. "You look—"

"Rough?"

His eyes scan over my damp cheeks and wrinkled clothes. "That's much nicer than what I was going to say."

I try to laugh, but there's a lump in my throat the size of a Skee-Ball, and the tears come again. Thick, ugly ones. I can't wipe them away fast enough.

I was taught not to cry in public. Royalty keep their chins high, shoulders back. Never let anyone see you break. People don't respect criers. They want strong leaders, not emotion.

But I can't help it.

"Léon's gone," I say, voice thick.

"Forgive me, Your Highness," Luc says with a wry smile, "but from what I heard, that's good news."

"Reiss ended things too."

He pauses, rubbing a hand over his buzz cut. "That's unfortunate."

"Very," I say shakily. I give him the short version. The party and the kiss and the aftermath in Willow Wood's quad.

He tilts his head. "You don't usually let people get to you."

A hysterical laugh bubbles out of my tight throat. "Luc, I know you're still new, but people always get to me. It's my whole history."

The prime minister, Kip Davies, schoolmates in America *and* Rêverie, Léon, Kofi. My papa. The list keeps going.

"I'm like the world's worst prince." I look over my shoulder toward the house, then whisper, "I'll never, ever be perfect like Anni."

Luc guffaws. When I glare at him, he says, "Sorry, sorry. It's kind of funny because, Your Highness, the crown princess isn't perfect. She'll be the first to tell you."

I stare blankly at him.

"I'm serious," he insists. "You two are a lot alike. Fearless. Stubborn. No fucks given."

"Um, Luc, that's the future queen you're talking about."

"I know, I know!" But he's grinning in a way I've never seen from him. "She doesn't give up. And neither should you."

I pull my legs to my chest, chin on my knees.

"Forgive me for being informal," Luc continues, "but you're badass. Black, queer, and powerful. Three things this world loves to hate. Don't let them win. Prove the assholes wrong."

He laughs. I do too.

Luc moves over to my chair. He unlocks his phone—hiding his lock screen, as if I'd steal his passcode—then opens his camera roll. The most recent photos are of Annika. She's on USC's campus. Shots of her from Fisher Museum of Art and Alumni Park, then the Village.

"She reached out to one of your mom's old professors to request a visit," Luc explains. "They talked for hours."

The next photo is a side-by-side: College Mom and Annika now, both wearing cardinal-and-gold sweatshirts, posing in front of the fountain outside Doheny Memorial Library.

"The princess might've mentioned that she hoped you'd spend more time visiting places your mom loved."

"Might've?" I tease.

Another quiet chuckle. "I haven't been around Her Majesty much, but I can see it. How much you're alike. She's a fighter. She takes advantage of every moment. That didn't come from being the queen, you know. She was someone before that."

Cautiously, I trace a finger over Mom's curls, her expressive eyebrows. This version of my mom didn't quit. She never let anyone stop her.

"Sometimes," I whisper, "I wish I was normal. Like, if my papa had abdicated and we grew up here instead. Had real friends. Went to a boring school, lived a boring teen life, fell in—"

I stop. If Luc notices me blushing, he doesn't comment.

"Am I wrong for that?"

"No," he says without hesitation. "But would you be who you are now?"

"Have you *met me*?"

He grins. "What's stopping you from being that boy *and* this one?"

"Um, the crown. Obligation. Tradition and rules—"

"Again, no disrespect, but the prince I know doesn't give a shit about any of that."

I fling my arms around, exasperated. "And look where we are! Stuck in America."

"You keep saying that like it's bad."

I chew my lip. It's not. I *like* it here. The house and the swaying palm trees and the sun stretching high above the Pacific. Willow Wood and no uniform policies and the fresh, salty air while sitting in the courtyard.

A cozy café and funnel cakes and sunset-pink hair.

"One LA boy has you this gone?" Luc says.

He did. He does. But now he's just another casualty of the life I was born to live.

Absently, I swipe to the next photo on Luc's phone. It's him and Anni in front of the famous Trojan Shrine. Luc's flexing his bicep. Annika's laughing, arms hooked around his neck.

"That's *cute*," I coo.

Luc locks his phone, repeatedly clearing his throat. "It's—uh. So. Well."

His stammering is interrupted by a clear, confused voice from the doorway.

"Why is Ajani cleaning scorch marks out of the oven?" Annika asks. "And what are you two talking about?"

Luc abruptly stands. "Nothing, Your Highness." Annika's eyebrow arches high when he bows. "Should I order dinner?"

He doesn't wait for an answer. Strides right past her, mumbling to himself.

Annika stares at me expectantly. I shrug. All this talking and story-sharing and *feelings* have left me starved.

I shout after Luc, "No tacos!"

15

After the final bell rings, I settle onto a bench in the courtyard. Department chair meetings have canceled today's rehearsals. Dr. Garza Villa doesn't trust us to handle things unsupervised. I don't blame them. Instead, I'm spending my afternoon editing my Sunset Ball speech on my phone.

Luc was right. Just because my current situation is a mess doesn't mean I should give up. That's not who I am. I've spent months letting everyone decide the prince I'm supposed to be. But maybe—maybe it's time I decide who *Jadon* is.

Show the world the real me.

I just need to figure out how to say it. I need to focus. I need to . . . stop looking up every time someone passes by, hoping for a glimpse of pink hair and a crooked grin.

No, I remind myself. He's not answering my messages. Doesn't show up in the quad during lunch. I don't see him in the halls. Forget about asking Karan or Lo.

I'm leaving. It's better this way.

"Wow. That's fucked."

Except, my gaze lifts at Morgan's voice. She's a blur, rushing by me, a very impressive feat considering the Doc Martens she's wearing. I pocket my phone and swipe up my messenger bag, jogging after her.

"No, no," she's saying when I catch up. "Stay. I'm on the way."

"Hey," I heave out. "Everything okay?"

Morgan stops short, hands on her hips. She stares at me like I'm a bug. Like she can't believe I chased her across the courtyard.

Neither can I.

"You seem upset," I say, breathing normally again.

"What gave it away, Benoit Blanc?"

I ignore her sarcasm. "Is it something I can help with?"

Her eyes narrow. "What is this?"

"What's what?"

"What you're doing. Your face is all . . . *concerned*. We don't do that." She stabs my chest with her index finger. "You don't do that."

"Ow!" I squawk indignantly, praying Ajani steps in soon. "Stop, you wannabe-mean-girl, heartless monster!"

"That's better." She pokes my ribs one last time before folding her arms. "Now why do you want to know what's going on with me? You never cared before."

"That's not true," I object.

She snorts. "You might be in the fall production, but your acting isn't *that* good."

I shake my head, but she's right. I had to be cautious. Keep her and everyone else at a distance. It's easier that way. But Léon was right about something too: it's time for me to get comfortable with being uncomfortable.

"I just want to make sure you're okay," I say.

She stares at me for a long minute. I tug on my messenger bag strap. Shuffle my feet.

"I have somewhere to be," she relents. "Not exactly the kind of place royalty go."

I cock my chin. "Maybe I'm not like other royals."

She laughs. Loudly. "Trust me, you don't want the smoke." Her fingers tug on her silver chain. She's out of uniform. It's the first time I notice the twinkling O charm on her necklace. "Besides, you don't have opinions on things that don't affect you. Remember?"

My fingers tighten around my bag's strap. I can't argue with her. As much as I want to. Because that's the Jadon I've been anytime a tough topic has come up—the good, reasonable, rule-following royal I was always taught to be. The one I thought Réverie would respect.

I stopped being me.

Luc's voice is in my head again: *the prince I know doesn't give a shit about any of that.* I stand taller. "Maybe I do. Have opinions. And maybe I want the smoke."

It wouldn't be the first time.

Morgan twists her charm, thinking. A beat passes before she says hesitantly, "It's a protest."

I don't stand down. Nose wrinkled, I say, "You know I'm not just some pretty prince who's afraid to get his hands dirty."

Her lips curve up. "So, you think you're pretty?"

"Of course," I say with a tiny huff. "I'm going with you. That's a royal decree."

Morgan finally grins. "One, fuck the monarchy. Two, you're driving."

In the car, Morgan explains what's behind the protest: a nearby public high school hosted an assembly honoring local heroes. One of the honorees was a drag queen. After, angry parents demanded to know why queer performers were speaking to their children without parental consent. Now, they're attacking LGBTQ-related after-school clubs.

"Some school boards have even passed proposals requiring educators to inform parents if their kids come out as trans at school." Morgan scrolls anxiously through her phone. She's been doing it since we left Willow Wood. "They claim it's to protect teens' mental and physical health when really it's—"

"Harming them," I finish.

She sighs, nodding. "This isn't new. Anti-queer propaganda has been popping off since forever. It's just never been this close to home."

"Is there anyone actually fighting for you? Someone with power?"

"Not enough." Morgan half-shrugs. "Most adults sound like Kaden. Or my stepdad. Go vote. Get legislation passed. Which is true in a lot of situations." Her voice lowers. "In the meantime, kids are on the streets. Kicked out. Not surviving."

"What about Grace's dad?" I ask.

"Vote," she repeats, deadpan. "Win this war the right way."

"I thought LA was different."

"Assholes are everywhere," she tells me. "Even in the prettiest, most progressive places."

I stare out the tinted window. Watch Santa Monica drift by in streams of neon signs and busy crosswalks. In palm trees wrapped in fairy lights. Groups ducking into cafés and tourist shops. Sunlight glowing on smiling faces as everyone shuffles to their next destination.

How could anyone want to exclude a person from this? How could you want to be anything but different here? Why is anyone hated for simply choosing to exist as themselves?

They don't belong here. She's not one of us. Never will be!

"Are you sure about this?"

Morgan's voice drowns out Barnard's in my head. I half turn to her, eyebrow raised.

"It's a small protest," she says, reassuring. "Students from all around. Friends and families." She tugs on her chain. "We're done with them erasing us. Silencing our voices. Pretending we shouldn't be here."

There's a fire in her voice like the one pulsing in my chest. She's nothing like the Morgan I'm used to: bored and disinterested. She looks pissed. Ready to fight. I don't know how I misjudged her.

But I won't anymore.

"I'm sure," I say.

"This could land you in a lot of trouble," she comments, like she's giving me a final out. "My mom's gonna lose her shit. My stepdad too. But you don't have to—"

"I don't," I confirm.

It's the Réverie way. *Neutrality*. But that's not me.

"Sometimes the only way to be seen," I continue, smirking, "is to burn down everything else around you."

The SUV slows in front of a campus half the size of Willow Wood. HOME OF THE MUSTANGS is broadcast across the digital welcome board. There's a thick crowd standing outside. At least a hundred people, signs raised, fists in the air. Blue and white lights from a group of nearby police cars shining on their determined faces.

"My prince," Ajani says while opening my door, "is this truly a good idea?"

I pause.

Ahead, the protestors' chants are like a drumline. Rainbow flags fluttering above their heads. Light blue, pink, and white stripes painted across their cheeks. Teens and adults. Jocks and drama geeks and drag queens, arms linked.

My heart beats to their noise. To their unwillingness to break.

I hear Léon: *How do you want them to see you?*

I hear Luc: *Don't let them win. Prove the assholes wrong.*

A grin splits my face. "It's a terrible idea," I tell Ajani. "That's never stopped me before."

Morgan leads us into the swarm. In the center, she stops to introduce a tall, fair-skinned girl with a black-and-blond pixie cut and a wicked grin. "This is Olivia," Morgan says, almost self-conscious. "She, um, goes here."

Olivia gives a playful eyeroll, unzipping her track jacket. Then, I see it. The charm at the end of her silver chain: an M.

And now Morgan's in my head: *As if I'd date anyone from our school.*

It takes every muscle not to laugh. But there's no time to interrogate Morgan. A sign is shoved in my hand. I'm nudged toward the front of the line. Within seconds, I've memorized the chants and I'm yelling relentlessly.

This. This is what I want. To scream about what matters. To be heard over the people trying to erase me, my mom, *anyone* that doesn't "fit" into their ideal world.

To stop standing aside like Rêverie always has.

What's the use in having power if you don't make a meaningful change with it?

Soon, news reporters arrive. Cameras zoom in. Uniformed officers watch us, arms crossed, but never moving closer.

Our numbers expand. Our voices grow louder. I keep my fist raised to the sky until the sun fades away.

❖ ❖ ❖

"Your Highnesses. I'm Ambassador Ime from the Réverie Embassy. Thank you so much for inviting me to this dinner."

Ime is a statuesque woman. Taller than me. She's in all dark green with a tiny Réverian flag pin. Ruby lips stand out against cool dark skin and elegantly bundled locs. After bowing, she shakes our hands.

"Wonderful to meet you," Annika says.

Ime raises an eyebrow while releasing my hand. "Quite the week you're having, Your Highness."

My face heats. I try for a laugh that comes out like a cough.

"It's my brand, right?"

Ime hums in a way that tells me she doesn't see the humor in my latest headline.

"Let us eat," she advises.

Senator Miller secured a private dinner inside a stylish, multicultural fusion restaurant. "One of Santa Monica's finest," according to the online reviews I read. Paper lanterns cast the space in crimson and gold. A long table draped in white linen awaits us. So do Grace, Kaden, and the senator.

He's a grayer version of his daughter—green eyes, strong cheeks, a blindingly white politician's smile. "This is fantastic," he says with camera-ready enthusiasm as servers bring out dishes. "All of us meeting for the first time."

Annika grins politely. "Our deepest gratitude for organizing this."

I almost gag. Somehow, I forgot what *Princess Annika* is

like. Eloquent, perfect posture, far from the girl I saw yesterday slurping boba in her pajamas.

"It's nothing." The senator waves her off. "This is needed.
What with everything happening these days."

I force myself not to roll my eyes. As expected, my appearance at the protest is everywhere. Me, clutching a sign. Me,
fist raised, shouting at cameras. Me, on constant rotation for
Kip Davies's nightly show.

At least my parents haven't called. Yet. Mom is at her wom-
en's retreat, while Papa is busy, again.

"It is nice to have such a wide range of promising influence
in one room," Ime comments, water glass lifted.

Kaden lets out an obnoxious yawn. Grace discreetly elbows him.

"Yes," Senator Miller agrees. "I rarely get to spend time
with my Gracie like this."

Grace's smile barely touches her cheeks. As if she's heard
this same speech dozens of times. She's in a simple black
dress, a pink headband holding her bangs off her face.

"I understand." Annika reaches out to tousle my curls. "It's
hard to let this one out of my sight."

In a hidden corner, I swear I hear Luc laughing.

"What can we do?" Senator Miller shrugs. "Serving our
people first is part of the job."

I nod robotically. Funny, I don't remember applying to be a
prince. It's been attached to me since birth.

Wistfully, Senator Miller adds, "She's all I have."

Grace's smile tightens. There's something unreadable in
her eyes. It disappears when Kaden touches her hand on the

table. The smallest brush. All the tension in her shoulders fades.

Huh. Kaden's actually useful. Shocking.

"You must miss Rêverie." Senator Miller's eyes are focused on me, not Annika or Ime. "Have you ever been away this long?"

There's a fist-sized knot in my throat. It's been almost three months since I saw home. Touched my bare feet to soft shores. I tug at my collar, wiggling around in my chair. "We *all* miss home," I get out. "Right?"

Annika, thankfully, nods.

Ime says, "Always. Especially my family. But I know the good I'm doing by properly representing my homeland here."

Thanks for the vote of confidence, Ambassador.

"Such an amazing country," Senator Miller chimes in, swirling his drink. The sharp sting of whiskey hits my nose. "The definition of excellence."

"Thank you," Annika says, dipping her head.

"Mmhmm." I'm so flustered, I cut into my chicken with the wrong knife. "It's great."

"I've always wanted to visit." The senator sips. "I was so fortunate to chat with Prime Minister Barnard on a couple occasions."

My knife clatters against the plate.

Grace tilts her head, mouthing, *Everything okay?* Even Kaden shoots me a weird, slightly concerned look.

Blood roars in my ears. The start of a flame in my chest. I hide my shaking hands under the table, my lips pinched.

"What a brilliant leader," Senator Miller continues. "Admirable. Passionate."

Annika clears her throat. "Rêverie appreciates his dedication."

Ime gives a small nod.

"A lot of my colleagues could learn from him," Senator Miller notes.

A surprised laugh escapes me. "You think so?"

"Mon Dieu," Annika whispers into her wine glass.

"The world needs more leaders like him," Senator Miller announces, undeterred. "He thinks about his country's values and needs. He's very selfless."

"I wouldn't call it that," I argue, barely holding onto my plastic smile.

In the corner of my vision, Ime is studying me.

Senator Miller leans back. "Reports show he's a big inspiration to your people."

"No, just his son," I mumble.

Annika pinches my hip. A warning. Ime's still watching.

"God, I hope not," Kaden gripes over his plate. "That guy was awful."

Another unexpected check in the Kaden Is Decent column.

"Listen, I get it," Senator Miller says. "Your generation is all about reaction. You don't trust the system. You want fast solutions. Change with no consequence."

Grace sits up, shoulders drawn, but she doesn't interrupt him. She doesn't say anything.

"Like that Morgan girl I warned Gracie about," Senator

Miller goes on. "What was she thinking? Showing up at that protest."

My eyes cut to Grace again. More silence. Like at the parties when Kaden and Morgan argued. Like anytime a complex topic comes up.

"*I* was at that protest," I say sharply.

With the expert air of a politician, Senator Miller effortlessly changes course. "I'm sure you were misinformed or coerced."

This time, I purposely drop my knife. "I wasn't fu—"

"For what it's worth," Annika jumps in, her voice calm, unlike mine, "my brother and I believe there are a multitude of ways to address political and social issues. Especially ones that affect those we care about."

Senator Miller nods, as if to say, *go on.*

"Sometimes change requires being involved," she says. "Standing on the front line."

Ime smiles, a glint in her eyes. Annika has that effect on people.

Senator Miller, however, laughs dryly. "That's what I mean. My staff has been working hard on laws, new proposals, to protect people. Change comes from the top. From patience. From trusting the ones *currently* in charge."

It's a loud, verbal slap. A reminder: Annika's only the crown princess. She's not queen yet.

Her genial expression doesn't falter. "Power is not defined by titles, Senator."

"Agreed." He grins confidently from across the table. "But it makes it a hell of a lot easier to get people to listen."

He doesn't wait for her response. Senator Miller waves down a server, asking about dessert options.

End of conversation.

Grace sits stiffly as Kaden whispers, "This isn't going great."

Ime examines her half-eaten dinner, peeking at Annika, then me, through her thick eyelashes.

Annika is steady, unmoving. Silent. A shell of the sister I grew up with.

"Restroom," I mutter, pushing my chair back. The force tips over my half-empty water glass. I don't stay to clean up the mess.

"You know," Grace says, startling me when I emerge from the restroom, "no one talks to my dad like that."

I sniff. "I'm honored to be the first."

She doesn't react to my sarcasm. Instead, she leans against a marble wall, sizing me up. I cross my arms, smiling coyly.

"Is there a problem, Grace?"

"I'm trying to understand you. You're all 'no comment' at school and parties, then you show up at a protest."

I shrug. "I contain multitudes."

"And just now," she continues like she's not satisfied with my answer, "with my dad—you looked like the Jadon from that video."

My teeth clench hard. "What's your point?"

"Is that the real you?"

The heavy silence between us is broken by my knuckles cracking. My hands ball into fists at my sides. Tension ripples through my body. Grace's eyes don't leave mine. She's waiting for an answer.

I refuse to give it. "Why weren't *you* at the protest?"

Morgan told me Nathan had an orchestra commitment he couldn't get out of. But she never said where Grace was.

"Isn't Morgan your friend?" I challenge.

She inhales, lips pursed. It's her turn to avoid questions.

"Don't pretend to know what happens between me and *my* friends."

"Don't pretend to know me," I hiss. "You have no idea what I'm dealing with—"

"I was eight when my mom died," she inserts. "Ten when the press said my dad rode the wife-died-from-breast-cancer sympathy train to his first election. Fourteen when a class-mate sold me out to the highest-paying media outlet."

My mouth snaps shut when reality sinks in. Her pink head-band, the ribbons she wore all last month. Her mom died from cancer, just like my pépère. Her whole world changed after that, just like mine. Her friend sold her out, just like Kofi.

I didn't know any of this about her. I never bothered to ask.

"I don't do a lot of things because of who my dad is," she says. "Because it's *easier*."

Her voice cracks. The smallest chip in the armor I've al-ways seen Grace wear.

"My friends are all *I* have," she goes on, sounding nothing like Senator Miller. Her eyes are shiny. "I don't always agree with my dad. But why fight him? Dealing with the backlash isn't worth it."

"So, you do nothing?" I ask.

"I play my part," she says with a stubborn chin lift. "Stay out of trouble. Study hard. Look perfect. Act like—"

"You don't care?"

"You're not the first person to think I'm cold. A bitch." She releases a harsh breath. "I do what I'm supposed to. For now. Until I'm at Harvard or Yale. Anywhere but here. Nate and Morg know I love them."

I narrow my eyes. "Do they?"

Grace pushes off the wall. "Where are *your* friends, Jadon?"

I pause. My hands clench and release at my sides. Jaw so tight, the ache vibrates through my skull.

Then, it finally hits me: "You never say anything. When Morgan brings up issues she cares about. When Kaden gaslights her in front of people."

Grace goes rigid again.

I recognize it. The person she's trying to be. I was her. Neutral and silent and trained to keep your thoughts to yourself. To let that fire rage inside of you until you burn out.

"Easier doesn't make it right," I tell her.

Her shoulders barely lift. "But it's how we survive. Being who people expect us to be. Keeping our real selves hidden."

I let out a long exhale. Try to calm myself. To remember the prince Papa expects me to be. But that's the problem too. I'm still cautiously containing the fire inside me rather than letting it burn freely.

Wildly.

"No." I shake my head. "I'm not that person. Not anymore."

I leave her. Stomp back to the main dining room where Senator Miller is boring Annika with his vapid carrying on. Sitting tall like he's on a throne he can't be knocked from.

"For the record," I interrupt, ignoring how quickly Ime's

head snaps in my direction, "I *chose* to be at that protest. Waiting for systems to fix things is why kids like me are without homes or support. Abandoned by their families. Dead."

Senator Miller straightens, caught off guard.

"Change starts with voices," I continue, "not with silence or your silly paperwork."

Kaden choke-laughs into his fist.

Ime clears her throat. "Your Highness, maybe we should . . ."

I can't hear the rest of her words. In my periphery, Grace appears in the doorway. She's still guarded, like the old me. Maybe it's time for her to see who she could be.

Should be.

I grin.

"You want true leaders for your precious Gracie to look up to?" I lean down to his eye level, shoulders straight, chin high. The way I was taught. "It's women like Morgan. My sister, the crown princess. My mom, *current* queen of Îles de la Réverie."

It's hard to tell, but I think Annika's lips twitch, amused.

"Your daughter should never look up to cowards like Prime Minister Barnard," I half-growl. "Or ignorant senators who hide from the real issues, like when his state is taking away basic human rights."

The restaurant is hushed. Kaden grins wolfishly. Against the wall, Grace hugs herself, but her eyes never leave me. Senator Miller is berry-red, stammering, spluttering. Annika finishes her water, and behind the glass, I can see her faint smile.

Ime stands, crumpled napkin in hand. She looks ready to say something. To condemn me like so many Réverians have.

But I don't care. This is the real me. Who I've always been.

"Enjoy your dessert, Senator," I say with a practiced grin and perfect posture.

Then, I stride out the main dining area without looking back.

16

"Walking, again?" Ajani says impassively. "They say it takes two months to form a habit—"

"This is not a habit," I promise. "I didn't want to be seen."

We couldn't walk out through the front of the restaurant. Samuel tipped off the press in advance about the dinner. Photographers were waiting outside. Instead, we exited through the kitchen. I left the waiting SUV for Annika and Luc.

"—and if this continues," Ajani is still saying, "I'll need better shoes."

"Fine," I say, exasperated. "I'll approve them at the next royal budget meeting."

"Which is?" She's testing me. We're both aware I only know about things when they're listed on my itinerary, usually the day of.

I tug out my phone. It's buzzing nonstop with texts from Annika. Messages like: A protest AND dragging an American Senator in the same week?! What's next? Setting the Hollywood sign on fire?

Then: Please forget I said that. Don't get any ideas.

Followed by: Be safe, okay?

I smile, replying with, as you wish Your Majesty, and a winky face emoji. She responds with a middle finger emoji. It's enough to finally make me laugh.

We pause at a crosswalk. It's dark out, but the neighborhood is dusted in ivory streetlamp glow. Without thinking, I guided us here. To a cozy row of Santa Monica shops.

To The Hopper.

Other than the still hanging Halloween lights, the interior is cast in shadows. An older man emerges, locking up. He turns, and my breath catches.

I've never met Mr. Hayes. Part of keeping our dating secret meant Reiss didn't formally introduce me to his family. This close, he's a taller, older version of his son. Same dark eyes, jutting lower lip. Deep wrinkles form in his forehead when he notices me and Ajani.

"Whoa. Shit, it's *you*!"

"No, wait," I quickly say as he starts to bow. "Please, don't do that."

He straightens, wiping his face. "Don't tell Dom I swore. I already owe him like twenty bucks from last month. Our plumbing was screwed, and I might've let some four-letter words fly and—Oh, I'm Greg Hayes. Reiss's dad."

I hold in a laugh. So, this is where Reiss gets his rambling from.

"Jadon," I say, offering my hand. "I was hoping to, um . . . see him?"

Mr. Hayes has a strong handshake. He also has a suspicious glimmer in his eyes. Like Reiss might've mentioned what happened.

Perfect.

"No, he cut out early. Working hard on that film project." A proud smile softens his face. "Kid's gonna be the next Barry Jenkins."

I nod, fighting the disappointment pooling in my stomach. What did I think? Reiss would still be here? That he'd see me and suddenly forgive me? That I'd get another chance—

"But my wife just texted," Mr. Hayes says, looking at his smartwatch. "We're having a late family dinner. You two hungry?"

The Hayes family lives nearby in a six-story building made of sharp geometrical lines and floor-to-ceiling windows. Laurel trees sprout up from the sidewalks outside.

"It's only a three-bedroom," Mr. Hayes explains while unlocking the front door. "Small for LA. The boys share a bathroom. Mornings are kind of . . . violent."

I press a hand to my mouth to hide my snort.

"Michaela?" Mr. Hayes calls out. "I'm home, babe. I brought guests!"

Around a corner, a voice says, "Greg, my hair's a mess. I haven't cleaned and—"

Mrs. Hayes has Reiss's cheeks and jawline, the same complexion. Her hair is hidden behind a silk scarf. When she sees us, the plastic bowl she's drying slips from her hands, clattering on the hardwood floor.

"Sweet Jesus!" she yells.

Soon, I hear a pair of bare feet. A wide-eyed Dominic takes us in before happily yelping.

Another hidden voice: "Why is everyone around here always so extra?"

Then, it's him.

Reiss freezes in the living room, a fluffy towel hanging around his neck. His hair has faded to a soft peach. He's shirtless, beads of water rolling down his brown chest, dotting the waistband of his ratty joggers.

As I wave sheepishly, he mouths, *Holy fuck.*

"Guess I should've called ahead?" Mr. Hayes says apologetically.

Mrs. Hayes gives him the politest *what the hell do you think?* stare I've ever witnessed. "Your Highness," she says, trying to bow, "I—"

"No, no, please," I urgently say. "Nothing formal. I'm just Jadon. I go to school with your son." I peek in Reiss's direction—*not* staring at his glistening skin—to see if he wants me to add more.

He's still too shocked to comment.

"This is Ajani." I wave behind me. "My Royal Protection Guard."

"RPG?" Mr. Hayes makes a face. "Like D&D?"

Mrs. Hayes exhales. "Welcome to our home, Jadon and Ajani. We'd be honored if you joined us for dinner." She side-eyes her husband like he forgot to mention that part. "Greg, help me in the kitchen. Dom, set the table. The *fancy* plates."

"Mama, we don't have fancy—"

"Now, Dom!" Before marching back into the kitchen, she adds, "Reiss, go put a shirt on! This isn't that type of party."

For a second, Reiss doesn't move. He watches me, his mouth a thin line. It's better than him yelling. Or kicking me out. He shakes his head.

"You look . . . nice." Then, he disappears down the hall.

A helpless smile tugs at my lips. While Ajani sits on a navy-blue sofa, I find myself curiously roaming.

The apartment's small but comfy. A coffee table layered in homework packets and drawings autographed by Dominic and thick books on filmmaking. A USC sweatshirt thrown over a wicker chair. A plastic bowl with leftover Halloween candy and Hopper paraphernalia. Reiss's canary-yellow tie peeking from under the sofa.

Inside Centauri Palace, there are dozens of rooms for show, nothing else. Quiet halls and soulless spaces. No sign that a family lives there.

It's not the same here. From the kitchen, I hear whispering:

"Michaela, it's okay."

"Greg, royalty is in our living room, and I *burned* the damn meatloaf."

"I'll run to the market. You can make him your special."

"I'm not making the prince sloppy joes!"

"I don't mean to be rude," I say, stepping around the corner.

Reiss's parents freeze. There's a slight smokiness in the air. On the stove, an oven mitt barely hides a charred dish. But I spot a bottle of honey next to a jar of Nutella on the counter. Two empty pans.

A grin takes over my face. "I spent lots of time with the palace cooks. Can I help?"

"Yes," Mr. Hayes says, delighted.

Mrs. Hayes smacks his arm. "He's a *guest*."

"It'd be rude to deny a prince."

Mrs. Hayes glares, so I say, "I promise not to burn down your home."

A stubborn line forms between her brows, the same one Reiss gets. She sighs. "What did you have in mind?"

I roll up my sleeves. "Do you have milk and eggs? Also sugar, flour, and butter? Oh, and a whisk?"

We work side by side, Mrs. Hayes and me. I walk her through the crêpe recipe Papa taught me. Mr. Hayes plays old-school R&B from a Bluetooth speaker. In the entryway, Reiss watches us. Sadly, he's fully dressed now, but I don't let that distract me while cooking.

Dinner is noisy. Breakfast at 9:00 p.m. brings out the best in everyone. While spreading Nutella on her crêpe, Mrs. Hayes doesn't hesitate to recount her sons' most embarrassing stories. Four-year-old Dominic stripping naked while in a plastic ball pit at a friend's birthday party. Ten-year-old Reiss vomiting over the side of the Pacific Wheel.

Chuckling, Mr. Hayes adds, "We were midair. At the very top! It got all over the poor guy operating the ride."

"Dad," Reiss says, pouting. "We're *eating*."

I raise my eyebrows at him until he facepalms, then says, "It's called acrophobia!"

"It's called eating too many churros," Mrs. Hayes corrects, giggling.

I laugh so hard my cheeks ache.

Crammed around the small dinner table, Reiss's family happily talks over each other. Point accusing forks at one another when a story is told wrong. I love it. But I miss when my own family was this close. Before Papa became king.

Dominic stares up at Ajani, awed. "Have you ever killed anyone?"

Mrs. Hayes gasps. "Dom!"

"No," Ajani deadpans. I can't tell if she's lying. Her poker face is too good.

"You look like a superhero," Dominic says while chewing.

Ajani's lips quirk. "Would you like to be an honorary member of Réverie's Royal Protection Guard?"

Dominic shrugs self-consciously. "I can't. Everyone says I'm too scared to be a hero."

Ajani clucks her tongue.

"Every hero is scared of at least one thing," I say, smiling widely at Dominic. "That's what makes them super. How can you be brave if you've never been afraid?"

Dominic's face lights up. Mr. Hayes tugs him close.

Across the table, a pair of dark eyes crinkle. I blush, staring at my half-eaten crêpe.

After dinner, Mrs. Hayes refuses to let me help with the dishes. "I have to draw the line somewhere." While Dominic shows off his drawings to Ajani, Reiss quietly leads me down the hall to his bedroom.

We're barely inside before his mom yells, "Door stays open!"

"Babe, that's a prince!" Mr. Hayes hisses.

"A prince who's also a *teenage boy* who's clearly into our son. Don't tell me you didn't see the way Reiss looked at him."

Pink spreads from Reiss's neck to his ears. "We can hear you!"

"And we can hear you, because the door stays open!"

Mortified, Reiss flops like a dead starfish on his bed.

His room's nice. Citrus-orange walls peeking from behind film posters. His laptop is collaged in stickers of movie logos and quotes. Hoodies piled on a desk chair. No sign of his sneaker collection, but there are USC brochures and leftover tickets from our trip to Playland Arcade on his bedside table.

"You saved them," I say, grinning.

Reiss sits up. Follows my gaze to the tickets. He shrugs, but doesn't say anything.

All the endorphins I felt ten minutes ago fizzle out. This is the Reiss I should've expected when I arrived. Distant. Angry. Hurt by what I did.

I rub the back of my neck. "Thank you. For not kicking me out."

"You surprised me." Another careless shrug. "Besides, my parents would kill me."

"They're sweet." My smile lifts. "And *really* funny."

"They're not bad, I guess."

"And Dominic," I start, but Reiss's expression shifts. Like he's fighting something, but he doesn't interrupt me. "Dom's amazing."

Awkward silence returns. Even with the muted voices from the other end of the apartment, it feels like no one else is here. Just me and him and the things we still haven't said.

I just want us back to how we were before. Not that he owes me that. Not that it ever works that way for me.

Reiss clears his throat. I trace my eyes over his face. It's still, but softer.

"Do you want to get out of here?" he offers.

"If Ajani finds out what you've planned, she's going to kill you."

"She wouldn't." Reiss flashes a confident smile while scanning a QR code on the e-scooter parked under a tree outside his complex. *An actual scooter.* It's all black with electric-blue accents on the deck and wheels. Reiss's grin slips a little. "Wait, would she?"

I shrug. "Probably not. She likes you too much."

"She does?"

"It's your sparkly personality and sense of humor and your"—with his back to me, I watch him bend over, unlocking the scooter with his phone—"ass . . . er, asking her what tea she likes."

"So, it's the free tea?"

I swallow, nodding even though he's not looking. I'm certainly not staring at how low those old joggers have slipped on his hips. Nope, not at all.

"Here." He passes me a helmet. "Safety first."

"Always," I say, then bite the inside of my cheek.

He climbs on, waiting for me to follow. After slipping on the helmet, I raise an eyebrow.

"Are we both, um . . . riding this one?"

He lets out a nose-scrunching snort. "You need a license to rent these. I'm guessing you don't have one?"

I smile. "Haven't even been behind the wheel of a car before."

"Figured. Come on."

Inhaling, I step on behind him. The deck is thin and short. We're *close*. My hands on his shoulders. His warm back pressed to my chest, and everything below that.

I try, "Is this legal—"

"Hold on tight," he commands, flipping the power switch, and I've barely repositioned my arms to hug him from behind before we're off.

The e-scooter isn't fast. We follow the bright green bike path up the road. There aren't many cars out. People are sticking to the sidewalks, where we're not allowed, according to Reiss. From here, Santa Monica is aglow—palm trees wrapped in bulbs, restaurants still glimmering, moonlight washing over the quiet streets. It's electric.

The breeze against my face. The way my stomach flips. I've never done something like this before.

It's like a scene from a movie. My favorite movie—*The Way He Looks*. When Leo rides on the back of Gabriel's bike for the first time.

An unexpected laugh spills from my mouth.

"Okay?" Reiss grins over his shoulder.

"Yes!" I shout as the city blurs into golds and reds and silvers. I rest my chin on his shoulder, breathing in his shower gel and the salty, damp air.

I'm not a prince. I'm not a headline. I'm a boy squeezing tightly to someone who makes me feel safe doing the most dangerous things.

It's the freest I've ever felt.

"Death by Chocolate." Reiss holds out his paper cup. "Here, try."

We're sitting on a bench on the far side of Third Street Promenade. After parking the e-scooter, he guided me to an ice cream shop, the menu filled with so many flavors, I couldn't choose. The freckle-faced girl behind the counter, who clearly didn't recognize me, picked mango sorbet. It's perfect—sharp but sweet. Still, it's nothing like Reiss's choice.

Thankfully, no one's around to hear the inappropriate noise I make. No one other than Reiss, who shifts around, biting his lip. It's just us. Helmets at our feet, thighs touching. Scooping ice cream from tiny wooden spoons into our mouths.

"Thanks," Reiss mutters. "For what you said to Dom."

"It's nothing."

"It is." He stabs at his melting mountain of chocolate. "Two years ago, one of the boys from his class had a sleepover. They watched horror movies. Dom's not a fan."

I grimace. "Me neither."

Reiss nudges my bicep. "Dom was so scared he hid in the bathroom crying until Ma picked him up. Some of the boys still make fun of him because of it."

A frown tugs at my mouth.

"I always want to protect him," Reiss says, a tight wrinkle between his brows. "Even when he's being a little shit. Which is constantly."

"As a younger sibling, I'm offended."

He ignores my fake pouting. "I never know the right thing to say. To make him feel better. To let him know it's okay to be afraid." He offers me his cup again. "But you did."

I swipe another spoonful, minimizing my reaction this time. "What can I say? I'm kind of perfect."

He shoves me, not before stealing from my cup. "Just say thank you."

But I don't. Instead, I say, "I'm sorry about Léon. I shouldn't have let it happen. The way he treated you. The way *I* treated you. You didn't deserve any of it."

He hums, spoon in his mouth. I sense he wants me to say more.

"This isn't an excuse," I preempt, "but my life's been a disaster since that video. I tried so hard to fix it. To get people to respect me. But nothing works. It's exhausting."

"What happened? To make you say what you said?"

I squeeze my eyes shut. I wish it was from a brain freeze. But it's from the memory.

"I was bored," I get out. "I was supposed to be meeting my tutor, but I ended up roaming around the palace. I heard voices coming from the Rouge Room. I thought it was my papa. I hadn't seen him in a week. But it wasn't."

My pulse picks up. It's like I'm back there, ear pressed to the mahogany door. Throat tight when I heard his voice. His words.

"It was Léon's dad," I say, choked. "He said . . . he said—"

Reiss rests a hand on my jumping thigh. "You don't have to tell me."

But I do. I need to tell *someone*. And now I know. Léon wasn't that person. It's Reiss, who always listens and calls me out and willingly lets me into his world.

I let the words come. Every sickening thing.

"I wasn't drunk at the party," I clarify. "I was *angry*. Kofi knew something was wrong. He always does. But he fucking let them record me. Then, he left me with the mess."

Reiss raises his cup. I dig in.

"This is why I don't have friends." I exhale. "No one wants to deal with royal drama. The endless bullshit. And no one sticks around long enough for me to—"

"Learn how to be a good friend?" he offers.

I nod, the melting ice cream cooling my temper.

"It's easier to keep everyone at a distance," I confess. "No one gets hurt that way."

"What about you?"

I shrug like it's nothing. "People will always have things to say about me."

I'm one of three Black princes in the entire world. The other two are much older. I'm also the first gay prince in line to the throne in my country's history. Every story written about a young, non-Black royal is a fluff piece compared to the ones about me. The media will never admit it, but I know why.

Reiss's forehead wrinkles. "That doesn't mean they're right."

"What's right and what people believe are two very different things."

He stirs his ice cream. Then, casually, he says, "I quit the essay hustle."

My eyebrows rocket up.

"Don't look so shocked. I have some integrity."

"Feeling up a prince in the back room of your parents' coffee shop?" I squint at him, then repeat his own words: "The jury's still out."

"Shut up." He smiles. "I need my scholarship. And recommendation letters from Willow Wood's faculty are worth more than a sick new pair of LeBrons."

"Bold statement."

"That's me." He scoops more chocolate, but instead of shoveling it into his own mouth, Reiss holds it toward me. "Super bold."

I take my time scraping the ice cream off his spoon, relishing the way his eyes never leave my mouth.

"Don't tell Karan I told you." He sighs. "But my short film? For Oceanfront Film Fest? It's about fear and how we're still beautiful as people in spite of it."

I tilt my head, curious, hungry for more.

"Karan's afraid of drowning," Reiss tells me. "Lo's scared of sea animals. Specifically dolphins, but other ones too. Dom hates scary movies."

The pool at Nathan's house. The fountain in Willow Wood's courtyard. Footage of him chasing Dominic around The Hopper in a Ghostface mask. All the places I've seen Reiss with his phone or Canon.

He explains how each shot is interspersed with footage of his friends, his family. Laughing. Living joyfully, without fear holding them back. The way he describes it warms my chest. In a good way.

"So, when you said that to Dom—" He pauses, smiling. "It was perfect."

I press my knee against his. "Do you want me to say it again?" I motion to his phone on the bench. "For the film?"

His eyes widen. "Seriously?"

I nod, despite the nervous sweat breaking out across my hairline.

"I'll only record your voice," he swears, scrambling to open an app. "No video."

I nod again, the knot in my belly uncoiling. I'm probably breaking a hundred NDA clauses. But for him? I do it, happily. Unapologetically.

After Reiss checks the playback, he pockets his phone. "Also, I was a little jealous of Léon. Like five percent."

"Wait. You were?"

His arms flail. Thankfully, he doesn't dump chocolate all over me. "This is all new for me! I don't know what I'm doing. How I'm supposed to feel. Fuck, it's my first relationship—"

He freezes.

I lean in. "Say that again. Your first—"

"I didn't say anything."

I slide my hand up his thigh. Chilled fingers against warm cotton. I wait until he has enough courage to look me in the eyes. "Reiss—sorry, do you have a middle name?"

He scowls. "Emile Dorian. Why?"

"*Two* middle names?"

"Don't royals have like sixteen names?"

It's my turn to make a face. "Counting titles? I have six."

"No thanks." He laughs quietly. "His Royal Arrogance is already a mouthful."

As soon as it's out, I can see the regret melt across his expression.

We stare at each other for a long moment. Even with his cheeks turning a violent shade of pink, his eyes never leave mine. The way he tips his chin higher, confidently, leaves my tailored slacks uncomfortably tight.

So, this is him. *Bold*. My lips curve up.

"Don't use that dimple on me," he warns.

"Reiss Emile Dorian Hayes," I start, "would you like to be my boy—"

"Isn't there a fancier title?" he interrupts. "Like Royal Suitor? A duke? His Royal Arrogance's—"

"Royal Attractiveness," I correct. "Royal *Adorableness*."

"Royal Assholeness."

"You'd be okay with everyone calling you His Royal Assholeness's consort?"

He fake-gags. "Gross. How about HRA's—"

"You called me Jadon," I interject, inching in. "In the locker room."

"Did I? That doesn't sound like me."

"You did," I whisper, my mouth a breath away from his. "I liked it."

"And I suppose as the prince's boyfriend," he says, smile unguarded, "you expect me to care about the things you like?"

"Couldn't hurt."

"I'll think about it," he says, before brushing his lips to mine. They're cold, but so soft. Flavored by chocolate. I'm urged on by the little noise at the back of his throat, by his hand guiding mine higher on his thigh. Our ice cream cups are forgotten on the bench.

Reiss barely pulls away to say, "Yes, I'll be your royal whatever."

"Boyfriend," I repeat, kissing him again.

17

On Monday morning, Ajani opens the rear door of our black Range Rover. I step onto the private sidewalk outside Willow Wood, fixing the cuffs of my blazer before reaching back. With a helpless smile, I grip Reiss's hand.

"Those seats," he gushes. "Soft as butter. It was like sitting on a cloud. And the individual climate controls—is that what your life is like every day?"

I shrug. "Mostly."

He shakes his head. "Ethically, that's a gross waste of money."

"Should I cancel the car for the afternoon?" Ajani offers.

Reiss spins to face her. "Don't you dare."

Her lips twitch up. Mine do too. It's hard to explain what this is like. The lightness in my chest, the constant crashing waves in my stomach. The hope and excitement and heavy fear.

I have an *American boyfriend*.

What does that mean for my plan? For going home?

I've done my best not to think about it all weekend. But Reiss has been busy editing his Oceanfront Film Fest project, and there's only so many hours I can spend practicing my lines for the play or writing my Sunset Ball speech.

Still, here he is—wearing a gray Willow Wood Academy hoodie over his Oxford. Crinkly-eyed smile. Holding my hand.

My boyfriend.

I look toward the arches outside the courtyard. "Are you sure about this?" I ask Reiss. "I thought you didn't like the spotlight?"

"I don't," he says, slightly defensive. Then, he beams at me. "But I like you. Sometimes. Listen, sacrifices are being made here."

"I'm so honored."

"You should be." He squeezes my hand. "How should we do it?"

My left eyebrow quirks. "Do what?"

"Walk in. As a couple."

I fight to keep the laugh in my throat. "You've really never done this before."

"It's not funny." His eyes narrow. "I want to get it right. So, arm around the back? Should I put my hand in your back pocket—"

"Is that just a reason to touch my ass?"

His face goes neon pink.

I casually rest an arm around his shoulders. "Trust me, it's not that hard." His cheeks go a shade darker, and it takes everything not to see what else I can get away with saying. Instead, I brush my lips against his ear, whisper, "Time to greet your loyal subjects."

"Hold on."

Reiss jerks to a stop. I tilt my head curiously. He's counting backward under his breath, still red-faced, looking down like he's waiting for something to happen and—

Oh.

Whatever resilience I had left dies in that moment. Head tipped back, I bark out a laugh while escorting him through the arches.

Inside the courtyard, conversations drop out. Bulging eyes track our stroll. Damien Cho from Lit and Composition is staring so hard, he crashes into a trashcan. Phones are covertly raised in our direction. I cheat my gaze toward Reiss.

He's grinning. I mirror him, proudly lifting my chin. The whispers pick up:

"No fucking way."

"Is that—is *he* who the prince was making out with?"

"Oh my god, text Becky. And Adam. They're gonna lose it."

On the benches, Nathan fist-pumps the air. "Hell yeah, PJ!"

I search for Morgan. We haven't talked since the night of the protest. She swore her mom was cool about her being there, even if her stepdad was furious. But she's missing. Next to Nathan, Grace lowers her Chanel sunglasses, her expression neutral.

I wonder if she gets me now. If she understands I'm tired of trying to win people over. That I hope she starts being the real Grace too.

Flashing my brightest grin, I shout, "Good morning!"

A beat. She arches one of her perfectly manicured eyebrows, the corners of her lips twitching. A small smirk.

The smile on my own face doesn't fade until the final bell.

Play rehearsals run more smoothly. For the most part.

We're off-book now. I still forget a line or two, but those extra practices with Nadia and Mia helped. Dr. Garza Villa side-eyes me a little less now. Dustin's still one lighting or sound issue away from setting himself on fire, but we've transitioned into dress rehearsals without having to cancel the production. That's a positive.

Backstage, I'm sitting in front of a vanity wearing a partially finished costume—a sharp emerald suit with black lapels.

Lo beams at their work while hovering over me with a makeup brush.

"Thanks for doing this," I say.

They shrug. "It's my job."

"Yeah, but." I shake my head. "It's weird. I feel like I'm *really* Mr. Green."

My eyes dart to the stage, where Mr. June gives Karan some tips. We're okay. He doesn't avoid me during rehearsals anymore, but he doesn't go out of his way to chat either.

Lo must notice my frown. "He'll get over it."

"Who?"

"Don't act." Lo tickles my cheeks with the brush. "Reiss explained everything to us. I'm cool. But Karan's great at holding grudges. Fucking Aries."

I chuckle.

"He was salty for two weeks when I missed his sixth-grade talent show performance," Lo goes on. "I had bronchitis!"

I recognize that look in Lo's eyes while they watch Karan talk animatedly with Mr. June—longing. "He's a good friend," they say.

"Uh huh. A *good* friend."

Lo ignores the smile in my voice, busying themselves with their makeup kit. They tilt my chin up to examine my face. A beat passes before they say, "Hey, what you did the other day? The protest?"

I nod carefully.

"That was kind of epic."

"You think so?" I ask.

"Dude, you're a *prince*. No offense, but I never see anyone like you show up like that. Not for people like me."

The corners of my mouth droop.

Lo picks up another brush. "Almost everyone's been chill and supportive since I came out." They pause, biting their lip.

"But when it's about the issues that really affect me—no one says or *does* anything. It's a 'me' problem. How fucked up is that?"

I sigh guiltily. "Very."

"Why are people trash?"

"Because secretly? They're scared." My chin lowers. "Not getting involved means they can protect themselves. They—" I think about what Morgan said before the protest. "They don't want that smoke."

Lo snorts hard. "Okay, what have you done with Prince Jadon?"

"I'm serious," I say. "Ignoring the issues doesn't make them go away. It doesn't mean you're not next."

For generations, that's how Rêverie has survived. Maintaining distance. Staying neutral. Pretending the world's problems aren't *our problems*. But they are.

And I refuse to be silent.

What's the point of being charming or approachable or the "good" prince Papa wants if I'm not the one my people *deserve*? Someone who will fight, regardless of how it looks to others.

"I did what everyone should."

Lo smiles. "Another country's prince fights harder for me than my own government. Way to go, America. Really leaning into that 'land of the free' bullshit."

Their fingers carefully pull on my eyelid, eyeliner pencil in their other hand.

I force myself not to flinch.

"Sorry." Lo eases back. "Is this okay? I thought—"

In the mirror, deep wrinkles line my brow. I've never worn makeup. Not even concealer for a pimple. My skincare routines and expensive face masks were all in the privacy of my suite. The palace stylists have always dressed me a certain way—like the polished royal you see on TV and in movies, a look I've been expected to maintain.

But is it what I *want*?

"I can stop." Lo begins capping the liner.

"No," I say. "Keep going."

"You sure?"

Slowly, I grin. "Time to stop being everyone else's version of Mr. Green, right?"

Lo brightens like that's exactly what they were going for.

As they apply liner, I sit perfectly still. Listen to all their Karan stories. First meeting to trading holiday traditions. Getting into theater because Karan liked it, then falling in love with being on the backstage crew. How makeup is fun, but their passion is rebuilding cars, and Karan's encouraging them to go to a trade school after graduation.

With a grin, I say, "If you asked him out—"

"You really want to go there while I'm holding a pointy object near your eyeball?"

I laugh. "Forget I said anything."

When Lo finishes, I stare at my reflection for a solid minute. What they did was subtle, but also . . . striking. It's me, but different. A Jadon I'm more comfortable with. The prince I *should* be.

Lo shakes my shoulder. "Amazing, right?"

"Yeah," I exhale, my chest light, my body relaxed. "Amazing."

"A protest." Papa's voice comes like the start of a storm through the laptop's speakers. Deep lines are etched into his brows, his eyes darkening.

He's in his personal office. Mom sits quietly next to him. Behind them, intricate designs are carved into the cypress walls.

"You participated in a protest!" He shakes his head. "With reporters present. Police. In America, of all places. What if something went wrong?"

"It didn't," I attempt.

"This time." His tone is like thunder. "You were foolish. Thoughtless. Your title means nothing to the wrong person there. Your life means nothing to them. Do you understand that?"

"Yes," I say through my clenched teeth.

"And that's not how a prince acts," he continues. "A prince of Réverie, no less. I taught you better. We don't handle situations that way."

We don't handle them at all. I command myself not to say the words. It helps that Annika's seated next to me. She nudges my knee. Reminds me that this isn't just Papa I'm talking to.

It's the king.

"Papa, I—"

"It's not your place to concern yourself with American issues."

"Simon," Mom says evenly, laying a gentle hand on his shoulder. "Let him speak."

Papa scoffs. "We had an agreement, Ava. He was to stay out of the headlines. Earn Réverie's *respect*," he asserts. "None of this has helped."

"Actually, Papa," Annika says. "It has."

My head snaps in her direction. She flashes a *trust me* smile.

"Since the protest," she begins, "people have been talking about what Jadon did. Good things." She unlocks her phone, then opens her camera roll. There's a series of screenshots. "I forwarded these to your equerry, Papa, but I want to read them for you."

Papa's frown deepens, but Mom grabs his hand, squeezing. Stiffly, he says, "Go on."

Over Annika's shoulder, I scan the photos. Comment after comment from all over the world. People talking about me and, for once, it's not awful.

It's incredible.

@HistoryHuhHenry: where are the other royals making a stand for queer lives like prince jadon??? hello @TheRoyalFamily!

@BmoreKings: Prince J did more for LGBTQIA+ folx than your favs have ever. RESPECT.

@PrinceSeb_Stans: OMFG PRINCE JADON REALLY SAID TRANS RIGHTS WITH HIS WHOLE CHEST! #LoveToSeeIt

@Genovia_Diaries: Have you guys seen the vid of Jadon hugging and taking selfies with protestors? He's so sweet! He's hot too 😍 Check out my Etsy page for new Jadon merch. link in my bio!

@AkioAndPrincessIzumi4Ever: Hey @Disney . . . more princes like Jadon, thanks! #MakeItOfficial #ThatsMyPrince

There are so many more, I lose track. Annika also has blog posts, articles from local and foreign presses. She must've spent hours on google sifting through the piles of bullshit usually written about me to find these.

"Paris. London. South Africa. Tokyo," Annika lists. "A Réverian professor in America wrote an article for the *New York Times*. She wishes heroes like Jadon were more visible while she was in Réverie. How she would've felt proud of who she was then."

My breath hitches, eyes wet.

"Most of these are from teens," Annika adds.

On-screen, something flashes across Mom's face.

"Isn't that what we want?" Annika asks. "For him to have an impact? Be the kind of leader his generation respects *and* admires?"

Papa clears his throat. "It is." His eyes land back on me. "But if you want to be political, son, then make a difference *here*. With your people. Join the Council."

I shake my head. He still doesn't understand. I don't want to sit at a table full of old, out-of-touch nobles and politicians too set in their traditions. Who want to do things like Senator Miller. Who think like Prime Minister Barnard.

A room where someone like me—born of Réverian and American blood—won't be respected, title or not.

"No," I say firmly. "That's not enough."

"Enough?" Papa repeats, incredulous. "Who are you to decide what's—"

"Maybe," Mom interrupts, squeezing Papa's hand again, "it's better we have this conversation in person? Thanksgiving break is coming up, right, Canelé?"

I nod once.

"Simon," Mom says, patiently, sweetly. "It's time."

Papa sighs through his nose, his mouth flat. "Agreed. You'll come home. To talk."

There's a finality to his words. The king has spoken.

But I'm not done. I spent too much time in America. Running from problems. Trying to be someone else. Letting everyone else decide for me.

That Jadon's gone.

I lean forward, determined face big on the laptop screen. "Fine," I say. "But we're not coming alone."

"This can't be real."

My lips smooth into a grin. It's the third time Reiss has said that. First, when the crew welcomed us aboard the jet. Second, post-nap, when we were soaring somewhere over the Atlantic. Now, minutes after the pilot has announced our forthcoming descent.

I rest a hand on his knee as we glide through a sea of clouds in the pinkish-blue sky. Across from us, Annika's reading another Jasmine Guillory rom-com. To her left, Luc is secretly weeping over an evicted contestant on *Paradise or Purgatory*.

"I work at my parents' coffee shop. I share a bathroom with my little brother," Reiss whispers, awed. "How is this happening?"

I laugh. "It's not that special."

"*To you*," he says, stabbing my chest with an accusing finger. "I still fly standby to visit my cousins. No free snacks. No Wi-Fi. Just a middle seat and a stranger snoring on my shoulder."

"How primitive," Ajani comments from behind us.

"It's a good thing you had a passport," I tell him.

It wasn't the most organized plan. Once I ended the call with my parents, I messaged my idea to Reiss. Then, after convincing Mr. and Mrs. Hayes to let him come to Réverie for the school break, we scrambled to get all the proper paperwork ready with Samuel.

"When I was nine," Reiss explains, scratching the back of his neck, "we were supposed to take a family vacation to Mexico."

Annika closes her book. "What happened?"

His cheeks flush. "I caught the flu from a classmate. Gave it to my whole family. We haven't had the chance—or money—to go since."

Annika tries to smile sympathetically, but it's closer to a wince.

I bump Reiss's shoulder. "Happy to be your first." When his eyebrows shoot up his forehead, I stammer, "Er, first *overseas* trip. First first-class experience."

Luc tugs out his earbuds. "Ignore these two." He draws an invisible line between me and Annika. "They were born with gold pacifiers in their mouths."

There's nothing rude about his tone. Beyond what's in his royal dossier, I don't know much about Luc's personal life. His mom is a former Royal Protection Guard who served under my mémère. Now, she lives on the other side of Réverie in a small, quiet city. He visits whenever possible.

He nods at Reiss. "Private travel *is* cool."

"Did you," Annika says, "just tell someone to ignore the crown princess?"

"I did." Luc sniffs defiantly.

Annika's eyes narrow, but the edges of her mouth start to lift.

"Your Highnesses," Samuel announces over Reiss's shoulder. "We're home."

Outside the window, the band of clouds disappears, and there it is.

"Îles de la Réverie," Samuel says in a serene voice.

Reiss inhales sharply. I squeeze his knee, beaming.

The island stretches like open arms. From the sea cliffs along the northern shore to the verdant countryside along its western coast. Mountains dip into thick forests. My eyes trace along the sugarcane fields Pépère would take us to visit. Over hillsides where horses roam in dancing grass.

"The centuries-old Réverie Islands," Samuel narrates for Reiss. "First inhabited by French settlers. A major port during the Atlantic slave trade. But battles between the French and British destroyed much of the land. Its people too."

In my periphery, Annika and Luc bow their heads, a tradition I mimic.

En mémoire. *In remembrance.*

We pass over untouched ruins. Shattered ivory buildings rising up like jagged teeth. Decayed churches and piles of crumbled brick.

"War came again. This time from our people," Samuel continues as cities blossom into view. "Réverians fought against their colonizers. For freedom. For the home they built from rough hands and tired legs. Led by Réné, our first king."

Modern shops are built around antiquated structures. Roads wind like still rivers. We pass over Académie des Jeunes Dirigeants, the vast emerald park surrounding it. The marketplace sits like a beating heart in Réverie's chest, breathing life back into my lungs.

"We are a people of survival," Samuel says proudly. "Determined. Strong. We are hope, for one another and the world we created for ourselves."

Goosebumps break out along my forearms.

It's easy to forget history. The places you come from. Where life ended so yours could begin. But it's just as simple to get tangled in the past. To accept the now as the happy ending rather than the next step to what can be.

"And here," Samuel whispers, a smile singing through his voice, "is where the light shines brightest."

Even at sunset, Centauri Palace glows ethereally. Towering peaks and white marble and gleaming windows. Trees circle the land like a gate. The Atlantic waits in the distance, a fluttering cape of blue extended from a crown. From our very own star.

Home.

18

"Do I look okay?" Reiss whispers. "To meet the king and queen?"

I grin. We've fallen into the traditional line of succession—Annika first, then me, with Reiss by my side. Our guards shadow close behind. Around us, the palace's staff efficiently collects our luggage from the Bentleys we rode from the airport in. Outside Centauri's entrance, a line of Royal Protection Guards bows as we approach.

"They're just my parents," I tell Reiss.

He snorts. "Yeah, no. Your dad was on CNN this morning. Mine was burning waffles. They're *not* just your parents."

A laugh tickles my throat. I give him a brief once-over: the collar of his Willow Wood Oxford peeking from beneath a black crewneck sweater, nice jeans, a pair of light purple Air Jordan 1 lows. Fading sunlight winks off his diamond-stud helix piercings.

"You look great," I say. "I'd date you."

"Oof, sorry." He frowns. "I kinda have a boyfriend."

"Hmm. What's he like?"

"Super arrogant. Loves pouting. Hates apologizing. Decent kisser, but the dimples make up for it."

"*Decent?*" I squawk. "I'll show you how *amazing* I can—"

"Crown Princess. My prince." At the top of the palace steps, Jean-Marc, my mom's most trusted chamberlain, gracefully bows. "All of Rêverie happily welcomes you home."

"Thank you," Annika says, perfect princess tone in place.

"Where's Mom?" I ask. "Papa?"

Jean-Marc's smile turns commiserative. "His Majesty and the queen are away. A prescheduled trip. They will return late tomorrow."

I try not to deflate. What was I expecting? My parents waiting for us? To cancel *another* appointment? Treat me like a priority and not a checkbox on their daily itinerary?

"We can't wait," Annika answers for both of us.

Jean-Marc nods. "This is Mr. Hayes, correct?"

Reiss waves awkwardly. "Mr. Hayes is my dad. Reiss is cool, your, um—royalship?"

Jean-Marc is in his late forties, tall and bald with dark brown skin and very expressive eyebrows. They climb his forehead.

"Interesting." With one subtle wrist flick, a chamberlain appears. Jean-Marc says, "Your suite is in the eastern wing. Henri will escort you."

"*Suite?*" Reiss gasps, jaw unhinged.

Barely holding in another laugh, I say, "See you soon," squeezing his hand one last time before he disappears behind the large glass doors.

Annika turns to face me. "Wow. Jade, you've got it *baaad.*"

"What?" I shake my head. "No, I—"

"So bad," Luc confirms.

"It's quite nauseating," Ajani notes, upper lip curled. The Royal Protection Guards behind her fail to hide their giggling.

"We've cleared your schedules," Jean-Marc announces, his own lips twitching. "In case you want to spend *extra time* showing Mr. Hayes around tomorrow."

I growl out, "I hate all of you."

More laughter follows as I storm away, face so hot I could be the primary source of global warming.

Rêverie's marketplace is luminous the next day. Ribbons of sunlight cut through the colorful canopies hung over stalls selling fresh produce and lush fabrics and pottery with intricate designs. Vibrant murals crawl up the sides of buildings. The air is fragrant with the scent of grilling meats and heady spices. Voices chase each other, in French, in English, in a collective harmony of people selling and buying and bargaining.

The rush hits like a tidal wave, nearly knocking me over. I've missed this space.

I half-turn to Reiss. "What do you think so far?"

It's late afternoon. I can tell he's still jet-lagged, occasionally rubbing his eyes or yawning. But now, his gaze dances around like he's overstimulated. He can't settle on one thing. His face glows at the laughter, the noise spilling from every angle.

"It's beautiful."

Ajani and two other guards navigate us through the crowds. It's a slow stroll. Every few shops, Reiss pauses to admire another shiny trinket.

"Is it weird," he says outside a teashop, "that I feel so safe here?"

I lift a curious eyebrow.

"Everyone looks like"—his eyelashes flutter when he inhales—"like me."

All around, there are gorgeous shades of brown. Rich dark complexions. Warm sepia skin and cool russet tones. Different faces, body shapes, each person carrying their own swagger. For once, Reiss and I aren't two Black boys in a pale sea, like at Willow Wood.

Here, Reiss doesn't stand out. He's one of us.

"No," I whisper, bumping his shoulder. "It's not weird."

He grins crookedly. "I'm glad I came."

"You are?" I don't mean to sound so shocked.

He pans his phone around. Snaps photos and records video. "Visiting another country? Kicking it at a palace over school break? Do you know how much this is gonna elevate my social outcast status?"

I laugh, head tipped back into the warm sun. "I've heard somewhere that reputation matters."

"Only on the internet."

I wish that was true.

As we pass through a busy café, eyes track us. It's happened since we arrived. I smile and nod politely, the way my mom would. Some return the gesture, faces glowing with surprise at seeing me this close, outside Centauri's walls. But others avert their gazes, whispering furiously when they think I'm not looking, whenever my hand absently brushes against Reiss's.

Prime Minister Barnard's faithful followers. The ones who don't know the real him. Or the real me.

During the flight, Samuel swore public opinion has changed. That our efforts are working. But I don't know. Am I more than pics and videos to them? More than polls and surveys?

When they look at me, do they see the prince they *want*?

"Oh, shit." Reiss holds up his phone. The screen lights up with a FaceTime call. "I forgot to check in with my parents. Dom's been dying to see what Réverie looks like. Is that okay?"

I bite my lip, grinning. "Yes."

"BRB," he says, answering as he stumbles to a quieter corner.

Ajani motions for the guards to follow.

I drift deeper into the market. Losing myself in familiarity. In my thoughts.

"So, it's true. He really let you come back."

I jerk to a halt. My spine tightens at the unwelcome voice. At the boy standing in front of me. The same twists falling in his dark eyes, mellow brown skin; thin cheeks and a long jaw. Height like a basketball player, which he uses to look down on everyone.

Kofi.

He smirks in that patronizing way of his. "Thought America was keeping you."

"Thought you were staying with me," I snap quietly.

"What gave you that impression?"

"You were my best—" I can't get the word out. Not only because we're in semi-public. Because it's not true. I'm not sure it ever was.

Kofi exhales a dry laugh. "I did too."

"Then why'd you leave?"

"Why?" He repeats it with a pinched face, like the question tastes sour. "What did you want me to do? Go against the king's orders?"

"How about not let someone record me during my worst moment—"

"You have a lot of those, Jadon—"

"—and release it to the whole damn world?"

"Here's an idea." He edges closer. "How about, for once, we don't make everything about you, Your Highness?"

His tone is like a sharp slap across the cheek. He's never talked to me like this—with overwhelming disgust.

At my silence, his nostrils flare.

"You still don't get it." Kofi throws his arms out wildly. "It was my fucking birthday—"

Ajani leans forward. "Watch your tongue. Or I'll remove it."

I lift my hand before she follows through on her promise. I want him to finish.

"You made *my day* all about you, like always," Kofi says, lowering his voice, but the rage is still brimming.

"We didn't have to talk about it," I argue. "*You* asked *me* what was wrong."

"Sorry for caring," he says without a hint of sympathy.

"You let total strangers into our booth."

"Yeah." Kofi scoffs. "Because it was better than hanging out with poor, sad Jadon again."

"They *filmed me*, Kofi." I shake my head, chest hot. "Invaded my private moment. I needed a friend."

"You don't know what that word means."

It's another sting to the face. He's right. We've been around each other for years, but I don't *know* Kofi. His favorite movie. His dreams or fears. I never asked.

Kofi was always this carefree force of nature I could go to when I was angry or frustrated. I was made of gasoline. He was the one holding a match. But were we ever more than just two boys watching our fire burn the world down?

I hear Grace's voice in my ears: *Where are your friends, Jadon?*

Judging from Kofi's impatient glare, I never had any.

"Mon Dieu," he whines, shaking his head. "You don't get it. I was tired of being your sidekick. Tired of making every little thing about you. I needed a break, so I let them in."

I thought it would be different. Hearing him admit it. Like it'd give me relief. But it only makes me angrier.

He laughs bitterly. "I didn't think one video would ruin the son of a king—"

"I'm a *person*," I seethe.

Tears prick my eyes. I didn't choose to be a prince. To grow up the way I did. But I chose loneliness and distance and making excuses for never fixing that. Because it was safer, comfortable.

But comfort doesn't last forever. And I don't want it to.

I want movie nights with Karan and Lo. Mornings in the courtyard with Morgan and Nathan. Scooter rides and pier walks and sharing hot chocolates with Reiss.

That's the kind of friendship I'm choosing for myself.

"You don't have to worry about being my sidekick anymore," I tell him. "About poor, sad Jadon stealing your spotlight. It's all yours. I hope you enjoy it."

I spin away. Walk back into the booming marketplace, where I find Reiss with an armful of gifts for his family.

"I went a little overboard," he says sheepishly. Then, he studies me. "Everything okay?"

I pause. For once, there's no unbearable heat in my chest. No fire waiting to get out. It's just me and Reiss. I smile at him.

"Yeah. I'm . . . better than expected."

His eyebrows crinkle in confusion. Whatever question he wants to ask is drowned out by voices chanting, "Jadon! Jadon! Jadon!"

It's a pack of beaming, sweaty kids half my size. Their

clothes are grass-stained. One boy spins a football on his index finger.

"You're back!" he shouts. "You owe us like a million games."

They all nod in unison.

I pivot to Ajani. She sighs, her face saying it all: *You're asking for trouble.* I am. But, this time, it's good trouble. Far from newsworthy trouble.

Turns out, Reiss is terrible at football. A fumbling, tripping, can't-score-on-an-open-goal mess. We run around for hours, breathless and drenched by the time we finish.

When the kids dogpile Reiss in the center of the field, my chest cracks at one thought:

I'm finally sharing my world with Reiss, like I hoped back on Santa Monica Pier.

Before we leave, I buy everyone crème glacée and promise another game soon.

Reality hits me again: this is my home. The place I was so desperate to get back to. America was temporary.

This thing with Reiss is . . . I'm afraid to figure that part out.

Centauri's eastern wing is always eerily quiet. It's only for guest chambers. I should be in my own suite on the other side of the palace. Then again, when have I ever done what I was supposed to?

The silent corridor's antique rug is soft under my bare feet. I move quickly. Sneaking around at midnight isn't new. I mastered it long ago, figuring out where the loose floorboards are, discovering secret rooms, places to hide from patrolling guards. I've never been caught.

"My prince."

Until now.

Wincing, I slowly turn to face Ajani and her suspicious glare.

"Sleepwalking?"

"Something like that," I squeak, throat tight.

She purses her lips, one hand behind her back. No doubt concealing the taser she's going to use before dragging my unconscious body back to my suite.

"Thing is," I try, "I was just looking for the, er—"

"Oh, please." Indignation flashes across her eyes. "Do I look that incompetent? Like I didn't know you were sneaking out with Léon all that time."

My jaw drops, eyes probably cartoonishly wide. *She knew?* All my careful planning. Ducking behind curtains. Crawling out open windows.

"Every single time," she says, as if reading my mind. "I won't speak of this if you"—she reveals what's behind her back: a plate of gooey chocolate cake drizzled in raspberry sauce—"never tell who's been stealing desserts from the kitchens."

"I saw nothing," I confirm.

"In your suite by sunrise," she commands, then disappears into the shadows.

At Reiss's suite, I knock twice before cracking the door. I messaged ahead of time. To make sure he was still awake.

The bedside lamp throws golden beams over the room's rich blues. Across the expensive furniture. Reiss sits in the middle of the baroque bed, legs crisscrossed. He's fresh from the shower, shirtless. I swallow as he uses a fluffy gray towel to dry his hair.

He mock-bows, a smirk flitting across his mouth. "Your Royal Arrogance."

I lean against the door. "Am I keeping you up?"

"Maybe." The corners of his mouth stretch higher. "I don't mind."

Warmth settles in my belly. I want to be near him. Touch him. Find new ways to make his eyes crinkle. But there's another thought chasing a chill down my spine:

What happens when Papa lets me come home, permanently?

Reiss clears his throat. "Can we talk?"

He's drumming his fingers on his knees. That nervous tic I recognize. Is he thinking the same thing? That this can't last?

I motion to the empty spot next to him, my eyes saying, *Is that okay?*

He nods.

Once I'm on the bed, he stretches his legs across my lap. Our hands find each other, fingers threading together. He chews his lower lip.

I say, "Is this a . . . bad talk?"

"What? No." Reiss's shoulders pull up around his ears. "I mean, I hope not? You said we should talk first. At the coffee shop. If I wanted to—*you know*."

It takes five seconds for my brain to recalibrate. I rewind through our conversations and laughs and arguments before—

Oh. That.

My back pressed against a shelf in The Hopper's backroom.

Fingers peeling up his shirt. In the shadows, mouths so close, talking about taking this to the next step.

"Fuck," he breathes out. "I made this weird. Karan warned me. No one talks about sex. It just happens. Talking about it is—"

"Great!" I interrupt, gripping his hand. "Sexy. Necessary."

His dark eyes stare at me skeptically.

Grinning, I say, "I promise it is. I told you consent is important to me. Communication is too. I don't want to read things wrong."

"You're not." His cheeks are bruised pink. "I—I want to."

"Me too."

He struggles to keep eye contact when he says, "I brought condoms and stuff." Vaguely, he waves toward his luggage in a corner.

I can't imagine the personal crisis he suffered through in the checkout line. Léon always took care of that part for us.

Touching his burning cheek, I whisper, "That's a great start."

He exhales shakily, eyes still lowered.

"It's okay to be nervous," I tell him, lips brushing the corner of his mouth. "There's no rush."

A sharp noise escapes his throat as I grab the back of his neck. Pull him in. Ease my mouth across his.

He's the first to deepen the kiss. He yanks my shirt up so quickly, the collar gets caught around my forehead. We're both laughing when I finally free myself.

"Okay so far?" I ask while guiding him into my lap.

He stares down at me through thick eyelashes. I rub up against him. Hoarsely, he says, "Y-yeah. Perfect."

His sweaty hand moves from my bare shoulder into my curls. A tentative tug.

"Can I—do you like that?"

An involuntary shiver wrecks my body. "Yes. What do you want to do?"

"All of it."

I laugh. "Me too. But this is new." I remember my own first time. The awkwardness and messiness and how fast it ended. I want more for him. "Tell me what you like first. What you're comfortable with."

He pauses, thinking.

I edge my fingers up his spine. His response is immediate—a breathy gasp. I wiggle to adjust my boner, then say, "Just tell me what feels good. Or what doesn't."

"What about other stuff?"

My eyebrow flexes in confusion.

"I mean, I've seen porn," he says, chin jutting. "Should we know who does what?"

I press a kiss to his sternum. He smells incredible. Like peppermint and . . .

Wait.

"Did you shower because—" I purse my lips. "You already thought this through, didn't you?"

He doesn't blush or fidget when he admits, "I wanted to be clean. Just in case."

Just in case. Those three words run like lava through my brain.

"We can talk about that," I say, easing him onto the mattress, swiping away the dozens of useless decorative pillows, "if you want to go there."

"You won't get annoyed if I ask too many questions?"

"I promise." My hands spread over the waistband of his pajama bottoms. "Can we start here?"

After a long beat, he nods.

I untie the knot. It's a clumsy, graceless effort, but we get there. Then he slides off my joggers, and my boxers too.

"Whoa." He pauses. I can tell he's trying hard not to stare below my navel. "You're not, um, like me? Down there, I mean."

I grin. "No."

"Cool, cool." He nods too many times. "Should I do anything . . . differently?"

This time, a full, stomach-clenching laugh rumbles out of me.

"I'll show you."

"Cool, cool," he repeats to himself. "One more question."

I raise an eyebrow.

"Why aren't we kissing?"

"So bossy," I whisper, lying on top of him, skin to skin.

I take my time. Quiet pecks across his collarbone. Long seconds with my mouth against his shoulder. His hands roam over my biceps. Map every piece of skin he hasn't explored while my heart thuds noisily.

I stop to whisper, "Are you still okay?"

"Beyond." He's restless under me. "Keep going. I'll tell you if it's too much."

I comply. Through every motion, every new touch, I study

his reaction. Wait for little cues. I never shy away from his questions or requests. He smiles appreciatively as we take breaks until he's ready to tell me what he wants next.

Reiss is the sea. I'm his shore. We meet in a soft embrace. In a thundering crash. In a rhythm only we understand.

Night stretches into dawn. Through a gap in the curtains, the sky melts from dull purple to a vibrant pink.

Sunrise.

I need to go. Ajani will literally kill me. But my legs are tangled in the sheets. Reiss is on top of me, boneless. Snoring into the crook of my neck. I trace his cheek with a finger, eyes heavy and gritty. I've barely slept, but this is worth it.

Watching him so relaxed. Knowing what we did. Dazed by this feeling in my chest, the words I'm scared to say out loud:

I'm in love with Reiss Hayes.

19

EXCLUSIVE: "HE'S NOT THE PRINCE YOU THINK HE IS"

For years, the world has obsessed over who Prince Jadon really is. The boy who caused a stir in Milan? The drunken misfit badmouthing a political leader on camera? What about the ambitious rebel protesting in America? In an exclusive *The Dish and Chips* interview, Kip Davies talks candidly with Kofi Baptiste, the prince's former best friend, about the Jadon in the news and the real him. You might be surprised by what you read!

I'm not nervous.

Behind the Rouge Room's mahogany doors, my parents are meeting. They got in late last night. Too late for a formal welcome. Also, I was a little busy with . . . well. Spending the night in a certain boy's guest suite.

This is the first time I'm seeing my parents in person in

months. The first time they'll see the real me. The first time they're meeting Reiss too.

But I'm not nervous. Nope. I don't anticipate projectile vomiting from the queasiness in my stomach in the near future.

"Your Highness."

I startle when Dion swoops in like he did this morning. All impeccable clothes and perfect sepia skin and confident smile. He bows, then says, "I present . . . Mr. Reiss Hayes."

He steps aside. Whatever's happening in my belly calms.

Reiss is in a black Oxford, the top two buttons undone. Fitted Burberry trousers match his loafers. His faded pink hair is trimmed and styled. He's as beautiful as he was last night. A dream I don't want to wake from.

"Hmm." Annika walks up, studying Reiss. Her gaze turns on me. "I see what you mean."

My face is as hot as Reiss's looks.

She squeezes my shoulder. "Are you good?"

Over breakfast, she gave me a small pep talk: *Speak from the heart, be respectful, don't fuck it up.*

After a deep inhale, I nod.

I can do this. I *hope* I can.

The doors swing open. Samuel greets us with a deep bow. "His Majesty and Queen Ava are ready for you."

I grab Reiss's hand. We walk toward the glossy lacquered table in the center of the room. Papa waits at the head, stone-faced, sitting tall in a sharp suit. To his left, Mom smiles when she sees Annika, then me. Her expression doesn't falter after Reiss comes into view.

He bows in the way I coached him on earlier.

"My children," Papa says with a faint warmness. "Welcome home."

"You too, Papa," Annika says.

I nod, trying to detangle the knots forming in my stomach as I sit.

Mom folds her hands on the table. "This is Mr. Hayes?"

"Reiss," I confirm with a wobbly voice. I clear my throat. "My boyfriend."

"It's an honor to meet you," he gets out, just as nervous.

Mom's grin widens. Papa's face remains unsurprisingly neutral.

Samuel rests a folder in front of him.

"Quite the journey you've been on, son," he says, reaching for his teacup. The air is spiced with a flowery scent. Darjeeling, his favorite. "Going to dinners with respected figureheads. Baseball games. Rehearsing for a school play—"

Something like pride rests in the corners of Mom's mouth at that last bullet point.

Papa flips a page. "You've also had time to be *seen* at Los Angeles landmarks." His eyes drift to Reiss.

Under the table, I grip his hand. "Yes, Papa, I—"

"And yet," he goes on like I never spoke, "nothing to prove you've earned Réverie's respect again."

My mouth flattens into a thin line, eyes narrowed.

"You're still in the news." He turns another page. A copy of today's *The Dish and Chips*. The interview with Kofi.

My stomach roils as Mom's expression slips into disappointment.

"Where is the prince I asked for?" Papa inquires. "Three months in America. Ample time to prove yourself. But all I see is a rebel protesting. Getting caught kissing this boy."

"His name's Reiss," I say, barely keeping the agitation out of my voice.

Papa is unmoved. He's the king right now, not the man who taught me to knead dough or flip a crêpe.

"And I *am* the prince you asked for," I say earnestly. "The one I should be."

"Which is?"

"Someone who cares." I look at Reiss. "Who fights. Speaks up. Who isn't always right, but knows change takes time." I watch Reiss's mouth curve up before staring at Papa again. "I'm proud of who I'm becoming."

Papa sighs into his tea. "But is Réverie proud?"

"They should be," I insist.

Mom smiles sadly. "Son, have you thought about whether your choices are fair to Reiss?"

His attention jumps to her.

My perfect royal posture falters. "W-what?"

"I know what it's like to be an outsider," Mom says. "The crown carries a lot of weight. Not just for you. For whoever you choose to be involved with."

A familiar flame starts in my chest. Climbs into my throat. The prime minister's words pollute my blood all over again. *She's not one of us. Never will be!*

"There will be negativity. From the press. From our people." She exhales. "Is Reiss ready for that?"

I pause, mouth open. Last night, all I wanted was to keep Reiss as close as possible. To never let go. But was Kofi right? Is it always about . . . me? Did I bother to ask if Reiss wanted all of this?

"Can *you* handle it, son?" Mom says.

"I'm not even the crown prince!" I look around the table. "Why does anyone care what I do? Who I date?"

Papa sips his tea. "You represent this country." He motions toward Annika. "Your sister works hard to put our people first. Our family first."

"Our family," I repeat, almost hysterical. "The family that doesn't even see each other?"

Papa smacks his hand down. "Ça suffit."

"No, it's not." I shake my head. "Thanks to *you* exiling me to America, this is the most I've seen my sister in a year!"

Annika frowns at me.

"Unlike you, she's busy being a proper representation of Réverie." Papa's voice booms in the room. "Why do you insist on ruining your future?"

"What future?" I laugh hoarsely. "The one decided by the monarchy? I'm your *son*. Not just a face printed on T-shirts in a souvenir shop."

"You're a prince."

"I'm a puppet," I argue. "And every time I try to be myself, someone cuts my strings."

Papa scoffs. "You learned nothing in America. You're emotional. Impulsive. Ungrateful. Disrespectful—"

"I'm *me*," I say through the thickness growing in my throat.

"Excuse me." The chair next to me shifts. Reiss stands, letting go of my hand. "Sorry, Your Majesty, but I don't want this."

"What?" I almost don't hear my own voice over the ringing in my ears.

"I can handle this. I'm ready," he says to my mom. Then, he stares down at me. "This is where you belong. Where you wanted to be. Right?"

I can't answer him, my hands trembling on the table.

"I'm not standing in your way," he continues. "Those kids we played with yesterday? They need you. Kids like Dom need you too. Someone to look up to. A hero, remember?"

"But what about—"

"How can you be brave if you've never been afraid?" His lips barely hold a smile.

Tears burn against my eyelashes.

Reiss faces Papa. "I'm lucky. My parents support my dreams. They let me choose my own path. Even when I mess up." He raises a defiant chin. "That's what great parents do. They don't force their children. They let them be who they are. Mistakes and all."

A beat of silence. I scramble for words, but nothing comes fast enough. Because, deep down, I know what's next.

But it still hurts when Reiss whispers, "I'd like to go home."

I stare at him, incredulous. Heartbroken.

"As you wish, Reiss," Mom says, nodding. "Ajani, please see that he gets everything he needs. Samuel, coordinate a flight home."

There's a moment where Reiss lingers over me. I still can't

find the right words to ask him to stay. He doesn't wait for them. He turns his back from me and follows Ajani out the mahogany doors.

And I let him leave.

"I've decided," Papa starts after too long. "You'll remain in Rêverie. Your exile is over. We'll discuss how to move forward with your royal duties later."

I finally blink. No tears fall. I stare at Annika, her chin lowered, fists balled on the table. Even Mom's regal posture has deflated. Silently, Papa finishes his tea, as if the last few minutes never happened.

The decision has been made. This is how it will always be.

But the fire in my chest is burning too hot. I'm done letting someone else choose for me. If I don't say this now, I might not ever have the courage again.

I stand on wobbly legs. "I know we have obligations. That putting your country first is some kind of royal tradition. But I miss my family," I choke out. "Not this formal bullshit we've become."

"Jadon," Mom sighs.

"Know your place, son," Papa scolds.

"I don't *have* a place, Papa! And no one's letting me find it. I'm always told *where* I belong. *What* I should do. *How* I have to exist. When do I get to decide?" I shout, pounding a fist to my chest. "When do I pick my own path?"

"When you grow up," Papa says plainly.

"You can force me to smile and wave. Be the good prince you were," I bite out, "but you'll never change who I am."

Unflinching, Papa lifts a brow. *Who are you?*

"I'm kind. I'm angry. I stand up for what I believe. For the people I love. I'm not perfect, but I'm *trying*." I sniff, ignoring how my voice keeps breaking. "This is the real me. It's a shame my own parents can't love me for that."

I turn on my heels and march toward the doors.

"Jadon." Papa's voice echoes like thunder from the head of the table. His position of power. "I didn't excuse you."

"I know, Your Majesty," I say over my shoulder.

And I keep walking.

"Redecorating?"

Brows raised, Annika hangs in the archway of my suite's bedroom. It's been two hours since we last saw each other in the Rouge Room. She looks as tired as I feel.

The world's still spinning. It's like I'm on a Ferris wheel that never pauses. Never permits me room to breathe. My vision is nothing but blurred images of Papa's angry scowl and Mom's disappointed shoulder droop and Annika's sad, lowered eyes. Or maybe that's the tears I refuse to shed.

He's gone. And I didn't stop him.

Annika carefully steps into the room. Over the wreckage I created the second I kicked in my suite's door. I couldn't stand looking at it. Clean, organized, every detail decided by someone else. Just like my life.

So, I tore down paintings. Tipped over pretty, expensive, useless furniture. Knocked over a vase or two. Ajani stood aside as I went from corner to corner. As I unleashed the last flames swelling inside me.

Now, in the aftermath, I sit on my bed. Fists curled in my lap. Exhaustion creeping into my bones. The fire extinguished. And nothing's changed.

Not a single thing.

The mattress dips. Annika doesn't push me to speak. She waits, the same way she did when our mémère died and I couldn't stop shaking, absorbing the pain of the first person I loved and lost.

She did the same thing when Pépère passed. That was shorter. Because the palace had time to prepare for the transition from funeral to coronation to losing my papa to his new duties. We went from being paraded around in all black to being paraded around with smiles and graceful waves. There was barely any time to mourn.

But through it all, Anni was there. Like she is today.

"Walking out on the king?" She half-laughs. "That's bold."

I exhale. "Had to level up after walking out on a senator."

Her shoulder brushes mine, and my stomach twists, thinking about what I said earlier.

"I'm sorry," I whisper. "I didn't mean it when I said—"

"Yes, you did," she interrupts, grinning wryly. "But I'm not mad."

"You're not?"

"As much as it kills me to admit," she groans, "I *am* always gone. Always being Crown Princess Annika first."

"I wish I was like you."

"You mean impeccably dressed? Funny? *Nice?*"

"No." This time, I nudge her shoulder. A frown creases my mouth. "Perfect."

She sighs at the ceiling. "Jade, I promise you, I'm far from that. I'm the first female heir in our bloodline. That's a lot of pressure."

Before her, every monarch's firstborn was a boy. It wasn't an intended tradition—to only have kings. It just happened. But then Annika came along, and Pépère made it known that one day, she would succeed Papa. She would be our queen.

"For years, I tried to be the best. Give them no reason to doubt me." She cracks her knuckles, then stops. "But they'll always doubt me. Because of misogyny. Misogynoir. I'll never be enough."

I shake my head, irritated.

"I don't want to be *their* queen, anyway." Annika shrugs. "They don't deserve me. I want to be queen of a Réverie I helped shape. Which is what I've been doing for the last year."

She unlocks her phone. Swipes through contracts and building plans. Discussions with leaders about creating more facilities intent on providing aid to underserved communities. Fighting antidiscrimination laws. Empowering women of color across the world.

"Holy fuck," I whisper. "So, you weren't just lounging by the pool? Sipping boba all day?"

"Oh, I did that too. It's called multitasking."

We share smiles.

"I can't change Réverie in a day," she says. "But I can start. I can stop giving up before I even try."

My eyebrows knit. "Wait. You were supposed to be helping *me* in LA."

"I tried! You're so stubborn. Just like Papa."

"I'm not like—"

Her sharp glare cuts me off. "You both get these ideas in your head. How things are supposed to go. Sometimes it's okay to admit you're in over your head." Her face softens. "Or just . . . *listen*. Not only to me. Yourself too."

I slump forward, drumming my fingers on my knees. A new wave of sadness moves through me when I realize I got that from Reiss.

"There's something else." When I raise my eyes, Annika's chewing her lower lip. Worry sits in the corners of her eyes. "I kind of have a secret boyfriend."

I nearly fall off the bed, flailing.

She winces. "I know, I know."

"Who?" I demand. "I'll have Ajani kidnap him and—"

Annika swats my knee. "No, you won't. Besides, Ajani doesn't need any extra motives to throw him off a roof."

I stare at her for a beat. And then—

"You're fucking joking."

She passes me her unlocked phone. I freeze at her background. It's the two of them laughing, arms around each other, standing in front of the reflecting pool on USC's campus.

My sister and Luc.

"That might be the other reason I was so busy in LA," she says with an anxious grin.

"H-how?"

"It happened last year—"

"*Last year?*" My screeching voice would usually alarm half the Royal Protection Guard. Ajani simply rolls her eyes, as if this isn't a surprise. As if she's known all along.

"It was unexpected," Annika says. "Me and Lucky—"

"No, no. Stop." I rub my temples, my brain unable keep up with all this new information. "His full name's *Lucky*?"

Annika's eyes narrow. My jaw clicks shut. I wave a hand in a *please continue* gesture.

"It works," she says. "When things are too much. When I'm sad or angry. Or need a reminder that I'm more than all of this. He's there. He likes *Anni*, not Crown Princess Annika."

A tender smile tugs at my mouth.

I know who you are.

People talk. I don't listen.

The things Reiss said to me the first time we really talked. He's never cared that I was a prince. He likes me as just Jadon.

Well, he did. Before today.

"How do you deal with the, you know, royal stuff?" I ask.

"I don't go around kissing him in front of busy piers!"

I facepalm.

"I only give the press enough to keep them satisfied. Sometimes, more." She sighs, her pristine posture unraveling. "It's a sacrifice. But it means I get those quiet moments with Lucky. My *relationship* is mine until I'm ready to share it with anyone else."

"What about Mom? Papa?"

"They know. Now." She makes a face. "I told them right after you stormed out."

I'm kind of glad I missed that. I like Luc, questionable reality TV show obsession and all. I don't think I could've controlled my temper if Papa said the wrong thing about him. Not that I'm good at keeping my anger in check to begin with.

"No matter who you are, you don't owe anyone every piece of you," Annika tells me. "It's yours. *You* decide what they get. What they remember you for. Not the crown. Not the people of Réverie. *Not* our parents."

The sharp burn behind my eyelashes returns.

Annika pokes my chest. "You decide, Jade. Only you."

I rest my head on her shoulder.

She whispers into my curls: "You don't have to be perfect. But you can't give up either."

Finally, I close my eyes. The hot tears slip out. Slice down my cheeks like a river of lava. But it's okay. Princes are allowed to cry.

I'm allowed to cry. Their rules never fit me anyway.

20

LIKE FATHER, LIKE SON

Prime Minister Barnard has been the subject of many
headlines for most of his career. From his leadership to
his commitment to uphold his country's beliefs to the
scandal where a prince, once believed to be a close
family friend, questioned his integrity. Recently, he
sat down to discuss a more personal subject: his son,
Léon. Watch this candid clip of the caring father talking
about "the son every parent wishes for."

All I want is to be left alone.

Yesterday, after Annika left, I cried again. And again. I
made up for too many years of turning my sadness into rage.
Now I want nothing more than to sleep in. Eat my weight in
canelés while streaming shows and avoiding the email I need
to send Dr. Garza Villa about not returning to LA in time for
the play's opening night.

Not coming back to America at all.

Except nothing I want ever happens.

There's heavy knocking on my bedroom suite door. Someone's muffled voice says my name through the wood. I stuff my head under the pillows. Try to hide from whatever needs my attention at this very moment. It doesn't last.

The pillows are snatched away. Ajani stands over me in full formal guard uniform.

I frown. "Unless this is about breakfast, then—"

"The king requests your presence," she interrupts. "Immediately."

"And I request another hour of sleep!"

My attempt to sink back under the covers is denied. Ajani yanks it away too. She ignores my whiny protests. The hardness of her stare sobers me. It's the same one she had when the video leaked.

"He wants you in the throne room."

I bolt upright. Big mistake. My body's so weak, so dehydrated, I almost vomit.

"How long do I ha—"

Ajani cuts in again. "Fifteen minutes."

Shit. I roll out of bed—another mistake. I crash onto the ground. "No, I'm okay. It's just a fractured knee. Probably threw out my back. Don't call a doctor or help me up."

"Fourteen minutes," she says, unmoved.

I miss the old Ajani. The one who cared at least five percent more about my well-being. Who didn't show up first thing in the morning with life-destroying news all the time.

I miss when my life *wasn't* just life-destroying news.

I'm still buttoning my shirt, forcing my left foot into a sneaker, as we rush down the Great Hall. It's terrifyingly quiet. No staff or chamberlains buzzing around. Only the occasional guard stops to eye me as I zip up my slacks. My brain's still mostly offline, but there's enough working cells to register one face as we round a corner.

I skid to a halt.

Head low, hands cupped in front, I watch him shuffle with a pair of Royal Protection Guards bookending him. A criminal's walk. His chest falls with an exhausted exhale. It's in the corner of his eyes too: the lack of sleep. He's frowning, shoulders heavy, clothes wrinkled—a side of him I haven't seen since his parents divorced and his mom left Réverie.

"Léon," I rasp.

He falters, then bows. "Bonjour."

"What are you doing here?"

He rocks on his heels. Like he doesn't have an answer. Or he's afraid to give it.

I step closer. "Here to welcome me home? Celebrate ruining my life? Brag to everyone about how you—"

"I was a shitty boyfriend."

My mouth snaps shut. His words hit like a foot to the stomach. "What?" is the only thing I can say.

"I was awful to you."

"You were awful to me," I repeat.

He ignores my stunned voice. "When I realized things weren't working between us, I ignored you. I *blamed* you. But it wasn't your fault."

I search for words, a reply, but he's not done.

"It was no one's fault." He brushes his hand over his hair. It's short again. Like when we dated. "We just weren't meant to be."

I swallow, nodding.

"When you wanted to be friends, I couldn't do it." He sighs. "I wasn't ready."

"I under—"

"No. Don't do that." His face twists with frustration. "Let me finish. It's lonely being who we are. Friendships are . . . hard. I should've at least listened."

I chew the inside of my cheek. I'm not sure which Léon this is. The one I fell for. Or the one from LA who betrayed me. The glassy eyes, sagging posture, that little tremble in his lower lip, tells me he's not sure either.

But he's figuring it out.

"I didn't want to come to America," he concedes, glancing down at the polished floor. "I let *people* influence me."

"Who?" I demand.

"It doesn't matter. I saw you on the news. It was"—he smirks—"inspiring."

My pulse speeds up. "What did you do?"

Ajani clears her throat. "My prince, His Majesty is waiting."

One of the guards says, "We should go," her hand gripping Léon's bicep. He's being escorted out. Whatever he did was serious.

"The protest," Léon gets out. He laughs, resisting the hands tugging him away. "Fuck. I finally saw who you were. We all did. C'était incroyable."

It was incredible.

He gives me one final heartbreaking smile before he's dragged away.

I'm rooted to this one spot in the Great Hall. Nothing makes sense. Nothing until the throne room doors open and I see who's waiting on the other side.

Suspended from the high ceilings are crystal chandeliers shining like constellations. The walls are deep brown with gold accents. Tall ebony sculptures line the room like guardians. A crimson carpet runs through the center of the mirror-finished floors.

The small dais at the head of the room holds matching thrones. Papa and Mom are perched on them. In the seats surrounding them are Annika, a straight-backed, scowling Samuel, and a man in a smart navy suit with dark brown skin, his semi-wrinkled face almost identical to his son's.

Prime Minister Barnard.

My skin prickles as I bow to my parents. "Papa. Mom."

"My son," Papa says, his tone formal, but not as cold as yesterday. He gestures toward Barnard. "I asked the prime minister to join us for this meeting."

Through my teeth, I say, "Welcome, Prime Minister."

"Your Highness." Barnard inclines his head, smiling smugly. "Praise be that you and the crown princess have returned to us safely."

Annika shifts uncomfortably.

In the beat of silence, I hear Samuel's heavy exhale. I'm not sure why he's here. I never get a chance to ask.

"I hope America was refreshing," Barnard continues. "A moment of reflection, perhaps."

My knuckles crack as my hands curl into fists. I force myself to shake out my fingers. I can't let him get the best of me.

"We're sorry to have interrupted your busy schedule, Prime Minister," Papa says for me.

"Anything for you, Your Majesty."

Barnard relaxes on his plush chair. His coal-black eyes never leave my strained face. I do my best not to fidget. Or set him on fire. He strokes his thin beard, then says, "Have I been brought here today for an apology?"

My eyes shift to Papa, pleading. *Please don't make me do this.*

He adjusts his cuffs like he's waiting for me to do as the prime minister has requested. I feel sick. Everything that happened yesterday—the words said, the tears shed—none of it matters.

It's still Réverie first. Jadon . . . never.

My dry lips part. Before anything comes out, Papa raises a hand.

"Yes, Jadon. It's time for an apology." He rotates on his throne. "Prime Minister Barnard. Apologize to my son."

The air is sucked from the room. Heads crane in Papa's direction. All but Samuel, whose steely, unforgiving glare is on Barnard.

So is Papa's, ringed by a fire I've never seen in him.

"What could you possibly mean?" Barnard thrashes an arm in my direction. "He's the one who—"

"I know what my son did," Papa says evenly. "But no one here knows what *you* did."

"W-what I've done?" Barnard stammers.

Papa lifts an eyebrow. "Only Jadon knew. Isn't that right, son?"

My hands are trembling so hard, my wrists ache. I swallow, looking into my papa's curious eyes. "You know what he said?"

"Samuel as well." He motions toward Barnard. "Thanks to *his* son."

Barnard's throat moves, but for the first time, he doesn't speak.

I did the right thing. That's what Léon said.

"Papa"—I fight through the tightness in my throat—"what did Léon say?"

"He contacted Samuel yesterday. Told him everything," Papa confirms. His eyes have turned to pools of regret. "We had Léon flown here overnight. I wanted to speak with him in person."

"Your Majesty," Barnard attempts.

"*Save your words,* Prime Minister," Papa demands.

"Simon," Mom whispers. "What's happening?"

I try to grab Papa's gaze. To stop him. She can't hear this part.

The edges of Papa's softened expression promise me this needs to happen. It's okay. He steps off the dais.

"The prime minister has some . . . *thoughts* on our queen's place in Réverie," Papa tells the room. "Whether she's worthy to sit on that throne."

Papa's tall, like me and Annika. His perfect posture gives him even more height as he stares down at Barnard.

"All things my son, the prince, heard you say." His jaw

flexes. "In the Rouge Room. Three months ago. Right before a certain video of him was released."

Barnard chooses silence over admission.

Papa shakes his head. "Then, you sent your son to America. Told him to regain Jadon's trust. Ruin his plans."

Barnard's mouth twitches. He's still quiet. But something flashes across his eyes—fear, I think.

"Because if Jadon failed," Papa says tightly, "you'd be right. Réverie's people wouldn't respect my son. They'd blame their queen, who's from America. Who—how did Léon put it?" He looks over to Samuel. *"Isn't one of us."*

Samuel nods, nostrils flaring.

Flustered, Barnard stands. He struggles to button his jacket. "My son's delusional. I'd never—"

"You did," I belt. "Don't you dare lie to him."

"Jadon." Papa's stern voice echoes. A warning. He folds his hands behind his back, turning to Barnard. "Are you denying it?"

Barnard's face pales. "Your Majesty," he stammers, *"please."*

"There will be a royal investigation," Papa tells him, ignoring his trembling jaw. "Your administration. Members of the Council. All will be called in. We'll dissect every conversation. Rest assured, I'll uncover every last detail."

Barnard's upper lip curls. The first tell. He loosens his tie, paces. His shoulders are slumped, heavy from guilt. He stops in front of the dais.

"The crown is a symbol. A reminder of who we are. What we've fought to protect since the days of King Réné." He points accusingly at Mom. "Queen Ava and your son don't represent those values. Our people will never respect them."

"How dare you," Annika spits.

I stare at Mom. She doesn't flinch.

"This country was built on the broken backs of those within," Barnard says, undeterred. "We were almost destroyed by those who don't belong. They're undeserving of a position of power here. To bring their corrupt values—"

"Ça suffit!" Papa roars.

Barnard shivers, lips pressed into a thin line.

Frowning, Papa climbs the dais, toward Mom.

"I'm sorry, Ava," he says. "Since the moment you came here, you've fought hard to be someone people love and respect. Our people. Our children. You're the queen we *all* need."

Mom exhales shakily. There's a shimmer of light across Papa's eyes. I guess even kings can cry.

"This is my fault." His gaze moves around the room. "I let this happen. But no more. For once, I won't be neutral."

He stares at me like he hopes I know this isn't just King Simon speaking.

It's my papa.

He walks over to Barnard. "You're relieved of your duties until the investigation is complete, Stéphane."

Barnard wavers like he's overwhelmed.

Chin high, tone dignified, Papa says, "No Royal Council of State. No UN relations. You will not step foot on government or royal premises. No more *corrupting* our people with the old ways. You're done."

"Wait, I—" Barnard looks past Papa's shoulder to me. And I

see it. The blazing ring of fear in his eyes. "You can't—"

"I can. And, as king, I will," Papa decrees.

In my periphery, I spot Samuel shift around like he's about to give Papa a standing ovation, but thinks better of it. He settles for a swift nod. Annika shifts over to Mom, kissing her temple. Mom's gaze falls on me. When her lips lift the tiniest bit, like she's proud of me, my chest puffs out.

Papa signals to the back of the room.

In seconds, two guards appear on either side of Barnard. They escort him away.

I watch as tired traditionalism loses to good old "burn shit down, ask questions later."

Since I was a kid, Centauri's gardens have been my favorite hiding spot. My private sanctuary. Hundreds of trees, from fig, to palm, to dragon's blood, to species I haven't identified yet. Colorful flowers swaying with the breeze. An air soaked in heady sweetness and pristine grass and salty ocean.

I'm sitting on a stone bench in the center. Not far from the tree I'd nap under. Nowhere near whatever's happening inside the palace.

After Barnard's removal, Papa excused us so he could talk privately with Mom. Outside the throne room, Annika squeezed me in a long hug. We didn't say anything, but we both know. There's been a change inside Centauri's walls. Inside our family.

Inside me.

I'm not carrying around the weight of what the prime minister said anymore. No longer worried about being Rêverie's perfect prince. Papa hasn't said what's next. Whether my time here is permanent. If I'll ever go back to America.

If I'll ever get to talk to Reiss again.

But at least my parents finally see *me*.

"I knew I'd find you here."

I barely hear her voice over the splashing ocean behind the palace. Mom hugs herself against the soft wind. She's abandoned her designer wardrobe for sandals and jeans and an old cardinal USC shirt. It's rare to see her dressed so casually.

"Can I?" She signals to the empty place next to me.

I scoot over. "You're the queen."

"Not right now, Canelé," she says, flopping down. "I'm just Mom."

Her shoulder rests against mine. I can't remember the last time we did this. Sat in a long, comforting silence. Let the high sun wash over our faces. She's always gone, and I'm always . . . alone.

"Oh. The staff found this." She holds up something. "After cleaning up the wreckage of Hurricane Jadon."

I grimace. Then my gaze lowers to the object: a strip of photos.

The one of me and Reiss from Playland Arcade.

"I figured you didn't want to lose it," she whispers.

I hear the smirk in her voice, but I can't look away from the pictures. Surprised faces. Heart hands. Reiss laughing. Staring into each other's eyes like that one moment was endless.

A familiar prickle starts behind my lashes.

In every fairy tale I heard as a kid, the prince is the one who saves the day. Slays the dragon. Finds the glass slipper. Wakes a sleeping beauty with a kiss. In reality, being a prince doesn't mean happily-ever-after.

There is no magic or luck or heart-stopping kiss at the end of the story.

Happily-ever-afters aren't for boys like me.

"I loved the pier," Mom says, wistful. "Walking through Palisades Park. Going to Venice. The aquarium in Long Beach—"

"Wow, Mom, did you spend any time in school?" I tease her.

She tips her head into the sun. "When I first moved to Rêverie, it was lonely. Your papa was so busy, even then. I was stuck here. Mémère worried I'd get into trouble if I left the palace."

"Did you?"

"So much." Her laugh is like Annika's—wild, unfiltered.

I brush my thumb over the photo strip. Across Reiss's pink waves.

"I was careful," she tells me. "I saw how people here looked at me. Talked about me. I wasn't one of them. No one in Papa's family had ever courted an outsider."

We both frown.

I hate that word: *outsider*. Another way of saying some-one doesn't belong. Who gets to decide whether this wasn't someone else's place all along? Why should anyone gatekeep someone else's joy or peace?

"When Anni and you came along," Mom says, her voice turning fond, "I did my best. I wasn't Long Beach's Ava Gilbert. Or USC's Ava Gilbert. I was someone else."

Her eyes turn to the palace.

"I know you tried to protect me from the prime minister." She sucks air through her teeth, a move some might consider unroyal. Not queenlike. But it makes me think of Nana's photos. The fearless Ava Gilbert I want to know. "But I've dealt with his type before. His words don't hurt me. I'm strong. It's my job to protect *you*. So you never feel . . . different."

Another word that screws up her face, like a bad taste in her mouth.

"Mom," I say on a long breath, "I've always felt different."

She frowns again.

"Not because of you," I clarify. "I never felt Réverian enough. I'm not the kind of prince they're used to. It was the same in America. I wasn't the right kind of person. I didn't belong."

"Canelé."

"I'm too angry. Or I don't smile enough. Too stubborn. Too gay—"

When I freeze, Mom squints. "There's no such thing. But we'll circle back to that later."

My shoulders sag. "Everyone thinks I act like—"

"A teenager?" she volunteers. "That's what you are. That's what I saw when you spoke to me and Papa yesterday. A boy."

I try to hide my embarrassed face behind my hands. Mom pulls them down to look into my eyes.

"Canelé, you're supposed to be messy. Sometimes difficult. Imperfect." Sadness pours over her face. "This world treats you like a man instead of allowing you to be a boy. They treat all Black children that way. Expecting excellence. Perfection. To grow up before you should."

Her eyes close, a tear clinging to her eyelashes. "We failed you," she says, voice breaking. "*I* failed you."

When she blinks, I stare at her, lost.

"It wasn't Papa who suggested you stay in America," she sighs. "It was me."

I let out a choked, surprised noise. "*You?*"

For months, I blamed Papa. His stiff tone. Unbending attitude toward everything. I used any excuse to direct my anger at him. But it was Mom's idea to keep me away from home.

"Why?" I ask.

"I wanted you to figure yourself out," she explains. "To have the freedom to discover yourself. Like I did at your age. And after high school. All through college."

This time, her laugh is wet, but her smile is big.

"Jadon, I fucked up so many times, your nana started making bets with the church ladies on when I'd call her for bail money."

"Mom!"

She snorts. "But my parents were there for me. Every single time. That's where me and Papa failed. We shouldn't have abandoned you." She squeezes my hand. "We should've loved you even when you were difficult."

I let out a tight, shaky breath. She gives me space to process.

"It helped," I confess. "I needed to be away. To—how'd you put it? Fuck up?"

Wind sweeps curls across her cheek. She tucks them behind her ear, smirking like she's not going to scold me, but also not to test her patience.

My gaze dips back to the photo strip. "I needed to find people who didn't hate me for being . . . me."

"Reiss is quite the spitfire." She nudges her elbow into my side. "Aries?"

"Scorpio, I think?"

She nods in a *makes sense* way. "I can see why you two work so well."

"*Worked*, Mom. Past tense." I do my best not to pout. Or cry. What for? It's over. This is how all my stories end.

"You love him, don't you?"

Mom's eyebrows are raised, as if she knew a long, long time ago and I'm just now catching on. That's the thing about moms. They're always ten steps ahead.

"Your papa fell in love with me in a *week*."

"Who does that?" I joke.

She shrugs. "I said the same things Reiss did. I don't want to get in the way. I have dreams. But he never quit." There's that fondness in her eyes again. "No matter how anyone felt about us, he was determined to make it work. *We* were determined."

I shake my head. "I messed up."

"That's what love is," she starts. "Messing up. Being un-afraid to get it wrong. Trusting the other person loves you for *trying*."

"But I'm here," I say. "He's in America, where I'm pretty sure Papa banned me from—"

Mom holds up a finger. "We talked about that. Plans are changing."

I lean back, stunned. Confused. Hopeful.

"And Reiss isn't in America." When my eyebrows start to droop, she adds, "I *might've* delayed his flight by, like, a day. 'Mechanical issues' is the official cause if anyone asks. He leaves in an hour."

I gape at her. "Why didn't you say anything?"

"Because I needed to know. That you were ready. That he was too."

My eyes stray to the photo strip. I am ready. I want this. I want him.

Mom bumps my shoulder. "Your name's on the passenger list. A car's waiting to drive you."

I swallow a laugh.

Mom planned this. Ambitious Ava Gilbert at her finest.

Her hand cups my cheek. "If this is what you want, fight for him, Canelé. For yourself." Every line, wrinkle, years of being what Réverie expects and who she wants, disappears when she smiles. "Go get *your* prince, Jadon."

21

I'm running.

Wind whips through my curls. My lungs are begging for relief—and a weekly cardio plan moving forward. I'm lucky airport security even let us through, considering I'm not *dressed* much like a prince right now: label-less black T-shirt, Burberry joggers, AJ1 mids with plaid accents.

But I'm not stopping until I reach him.

"I came prepared!"

Ajani matches my pace, not nearly as breathless as I am. She points to her sensible pair of Nike running shoes. Impressive on such short notice.

We're on the tarmac now. The airport attendants offered an official royal car. But there wasn't enough time to wait.

The engines are whirring. All luggage has been loaded. In the distance, the airstairs are still down. I see Reiss, flanked by two Royal Protection Guards, their backs to us.

I force one last burst of energy into my burning legs.

"Wait! Wait!"

The guards spin around, moving into defensive formation. A sweet-faced attendant at the top of the stairs frowns as I frantically wave my hands. Ajani catches me before I fall over and eat hot tarmac.

"Reiss Emile Dorian Hayes!" I shout until my throat goes raw.

He turns, eyes bulging. "Jadon?"

I stop in front of the guards. When they recognize me, they bow, parting from Reiss's sides. Then, it's him. Confused, but here and not angry and so, *so* close.

"Sorry," I gasp out, heaving. "Not much of a runner."

Ajani snaps her fingers. In a flash, the attendant is down the stairs, passing me a cold bottle of water and a towel.

I dab sweat from my brow, then gulp half the bottle.

Droplets dribble down my jaw. Over the front of my T-shirt. "How do people do this in the movies?"

"It's fake," Reiss says impassively. "No one does this in real life."

I nod, swallowing more water. "I need to tell you something."

He scowls. "And you couldn't message me? Or . . . I don't know. Maybe said it at the palace. *In front of your parents.*"

I grimace. "Maybe?"

He crosses his arms, unimpressed by the fact that I ran across a literal airstrip to reach him.

"I—"

The rest of the words don't come. My chest aches from more than just sprinting. From three months of hell and regret and countless mistakes. From wanting something so bad, it's going to destroy me if I can't have it. If Reiss walks away.

But I can't give up now.

He exhales an irritated breath. "Well? What is it?"

"You never asked me what I was afraid of," I blurt out.

Reiss's eyebrows wrinkle with confusion.

"For your film," I tell him. "You never asked."

"Why would—"

I cut in, urgent. Desperate. "For years, I've been terrified I'm not good enough. For my parents. Rêverie. The whole world. I'll never be the royal they expect."

A frown overtakes his face.

"And I don't care anymore." I smile, weak at first. "No matter what, someone will always think I'm not good enough. But you—" My voice cracks, even through the grin. "I can't stop caring about what you think."

The corners of his mouth twitch up.

"You're bossy. Terrible at football," I start counting off. "You break the laws. Decent kisser for a beginner—"

"My prince," Ajani stage-whispers, "This *isn't* helping."

But it is. Reiss's shoulders are shaking. His cheeks are tinting that memorable shade of pink he gets when he's amused.

"I'm scared," I continue, "of not being enough for you."

White teeth catch the corner of his lip, pulling. It's like he's fighting a reply.

"I'm tired of the rules. Of being who they want. I *like* me." My chest warms. But not like it has for years and years. In another way. A freer way.

"I'm angry. Bad at apologizing," I list off. "Arrogant—"

"Don't forget adorable," Reiss whispers.

My lips inch higher. "I like Death by Chocolate ice cream. Funnel cake. Those delicious cinnamon rolls." I dare to step closer. He doesn't retreat. "I like standing up for what I believe in, even if that makes me the world's worst prince."

"You really are awful at it."

"I like that you're so far from perfect, it's funny."

"Is this still an apology?" he asks flatly.

"I like that you listen. Call me out. You have dreams," I continue, undiscouraged. "You go after what you want. You don't quit. You don't let *me* quit."

Cautiously, I lean in. Rest my forehead against his. I stare into his dark eyes, synchronizing my breath to his.

"But, Reiss, I'm not afraid to say," I whisper, voice almost giving out, "I *love* you."

His breath hitches.

I say it again: "I love you."

A beat. His gaze doesn't leave mine, but I can see it behind his eyes. He's thinking. Considering every moment we shared. Everything I just said on this tarmac with strangers around, in front of an idling jet.

I count the seconds—three, five, ten—and I don't know what I expected. Nothing in my life changes. The ending's always the same.

It takes all my strength to pull back, but just as I do—

"I love you too," Reiss says.

And then, when I'm speechless, too stunned to absorb his words, he whispers, "I love you, *Jadon*."

My head tilts. Reiss closes the gap once more, and then his lips slide across mine. Smooth, soft, slow. Like a wave. Like the sea returning to shore.

We only quit when Ajani clears her throat over the engine's noise. "We're delaying takeoff, Your Highness."

I ease back. "Shall we?"

When we're in the air, our hands tangled, I say, "I hope your parents don't hate me. For keeping you away so long."

"They don't." He smiles conspiratorially. "You haven't seen the news, have you?"

When could I? I've spent the day being surprised by an ex, watching the prime minister's career crumble, being given love and life advice from my mom. Oh, and telling a boy I love him for the first time.

"Been a *little* busy," I say.

He googles my name. As expected, I'm trending. But it's not as bad as I anticipate.

Almost every article is about me and Reiss.

"I called Ma last night," he says as I scroll. "Reporters have been camping outside the café. Your loyal fans too. Everyone's dying to get a photo."

Eyes crinkled, he adds, "It's helping business. Just like when my dad proposed."

"Wow," I exhale.

"Dom's so excited," Reiss says fondly. "All his classmates love that his bro's dating a prince. No one's teasing him. Calling him a coward."

I grip his hand tighter.

"And this is okay? Your family being in the spotlight?"

He sighs, shrugging. "The one time the headlines are about me, and I have to share them with a prince."

I lean across the armrest, my nose brushing his. "Then I guess now isn't the time to mention I *hate* these photos of me? I mean, seriously. They didn't even get my dimples."

He groans against my lips, kissing me as the jet lifts us closer to the stars.

"And if you want to know who killed Mr. Boddy," I say with a teasing grin. I step over Karan's splayed body, staring into the dark. "It was me. Special Agent Green. In the hall. With my revolver."

Noel, the police chief, steps into the spotlight. "Great work, Green. Okay, officers, round 'em up!"

The orchestra plays as the curtains close. From the audience, I hear screams and laughter and chanting. Everyone gathers center stage. My heart is still thudding behind my chest when the curtain peels back. The house lights come up, and I finally see it.

I finally see . . . *them*.

A sold-out auditorium giving us a standing ovation. Their clapping cracks like thunder in an endless storm. I'm holding hands with Nadia and Mia as the cast bows over and over. Someone shoves Dustin forward until he's under the spotlight, hyperventilating at all the attention, but grinning so widely it looks permanent.

Backstage, Mr. June dances around in a sparkly pair of heels. Dr. Garza Villa shakes an elegant paper fan, proud tears wetting their cheeks.

It wasn't perfect. Vivian nearly fell offstage after tripping on a prop. Calvin missed his cue after intermission because of the line to the restroom. I forgot a line—or four. But we did it.

Opening night for Willow Wood's fall production wasn't an utter failure.

In the front row, my eyes land on Annika, hands cupped around her mouth, shouting. Luc whistles. Samuel got special permission from Headmaster Parker to record everything for Mom. And then there's Ajani, arms crossed, expression stony except for the tiny flinch at the corners of her mouth. Like she's fighting hard not to smile.

They're all here. My little Palisades family.

The cast steps aside. We let Karan take over center stage. He bows deeply, beaming brighter than any spotlight focused on him.

The noise level intensifies. I think the loudest cheers might be from his parents, who are also in the front row, waving bundles of flowers in the air. Or maybe it's Lo, who is pink-faced, but shamelessly screaming from backstage.

No, the loudest voice is mine.

I yell until my throat is raw and achy. Until he knows this is his moment. That no one deserves it more than him.

Hollywood, eat your fucking heart out.

I skip the cast party.

Before I leave, Nadia and Mia whine about how important it is. But, for once, I'm not ditching extra social time with my classmates because I don't want to be around them. Because I don't *like* them. I'm not maintaining a safe distance because it's easier than letting people in. This time, there's somewhere I need to be.

Someone I need to see.

"How'd it go?"

We ask the question at the same time.

It's dark outside, the sky over Willow Wood a blanket of indigo, but the quad's fountain is lit up. An ivory glow swims across Reiss's face. He's wearing the same clothes I've more or less seen him in for the last three days: worn-soft joggers, BASED ON A TRUE STORY T-shirt, a grungy beanie covering his hair. But there's something different about him. Something I've noticed since our return from Rêverie.

He grins fondly. "Did you mess up your lines?"

I ignore his question, too anxious for an answer to my own. "Did you finish?"

The moment the jet touched down, he holed up in the video lab. Or his bedroom. Working hard on his Oceanfront Film Fest submission. We've mostly seen each other in passing. Through brief FaceTime calls.

I made him promise to miss the play. Spend his time editing. The deadline is midnight.

He shrugs nonchalantly.

"Ugh." I step forward. "Just tell me."

"Is that an order, Your Royal Arrogance?"

I edge closer, smirking. "Yes. As your future king—"

"Excuse you. You're just the spare," he says wryly. "Also, America isn't a monarchy. There was a whole war. You should really learn your history—"

"Reiss Emile Dorian Hayes," I interrupt in my best commanding King Simon voice. "Stop rambling. Answer the question."

He rolls his eyes. "Yes. I finished."

I don't hesitate. The quad's empty, but it wouldn't matter. The public knows about us now. I don't care if someone's hiding in a bush, under a table, with a long-range camera. I haul Reiss into my arms, swinging him off his feet.

"Ew," he halfheartedly complains as I press small kisses to his neck and jaw. "I haven't showered in like forty-eight hours."

"You did it! You did it!" I chant against his skin.

He laughs, a hand in my curls.

We spin and spin. It's dizzying, but not as nauseating as the thought of almost losing this. Or how I almost never had this.

Too angry, too stubborn after Papa exiled me here. Swearing I'd never fall for an American boy.

Funny how life never goes the way you expect.

When I lower him to the ground, Reiss says, "Now answer my question. How'd you do?"

I settle my hands on his hips. Draw him in. While he waits, his eyes flit from my dimples to my lips, then back again.

"I was—" I pause, considering. *Good? Great? Managed to make even Dr. Garza Villa laugh so hard, they almost fell over?*

I settle on: "I was me."

Reiss crooks an eyebrow. "What does that mean?"

"It means," I singsong, grabbing one of his hands, "I want to celebrate! I made a call."

"*You* made a call," Reiss says, doubtful.

"Fine," I huff. "Samuel made the call. He arranged a special after-hours tour of USC's campus. The film school too."

There's a glow behind his eyes. A hypnotic swirl of hickory and obsidian and awe. It makes my stomach flip.

"I thought it'd be nice?" I say, almost bashfully. "You get a closer look at what your future could look like. And I get to see some of my past. The life my mom experienced."

It's been on my mind since we talked. Since Annika suggested it months ago. It's time I started discovering who I am. Who I *can* be here. Even if it's not permanent.

"You—" He swallows. "You did that for me?"

"For us," I clarify, then grin smugly. "Being a prince has a *few* privileges."

His lips purse. "Only a few?"

I hold up my thumb and forefinger, a tiny space between them. "So?" I prod.

Reiss gives my hand a squeeze. "Let's go."

"Go where?"

The new voice startles me. Approaching us, the silvery moon leading them like a spotlight, is Karan and Lo and—

I tilt my head. "Nathan?"

He beams, skateboard under one arm, his other hand gripping a violin case. All my nerves during the play made me forget he was in the orchestra tonight. "PJ! Or should I say, Mr. Green?" He does a comically bad eyebrow wiggle.

I snort despite myself.

Lo squints at us. "You two sneaking off without us?"

"I'm *hurt*." Karan clutches his chest. "Betrayed by my own bestie, who didn't even show up for my breakthrough performance."

Lo sighs. "He's gonna be salty about this until graduation."

"You. Owe. Me," Karan says, emphasizing each word by stabbing Reiss's chest with his index finger. "What's the move? In-N-Out? Movie night?"

He's looking at me. There's no resentment for what happened with Léon in his expression. We haven't discussed it. Reiss mentioned clearing things up, but I still owe Karan an apology. Maybe not now, but soon.

I stare at Reiss.

He bites on a smile, shrugging. An *it could be fun* shoulder lift.

I was hoping for some alone time with him, exploring the

campus. Holding hands as we walked through quiet halls. Posing for a selfie in front of the reflective pool like Annika and Luc did. But that can wait too.

I turn to the others. "Would you like to join us on a private tour of USC?"

A beat passes.

Karan sucks in a loud breath. "I don't know, bro. As a future UCLA alum, that's high-key disrespectful—"

Lo elbows him hard in the ribs. "We'd love to."

"Yeah. Sure." Karan coughs, a mix of anguish and adoration directed at Lo. "I'm down."

Reiss laughs into my shoulder.

In the background, I spot Nathan slinking away, chin lowered. Like he's aware this isn't his circle of friends. Like he doesn't belong.

"Hey." I catch his elbow. "Do you want to come, Nate?"

I don't realize why his entire face goes fond, a tenderness behind his eyes, until I think about what I just said.

That I called him *Nate* instead of Nathan.

An unexpected grin pushes at my cheeks. "You in?"

He shakes out his shoulders. "Most def." Then, he squeezes between Lo and Karan. "But only if I can get some audio for my next podcast. Tell me, Mr. Boddy, what's it like being a Bruin stepping into Trojan territory?"

Karan juts his chin. "Well—"

"Oh, shit. Wait. Let me get my phone out."

It all happens so quickly. Lo gliding through the quad on Nate's board. Karan waxing philosophically to Nate about his theater journey. Reiss tucked under my arm as we walk toward the waiting SUV. My heart backstroking through an ocean of warmth and affection and a freeness I can't name.

Looking to my left and right, knowing I'm not alone. That I have real *friends*.

That I can be just Jadon.

22

PRINCE JADON SPEAKS: "WE'VE ALWAYS BEEN HERE, BUT I'LL MAKE SURE THEY REMEMBER US."

In an exclusive interview, Îles de la Réverie's Prince Jadon sits down for a second time with *TeenBuzz*'s Khalia Matthews to discuss discovering more of himself while in America (including meeting his new boyfriend), life as a Black royal, and leaving his own mark on his family's legacy.

"Is all this"—my eyes trail over the copious amount of food spread across the marble kitchen island—"really necessary?"

"Typically? No." Reiss smiles shyly.

There's a tray of hot dogs. Grilled vegetables on skewers. Stuffed peppers next to lightly charred corn cobs and seasoned fruit speared by toothpicks. A bowl of something called potato salad that I'm very wary of. In the center, a tower of sliders—a Mrs. Hayes specialty.

The whole house has an air of spice and smoke, but next

to me, I inhale earthy sweetness. Reiss worked a shift at The Hopper earlier. His parents left the café open long enough to serve the Saturday morning rush before shutting down for the day. With all the added attention from our relationship, business is great. They can afford to leave early.

"But," Reiss goes on, "this is how my family celebrates things."

It's been less than a week since he submitted his short film. He still won't show it to me, but the preliminary results are in:

He's been selected as a finalist. One step closer to achieving his dream.

I press a kiss to his temple. "Fine. But I'm not touching that potato monstrosity."

He laughs. "Promise not to tell my dad."

It's his family's first time at the Palisades house. I stare out at the main lawn. Luc's eagerly explaining *Paradise or Purgatory* to Mrs. Hayes. On the lounge chairs, Mr. Hayes, in a frond-print shirt and board shorts, shares boba with Annika. Dom splashes around in the pool while Ajani sits on the edge, bare feet soaking in the water.

She can pretend all she wants, but I can tell she has a soft spot for Dom.

In the foyer, Samuel paces. Constantly staring at one device or another. Maybe he's searching trending topics to see if my name pops up. Nothing's come out about the prime minister yet. The worst headline about me is Kofi's backstabbing interview with Kip Davies, but I have a plan to counter that.

Maybe that's what Samuel's checking. Maybe—

The doorbell rings. I crane my neck. In Samuel's haste to answer, he drops his phone.

"Who's that?" Reiss whispers.

I try to shrug, but my shoulders are too tense. The last time an uninvited guest showed up, it was Léon.

But it's not him.

Somewhere behind me, Mrs. Hayes gasps out, "Sweet baby Jesus!"

Every muscle inside me goes cold. Even with the sunlight backing them, I recognize the perfect posture. The regally lifted chins.

It's Papa and Mom. The king and queen of Réverie. In the Pacific Palisades.

"Greg!" Mrs. Hayes whisper-shouts. "Get in here! Dom, out of that pool. It's the—the king and the—"

"Mom!" Annika cries. "Papa!"

She rushes past me, barefoot, skipping all formalities to haul our parents into a hug. Papa laughs. Mom squeezes her tightly, staring at me over Annika's shoulder.

I'm speechless. Motionless.

"Why is my hair always a mess when royalty shows up?" Mrs. Hayes murmurs.

Papa escapes Annika's arms. He smiles as he approaches.

"Bonjour, son."

"Papa." My throat barely works. "What're you doing here?"

Mom sidles up. She reaches out, touching my cheek. "I missed home. My *first* home. It's been too long." Her fingers brush my ear. "And we wanted to see you."

"Both of us," Papa confirms. There's a hesitance about him.

An uncertainty I've never seen before. It's because of me. Because of how we left things in Réverie.

I let out a quiet breath.

"I made Samuel swear not to tell you we were coming," Papa adds. In the background, Samuel bows with a small smile. "Sorry we missed your play."

"We were—" Mom begins.

"Busy," I fill in.

"We're here now," Papa asserts. His hand finds my shoulder, squeezing. "If that's okay?"

It's not an order. He's not telling me. He's asking for permission.

"Y-yeah." I shove down a surprised laugh. "I mean, yes. I'm glad you're here."

His grin is the size of the sun. It's not a king's grin. It's my papa, goofy and inelegant and kind. "Also," he says, eyes shifting. "I owe Reiss an apology."

By my side, Reiss hiccups. "Sorry, what now?"

Behind him, his parents stand tall. Protective. Dom's dripping on the hardwoods, but even he looks ready to defend his brother.

"Our last meeting didn't go as planned," Papa says. He doesn't frown at Reiss's derisive snort. "I'd love to start over. Have a *real* chat. With my son's boyfriend."

Mom adds, "With his . . . family? If you'll have us?"

Mrs. Hayes tries to match Mom's textbook posture. She looks at her husband, then Reiss, waiting for his small shoulder lift. "We'd love that."

"You've gotta try my potato salad!" Mr. Hayes announces, breaking the tension.

His wife glares at him in a *you did not just offer a queen potato salad* way.

Reiss grabs my hand. He's biting his lip, nervous. I hope he can read what I'm saying with my eyes:

I won't let them hurt you again.

After a small beat, he nods.

"I heard you're interested in USC," Mom says to Reiss. "Film school? The president is a good friend." She winks. "I'd be honored to write you a recommendation letter."

Reiss's eyes widen, his face glowing. I know he's in good hands.

He walks outside with Mom. Annika and Luc join Dom in the pool. Mr. Hayes slings a friendly arm around Papa's stiff shoulders, regaling him with his potato salad recipe. Mrs. Hayes shakes her head, on the way back to the grill.

Ajani joins me by the kitchen island.

"Did you know they were coming?" I ask.

She gives an unenthusiastic shrug. "You needed this."

I did. My parents in America. Watching my papa nod as Reiss tells him and Mom all his goals, hands moving around animatedly. Annika smirking at me from under the California sun. My two worlds colliding.

"How—" I start, half-turning to her. "How did you put up with me all these years?"

She's quiet for a moment. I worry I've crossed a line.

But she grins and says, "Because I know greatness. I've

seen greatness. It always starts with mistakes. With failure. With growth. You shouldn't be ashamed to be a rebel, my prince. Rebels won our people's freedom. Celebrate who you are."

It's the most consecutive words I've ever heard Ajani speak. The most affection I've heard in her voice. But it's not the first time I knew she loved me.

Sometimes, we don't need words for that.

Evening comes quickly.

Outside, the Hayes are gathered on plush sofas surrounding the glass fire pit. They're joined by Annika, Mom, Ajani, and Luc. From the looks Reiss gives me every few seconds, orange light dancing over his smile, I can tell Mom's showing him baby photos on her phone.

I'm with Papa in the gourmet kitchen. It smells like rum and vanilla. There's a smear of flour on his cheek. He's teaching me how to make canelés, the one recipe we never got around to when I was younger. Before royal obligations were all he had time for.

He rolls up his sleeves. "Do you bake much here?"

"Kind of." I coat copper molds with beeswax, grimacing. "I burned macarons."

Fondness scrunches his eyes. "A family tradition. I've ruined plenty of batches in my life."

I pour batter into the molds. Typically, it needs to chill for at least twenty-four hours. But I'm not aiming for precise. With my baking. Or my words.

"Nothing comes out perfect the first time," Papa says.

I raise my eyebrows.

"About what you said—" He wipes his cheek with the back of his wrist. "Me forcing you to be the prince I was?"

I start to wince. He chuckles.

"No, no. I get it. But son, I wasn't a good prince," he tells me. "Not at first."

I roll my eyes playfully. "Lies, Papa. I've seen photos."

"Photos and video don't tell the whole story." He scans my face. "Do they?"

Together, we transfer the molds onto a baking sheet.

"We didn't have social media then," he goes on. "All my missteps weren't blasted over the internet. Plus, your pépère was as tough as he was kind."

Something I'll always remember about Pépère—his infectious smile.

"He taught me a lot." Papa sighs. "So have you."

"I did?" I say with slight cynicism.

"Traditions don't dictate everything. In order to rule, you have to follow your heart. Take a stand. Be a little fearless."

I gape at him. "You got all that from me yelling at you?"

"Yes! I did." He laughs. After placing the tray in the oven, he adds, "I also talked with Ambassador Ime. You left quite the impression on her."

My nose wrinkles. I forgot about the dinner with Grace's dad.

"A good one," Papa assures. "She likes your . . . fire."

I set a timer on my phone. He leans against the island, waiting for me to speak.

Be a little fearless.

"Do you know what it's like?" I finally say. "To have a king—your papa—tell his *gay* son he's not the kind of prince his country deserves?"

His face falls. "Son. I didn't mean—"

"I know." I bite the inside of my cheek. "But it still hurt. For months, I didn't think being me was enough. I tried to be someone else. But I can't be."

"No, you can't." Papa smiles sadly. "You *shouldn't*."

He surprises me by grabbing my hand. His is wrinkled, a little cold, but still bigger. Still strong and gentle. A hand that guided me through the only moments where I felt like *Jadon was enough*—in the palace kitchens, just us, away from the world.

"I want to go to university," I confess. "In America."

Papa stays quiet. He grips my hand tighter. *Tell me more.*

"I want to pursue baking. Or acting. Maybe something boring." I laugh. "I want to study politics too."

A subtle eyebrow raise, but he still doesn't interrupt.

"I want to do more for Réverie," I say. "For people like me. I can't do that in the palace. Or on a council. I need room to explore and learn."

Papa's gaze turns to the main lawn. To Mom giggling with Reiss.

"Like I did."

I grin. At least I know where I got my stubborn, romantic heart from.

"Annika's the next queen," I say. "But I want to build a

Réverie I'm proud of too. I'm done with the past. I don't always want to be neutral."

Papa exhales, shoulders dropping. "I don't want that either." He clears his throat. Stares into my eyes. "You'll stay here. Finish your education. Annika will stay too. She wants to establish a stronger Réverian presence. That girl has your mom's drive."

"She gets it from you too," I tease.

He smirks. "Samuel will remain here to help as well. He's quite fond of you."

Again, I'm caught off guard. Not just by Papa's revelation. But because I like Samuel too, when he's not secretly inviting my ex to LA.

"He showed me your Sunset Ball speech," Papa comments. "I have some notes."

I groan, embarrassed.

Papa laughs again. "Don't worry. You're on the right path."

Am I? I still don't know if I've found the exact words to tell the world who I am. What my country—and America—has given me.

Papa hauls me into a hug. He smells like sugar and butter and Darjeeling.

Like home.

"You don't have to get it perfect," he says into my curls. "You can be angry. Kind. You don't need to be me or anyone else, son. Just be Jadon."

I exhale into his shoulder. Tears slip from my eyes as he squeezes tighter.

"I'm so sorry, son. For not listening. For everything." It sounds like he's crying too. But happy tears. Like we're finally okay. "Promise me you'll visit Rêverie. You'll come see your mom and me. Promise."

And I do.

The Sunset Ball is an absolute spectacle. Chic suits and glamorous gowns. A long, blush-pink carpet draped across the Getty Center's front steps.

I climb out of the Bentley. Photographers scream my name. Camera flashes shimmer against the darkening sky like exploding diamonds. But it's not only my attention they're scrambling for. It's the boy next to me, whose hand I don't hesitate to grab, threading my fingers through his.

Reiss grins nervously. I've done a million of these things before. But this is his first real taste of dating a royal.

"Don't worry," I say into his ear. "You look great."

He's wearing a custom-made Tom Ford suit in a familiar shade of cardinal. His gold tie pops against a black button-down. At least he's getting used to the designer wardrobe, having a stylist stand over him to fix his hair. It's freshly dyed. Pacific blue.

"It helps," I add, smirking, "that you're standing with me."

He squints against all the bursting light. "Is that so, Your Royal Arrogance?"

My nose wrinkles. "It is. Now, come on. You're blocking my dimples."

His mouth flexes into that crooked grin.

Ajani escorts us through the storm.

Inside, the main lobby is crowded with guests. Models and actors and political influencers. I don't search for Grace. We haven't talked since that night with her father. I'm giving her space to figure out who she wants to be, the same way being banished to LA gave me that chance.

As corks pop and the orchestra tunes up, I find us a quiet corner. My stomach churns anxiously. A million conversations are happening at once. In thirty minutes, I'll give my speech, right before the dinner. Bile crawls up my throat.

Annika's not far away. Standing in a gorgeous off-the-shoulder Carolina Herrera number, surrounded by the cast of a popular Netflix series. Nearby, Luc trades glances between her and me. His subtle eyebrow lift asks, *Do we need to get you out of here?*

With a small head shake, I smile his way, grateful.

He's not the only one who's noticed my pale face and tight shoulders.

Reiss squeezes my hand. He catches Ajani's attention. "Can I borrow him for a minute? Or, like, fifteen?"

Her eyes narrow with distrust.

"His, uh," Reiss stammers, "bowtie needs fixing."

I look down, frowning. I'm not wearing a bowtie. The all-black Prada suit Dion chose didn't require one. In the lobby's light, the gold accents threaded through the suit jacket sparkle.

"Ten minutes," Ajani says stiffly. "Not a second more."

Reiss beams. "I'll take it."

Before I can ask what's happening, Reiss hooks an arm

in mine. He drags me through a maze of faces. Around the champagne fountain. Behind a thick curtain where the noise is softened to a dull hum.

"What are we—"

My words are cut off as Reiss guides me against a wall. His hands splay on either side of my head. He grins slyly, something familiar flashing in his eyes.

"You're tense," he says.

I inhale a tight breath. "A little, yes."

"Cool. I'm here to help."

"Help?" I parrot, confused. Until his gaze drags over my mouth. His body presses against mine. One hand leaves the wall to run through my hair, down my cheek. "*Oh*. You want, um, to do that?"

His eyebrows wiggle, part amused, part serious. I can't blame him. Between the play and Oceanfront Film Fest and my parents' surprise visit, we haven't had any alone time. Not since Centauri Palace. It's crossed my mind too.

Just not *now*.

"It'll calm you down," he swears, suddenly an expert. I laugh when his head dips, soft lips tracing the skin under my jaw.

"What if . . . you know. The press walks in?"

"They won't." He grabs my waist. Angles my hips until I can feel him fully. "It's a big night. You're stressed about the speech. Just let me—"

"Hi, boys!"

Reiss flies back. I'm frozen as the curtain peels back. A fraction of light seeps in, highlighting the floral-embroidered gown Morgan's wearing.

She lifts a playful eyebrow. "Am I interrupting?"

"Not at all," I sigh, thumping my head against the wall. "Wait. Where have you been?"

We still haven't run into each other post-protest. To be fair, I've missed mornings in the courtyard to be with Reiss. But I haven't seen her in Willow Wood's halls either.

"Busy," she says nonchalantly. Morgan and her secrets.

I cross my arms, unwilling to let her deflect.

With an annoyed huff, she adds, "After, you know, *being on the news*, I had a big blowout with my stepdad. He wasn't happy about the protest." She looks down at her teal nails. "He yelled. I yelled. My mom threatened to take us on Judge Judy."

She's quiet for a beat. Her hard exterior softens in the shadows.

"My stepdad cried," she whispers. "He said it's fine if I want to fight for the right thing, but I'm a Black girl. In the city. Surrounded by cops. He didn't want anything to happen to me."

Reiss lets out a low breath. I do too. I remember Papa's words:

Your title means nothing to the wrong person there. Your life means nothing to them. Do you understand that?

I do now. It's not who you are. It's *what you are* that threatens them.

"Anyway." Morgan quickly wipes her eyes like the tears were never there. "We got off on the wrong foot. Me and him. So, we're spending more time together. Starting over, I guess."

I smile. I know what that's like too.

Her eyes drift over to Reiss. "I see you're doing the same thing," she says coyly.

I stare at him too. "I am."

"Good for you." In her hand, her phone chimes. "Ugh. Sorry. It's Grace. God, I regret agreeing to be her plus-one. She wants to know if you're okay?"

I blink owlishly. "Sorry, what now?"

Morgan lets out a real laugh. All high-pitched, nose wrinkling. "I heard about the dinner. She's . . . not everyone's flavor of intensity."

"She's not all bad."

Morgan tilts her head, stunned. "Plot twist."

I shrug, then laugh quietly.

After a short text and locking her phone, she says, "I'm glad you two get each other. She gives great birthday gifts. And she introduced me to my girlfriend, so—"

We share a look. Morgan's lowering her walls. I can do the same.

"I'm sticking around," I tell her. "You have to deal with me for another semester. Probably longer."

She shakes a hand at the sky like she's cursing some divine being. It's all a show. I can tell she's happy.

"I'm gonna go. See you Monday?"

When I nod, she unleashes a beautiful, sincere smile. Something I could get used to. "Don't do anything I wouldn't do," she warns us, then she's gone.

"Wow," Reiss says, for both of us. "You have some strange friendships."

I squawk. "Sorry, have you met Karan?"

"Unfortunately." He tugs on my jacket. Presses fully against me again. "Now, where were we—"

"Well, well. This is interesting."

Fuck my life. I'm living an actual nightmare. The curtains part again, another shaft of light creeping in before I see him.

Léon, wearing head-to-toe Armani like a well-dressed demon.

Smugly, he says, "Réverie's prince loves a scandal."

I'm about to ask what he's doing here, specifically *here*, at the Sunset Ball, in the one hidden space where I'm trying to spend time with my boyfriend, when I notice it. The unsteady line of his mouth. Uneven edge to his shoulders. Fingers wiggling at his sides. To anyone else, Léon's poker face is strong, but not with me.

We've known each other too long. He's nervous.

I cock an eyebrow, waiting expectantly.

With a long-suffering sigh, Léon says, "I'm not banned from Réverie. Only because of you."

A small smile tugs at my mouth.

While Papa was here, we discussed the prime minister. The conversation he had with Léon that started it all. I didn't beg on Léon's behalf, but I reasoned. Yes, he was shitty, but so was I. He shouldn't be punished for his papa's crimes.

He deserves a second chance.

"You said I inspired you," I say.

"You finally stopped caring." He grins. "You didn't do it their way. Like your papa would. I needed to see that." He runs a shaking hand over his hair. "To know I don't have to do things their way either."

"So, you ratted out your papa?"

"I did the right thing," he says with an earnestness I've rarely seen from him. His eyes slide to Reiss. "I'm sorry. For—"

"Being an asshole?" Reiss suggests.

"Yeah, yeah. That." He laughs roughly. "You're not so bad."

Reiss sniffs, his glare unrelenting, but his mouth lifts. Just a little.

Léon pivots back to me. "So, now that we're best friends," he says, rocking on his heels, ignoring my mocking expression, "what's the deal with Nate? Is there a chance?"

"Chance for what?"

Léon groans in that petulant way of his. "Can I ask him out? Is that . . . cool?"

I stare at him for a moment.

What we had together wasn't meant to be. We were better friends. As two boys who needed to know we weren't alone. But just because we didn't work romantically doesn't mean I should've sworn off future relationships.

First love doesn't mean last love.

Our pasts don't define what our futures can be.

"Go for it," I tell him.

His confident, fearless smile turns into something genuine. Vulnerable. He bows to me, then Reiss.

"Good luck out there, Your Highness."

Léon is barely on the other side of the curtain before Reiss is on me. Undoing buttons, easing a leg between my thighs. Hungry lips under my jaw as he whispers, "I'm proud of you."

I laugh breathily, ready to kiss him.

It never happens.

Ajani's voice says, "My prince. Time's up."

"What happened to ten minutes?" Reiss complains.

"I gave you twelve."

He slumps against me. I tip my head back, guffawing. How appropriate. Royal obligations ruining my one moment with Reiss. But that's okay.

Three months ago, I didn't think any American boy was worth this. That *I* was worthy of any of this.

But I am. He is. We are.

I press a kiss to his forehead. "Ready?"

When we step into the main hall, I almost don't hear his "You're lucky I love you." It's noisy as guests move toward the ballroom. His hand in mine is a welcome feeling. Like the tide meeting the shore. Like this is how it was always going to end:

With us, together.

Over the speakers, I hear:

"Distinguished guests of the Sunset Ball, accompanied by his date, Reiss Hayes, please welcome His Royal Highness Prince Jadon of Îles de la Réverie, *our* prince of the Palisades!"

EPILOGUE

Bonsoir. Good evening.

Most of you know me as the prince of Îles de la Rêverie. Son of King Simon and Queen Ava. Some of you know me from what the press writes about my life. What you see on the news and internet. But tonight, I want to tell you about the real me.

I was born on a beautiful island with a rich history. My papa taught me to bake before I could spell my own name. He taught me to knead and shape and pour my heart into creating something. My mom—who was born here, Long Beach to be specific—taught me compassion and strength. They both taught me to be the kind of person the world would respect.

My sister—the crown princess—thinks she taught me to be funny, which is why I didn't let her write this speech.

My country, my people taught me community. Resilience. My ancestors taught me that, from ashes, you can build a constellation.

I was ten years old when my papa became king. I was barely a teen when the headlines decided I wasn't worthy of my title. I didn't look or act like the type of prince they wanted.

I wasn't worth giving a chance.

Months ago, I came to America trying to be that perfect prince. Regal. Smiley. Worthy. I tried to live by their rules. To be who they wanted before I knew who I could be.

But isn't that what this journey is about? The discovery. Mistakes and growth. Love and heartbreak. Forgiveness. Making our own choices. Creating our own rules.

I come from a country that has survived centuries on traditionalism. Neutrality. While in America, I learned that tradition shouldn't mean contentment. You can't choose comfort over inconvenience. You can't be silent because it's easier.

I learned to use my voice. To stop standing aside while the world burns around me. To turn my own anger into action. It's our duty to each other to protect communities, even if they're not our own.

I learned that, despite my title, this is still my life. I get to decide how much of it I share.

People will always find a reason to hate you for what you are before they know who you are. We cannot let that stop us. Without fear, how can we ever be brave? How can we ever become who we're supposed to be without first acknowledging who we are now?

I'm here tonight to tell you this: I no longer want to be anyone else's definition of a perfect prince. A perfect human. I refuse to knead and shape and pour myself into anyone's mold. You shouldn't either. Why change who you are to fit someone else's expectations?

This is who I am—a boy who loves the ocean. Who has an insatiable sweet tooth. Who loves to laugh and be challenged and, sometimes, cares too much about his sneaker collection.

I'm also moody. I make mistakes. I'm a boy who is awful at apologies.

I'm a prince, and I'm not perfect.

I'm discovering more and more about who I want to be. I hope you'll allow me that grace. I hope you'll give yourself permission to do the same.

Our legacies aren't decided today. Or tomorrow. We have the power to create our own traditions and rules.

I hope you know you're worthy, no matter who you are.

Acknowledgments

When I sat down to write this book, I was so nervous. I was terrified I couldn't pull it off. After all, who was I to write a book about a royal when I'd never felt like one? When I'd never seen myself as a Prince Charming? But I had countless people in my life—before, during, and after writing Jadon's story—who reminded me I don't need a crown to be great. I just needed to be . . . *me*.

This isn't an exhaustive list of people I want to thank for believing in me, but it's a start:

Thank you to my fearless agent, Thao Le, who gives me so much confidence with her ALL-CAPS replies to all my silly ideas and always finds a way to fix the bad ones. To the phenomenal team at the Sandra Dijkstra Literary Agency for fighting tirelessly to ensure books like mine have a space in this world.

To my always-ready-with-a-GIF editor Dana Leydig, who forever sees my vision and helps me get there, and who gives each of my books the utmost care. To Maggie Rosenthal for helping me through the drafting phase, championing me, and having exquisite taste in sneakers.

To the coolest publicist around, Lizzie Goodell—seriously, how are you so awesome?

To the wonderful team at Viking Children's/Penguin

Random House: Tamar Brazis, publisher; managing editors Gaby Corzo and Ginny Dominguez; copyediting/proofreading: Andy Hodges, Krista Ahlberg, Marinda Valenti. Rebecca Waugh, Emily Parliman, Desiree Johnson, and all the lovely people at Listening Audio. James Akinaka, Felicity Vallence (my *Young Royals* partner in crime!), Shannon Spann, Alex Garber, Emily Romero, Christina Colangelo, Danielle Presley, and everyone in Marketing. To the magnificent PYR Sales team for all that they continue to do. To the all-stars in Design: Kaitlin Yang and Theresa Evangelista (cover design), Kate Renner (interior design). Thank you, Natalia Agatte, for bringing Prince Jadon and Reiss to life with your incredible cover illustration.

To Adib Khorram and Lana Wood Johnson for helping to brainstorm titles, introducing me to *Ted Lasso*, and all those times I needed to be reminded to "Believe!" To the best drafting buddy, Preeti Chhibber—thanks for all the pizza and laughs and "we should be writing, but . . ." moments.

To Dustin Thao (my forever NYC tour guide) for the beautiful blurb.

I'm very lucky to exist in a world with so many authors who inspire me and write the kind of stories readers need. I wish I could name them all . . . but we'd need another three hundred pages for that. Still, thank you for making a space for me. For being brave in a world that doesn't always accept us.

To the city of Santa Monica for giving me a second home and a place to exist as my weird self.

To my family and friends, especially Mom and Dad, for allowing me to countlessly mess up before discovering who I wanted to be.

To the booksellers, librarians, educators, artists, and reviewers who continue to uplift my stories—I can never say "thank you" enough. To my Atlanta bookstore crew: Brave + Kind Books, Charis Books & More, Read-It-Again Books, all the Barnes and Nobles, the team at Books-A-Million in Canton. To the staff of Little Shop of Stories for constantly welcoming me into their cozy world like I'm one of their own . . . thank you for making the hard days worth it.

Finally, thank you, reader! You make this possible. You remind me that these stories matter. That *community* matters. That we don't have to fit anyone's mold to be "worthy."

Remember: Never live by their definition of greatness. Create your own. And never, ever let them take your crown.

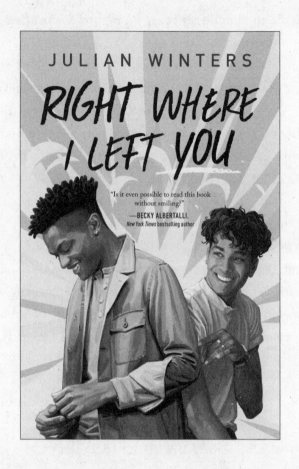

JULIAN WINTERS

RIGHT WHERE I LEFT YOU

"Is it even possible to read this book without smiling?"

—BECKY ALBERTALLI,
New York Times bestselling author

"Some books are downright fun, and *Right Where I Left You* is one . . . Winters sends a quiet but important message that queer Black and brown kids deserve to live happily ever after too . . . Winters weaves all of these threads—the romance, the relatable anxiety, the message—into a book that, like a crush, you won't be able to get out of your head."

—*The New York Times*

"As close to perfect as books get . . . Winters somehow strikes the perfect balance between hard-hitting topics and funny moments that make this novel work so well."

—The Nerd Daily

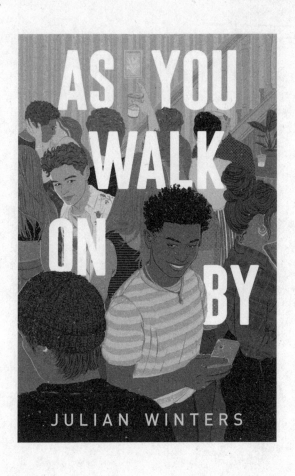